The Many Dates
of Indigo

AMBER D. SAMUEL

The Many Dates of Indigo

 by wattpad books

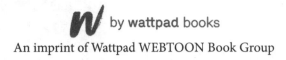 by **wattpad** books

An imprint of Wattpad WEBTOON Book Group

Published in Canada by Wattpad WEBTOON Book Group, a division
of Wattpad Corp.

36 Wellington Street E., Suite 200, Toronto, ON M5E 1C7 Canada

www.wattpad.com
First W by Wattpad Books edition: December 2022

ISBN 978-1-99025-928-9 (Trade Paper original)
ISBN 978-1-99025-929-6 (eBook edition)

Library and Archives Canada Cataloguing in Publication information
is available upon request.

Printed and bound in Canada

10 8 6 4 2 1 3 5 7 9

Cover design by Leah Jacobs-Gordon
Author Photo by Amber Samuel

For my Mama and Granny.
I miss you both and will always love you.

Prologue

Hair done. Nails did. Makeup flawless. Indigo stood in front of the floor-length mirror, the epitome of stunning. Her box braids hung over one shoulder, while diamond studs sparkled in her earlobes. Her champagne-colored wedding dress hugged her curvaceous body. She knew she looked good, but there was just one more thing she needed to complete the look. She effortlessly slid the gold band topped with a flawless diamond onto her ring finger. Indigo locked eyes with her reflection. Her copper irises sparkled.

One hundred and fifty people, including her husband-to-be, were already at the rustic yet elegant renovated barn, congregating and nibbling on appetizers, anticipating her arrival. Emotions bombarded her system: Love. Nervousness. Elation. Stress.

It felt like ages ago, the day she'd decided that she was done with single life and determined to find the one person she wanted to share her life with. She'd never been one of those people looking for her other half. She knew she didn't need completing because she was already whole. She was fully herself, and she was seeking an individual who loved every iota of who she was, even the stubborn, flawed parts of herself.

At this present moment, she was sure she had found that person. The one man who could be a haven during a storm, a confidant when worry weighed her down, and an encourager when she doubted her own dreams. Someone she could build a future with, start a family with.

"Okay." She took a deep breath, grabbed her bouquet off the vanity, and turned to her two bridesmaids. "It's time for me to go get married."

Chapter 1

I'm over this shit, Indigo thought to herself as she watched Saxon rip the pink wrapping paper off the umpteenth gift like the Hulk's sister. Only it wasn't Bruce Banner's sibling; it was hers. It wasn't her older sister's glee as she gushed over another set of pastel booties that had caused Indigo's current irritation. It was the glances and whispers she'd received while being the dutiful daughter.

Months shy of her thirtieth birthday—almost three months, to be exact—concerns for her health and well-being had shifted to interest in her relationship status and womb. No, her family didn't just outright ask her who she was dating or when she was planning to get pregnant. There were subtle hints cast here and there.

"Indigo just loves the single life," Aunt Maureen whispered to her cluster of church friends. There was a big nugget of truth in the statement. Indigo did love being single. Being able to do what she wanted, go where she wanted, eat where she wanted, and not have to let another soul know every detail of her weekly or daily plans was bliss for an independent spirit like her, but it was growing tiresome. She wanted someone to care about her itinerary and yearn to be added to her schedule permanently. She was also growing tired of being ultra-independent. She loved being a boss and taking care of business, but she also craved being pampered, adored, and loved.

"Still no ring," Cousin Tracy harped as she inspected Indigo's left hand after giving her a bear hug. That one hurt because even though Indigo prided herself on being an original, she *had* had an engagement ring picked out before the age of ten. It had happened during a simple stroll down the sidewalk of the River Oaks shopping district. She and her best friend, Tate, had walked behind their mamas, who'd talked about whatever adults talked about in the '90s, when a glimmer from a sizable cushion-cut diamond ring in the window of a jewelry store captivated all of her interest. Her mama calling her name snatched her out of her trance, but she never forgot the gem.

Sure, she had a bank account fat enough to buy herself the ring, but she wanted all the things the ring and the moment stood for. She wanted a man who would be her partner for their lives' journeys, and her past search to find one had left her with scars.

Presently, Indigo was on her third glass of wine and considered drinking straight from the bottle. Instead of risking a hangover, she snuck out of the living room. As she put distance between herself and the overcrowded room of cooing women, she felt the pressure fall off her shoulders. She sought refuge in Saxon's kitchen, the place she'd spent many evenings before buying a house in the same community, needing the sweetness of freshly baked desserts for a sugar high.

In all his six-foot mocha glory, her brother, Harrison, stood by the island, whipping pink food coloring into creamy, pillowy frosting. A platter of vanilla cupcakes sat in front of him, causing Indigo's mouth to water. She wanted to snatch one immediately but knew to wait. He hated when people tried his treats before they were finished. Presentation was everything to him. Ensuring people and things looked beautiful was something they shared.

"I thought you would've left by now." He judged the tint of the pinkness and decided to add some more into the bowl.

"I thought you weren't coming," Indigo groaned, climbing atop the barstool.

"I wasn't," he declared. Being the only brother had perks, but being the only baker in the family had drawbacks. "But Saxon ambushed me at the bakery and had a meltdown." He stopped stirring to give Indigo a fake smile. "So, I'm here. I had to cancel my date because of your sister."

"Our sister," she corrected before taking another swallow from the almost empty glass. "Wait! You had a date?" she asked, getting a nod from her little brother, the youngest of the trio. "With the Tinder chick?"

Harrison glared at her. "Her name is Tulip."

Indigo's nose turned up. "Like the flower?"

"And your name is what?" He snickered. "A color."

She flashed him her middle finger. "A bold, beautiful color with deep meaning."

The sunlight pouring through the window hit the red garnet in her ring. The lotus-shaped jewel had been a gift for her nineteenth birthday from Tate. It wasn't the most expensive piece of jewelry she owned, but its meaning was priceless.

Her hand gesture did nothing to erase Harrison's smirk. "It's a hippie name."

"You mean independent thinkers." Indigo shrugged, raising the glass to her mouth. "Who created their own paths, not giving a damn about what others have to say."

"Maybe that's why you're not married." He smeared frosting on a cupcake. "You're free-spirited at heart."

She didn't see anything wrong with being a free spirit. She'd never wanted to follow the crowd or do things just because everyone else was doing them, but this wasn't a matter of following the norm. She felt the clock ticking, and it wasn't in her favor.

And no one let her forget it.

"You're about to knock the hell out of twenty-five, and I don't see anyone giving you grief about getting married."

"Because I'm putting in an effort." He drizzled pink sprinkles onto the cupcakes. "Going on dates."

"And I'm what?"

"Checked out entirely."

"I'm just busy." She slapped the countertop. "I don't think you people understand how much work goes into being—"

"*A boss.*" Harrison cut her off, and she rolled her eyes. "We all know that's an excuse. Mom's a corporate lawyer, and she still had time to hook Dad."

"Well, Baker Bob, Dad was a partner at the firm Mom worked at." She straightened herself on the stool, getting serious. "I own a shoe store, and I don't see too many straight, unmarried guys buying Louboutin and Jimmy Choo."

She had been propositioned by numerous married men, but that was neither here nor there. She didn't fancy being a mistress. Plus, she didn't like to share; having two siblings had given her that trait at an early age.

"For starters," Harrison said, wiping the sugar off his hands, "you can stop saying no when someone asks you out."

"So, you're telling me that I should say yes to the idea of hanging out with a stranger?" She shook her glossy curls. "Seems like fraud."

The last time she'd spent time getting to know a stranger who'd found her attractive and engaging, he'd turned out to be an actual scammer. He still wrote to her from time to time.

"It's not!" Harrison threw up his arms. "'Cause that's how strangers become unstrangers."

"Unstrangers?" She burst out laughing. "That's not a word."

He looked at her blankly. "That's not an antonym for stranger?"

"No. Not at all." She stared at him, making a mental note to buy him a thesaurus for his birthday.

He shrugged. "Well, fuck, I'm not an English teacher. Saxon is. All I'm saying is . . ." He pushed her hand away as she reached over the island for a cupcake. He handed her the icing-covered spatula instead. "Say yes to a date once in a while."

She twisted her mouth, savoring the sugar on her tongue.

"And don't overthink it," Harrison insisted while lifting the tray of identically frosted cupcakes. "Just go with the flow."

"That's easy for you to say," she said, hopping off the barstool and following him back into the madness.

Indigo wished she could date as easily as Harrison. Unlike him, she had wounds that still lingered from bad relationships.

• • •

"Enjoy the rest of your Sunday!" Indigo stood in the doorway, happily waving to the last guest as they headed down the now vacant driveway.

"Mmm, this is good." Harrison slouched in one of the living room's striped armchairs with his legs propped up on the coffee table. "Mama, you put your foot in this gumbo." He shoveled in another spoonful of the swampy chicken-and-sausage delicacy that was reserved for special occasions.

It was also Indigo's favorite. Unfortunately, Indigo hadn't had any since she'd been too busy to stop and eat. Slurping the spicy juice from the crab legs was the best part, but now she was just too tired to fight with the crustacean exoskeleton.

"Thanks, baby," Stella Clark, the matriarch of the Clark clan, said. She headed for the stairs, arms full of vibrant yellow baby blankets. "You better get you a bowl to take home before Xavier gets back."

Saxon waited for their mama to climb the last step and round the corner before she peeled her lips apart. "Keep your paws away from that pot." She pointed her finger at Harrison while sitting back on the couch, stroking her round belly. "That's Xavier and the kids' dinner. You can go to Mickey D's to fill that bottomless pit of yours."

"Anyway, you need to stop stuffing your face." Indigo pushed the back of Harrison's head, sending it forward and almost into the bowl he was cradling like a newborn. "And help us get this stuff to the nursery." She gestured to the baby paraphernalia that cluttered the usually immaculate living room. "I don't want to be doing this all day."

"What else do you have to do?" Harrison and Saxon chirped simultaneously.

She narrowed her eyes at them with her hands on her waist, blocking the television screen that Harrison had commandeered, switching it from soundscapes to *Atlanta*. "Better things than stockpiling your already packed nursery." Indigo slid her bare foot across the hardwood floor. "This isn't how I wanted to spend my last off day of the week."

"Damn!" Harrison dug his spoon into the bowl. "Tell us how you really feel."

Saxon cradled her round belly with a sneer. "What's the matter with you? This is your niece. You don't want to be here for your sister and your niece?"

She wanted to ask how many baby showers she had to attend. Shouldn't being in attendance for the first two have filled her quota? But knowing how hormonal and expressive her sister was, the question would only lead to waterworks and their mom hurrying downstairs, ready to give a tongue-lashing to whoever had made the mother-to-be upset.

"I want to be here," Indigo said in a soft tone to erase the now downturned mouth and big eyes her sister was giving her. "I just don't want to be here all day."

Harrison huffed. "Lies. So many lies your teeth should fall out."

"What?" Saxon cocked her head in his direction. "Lying about what?"

"Stop instigating, you little scoundrel." Indigo tossed a cute plush teddy bear at him, but it sailed past his head by a country mile.

Saxon glanced between the two of them with suspicion, reminding Indigo of the days their big sister had been tasked with watching her siblings while their parents worked late, and they would plot to break the rules. "Are y'all keeping secrets behind my back? What is it? We have a code, remember." A code they'd crafted when she went away to college. Austin was far away, and she hadn't wanted to be left out and miss anything in their tight-knit trio. "Spill it, now."

"There is no secret." Indigo dropped to her knees by the coffee table, busying herself folding a pile of onesies. "Chill out, Sax."

Harrison swallowed his spoonful of gumbo. "She's pissed that she's still single and everyone around her is moving on."

"That's the last time I'm having a private conversation with you, Harriet." Indigo gave him the evil eye.

Harrison shrugged, shoveling another helping of food in his mouth. Her threat didn't faze him. He knew it was empty.

"Indigo . . ." Saxon said in a motherly, tender tone that clawed at Indigo's insides because it always had a way of dismantling her defenses, causing her to divulge more than she wished.

"Saxon, don't start." She was smoothing her hand over the polka-dotted onesies, trying to free them of the wrinkles that had set in from being bunched up. "We're not going there, remember?" She peeked at her sister with a pointed look.

"See, that's your problem right there." Saxon sternly jabbed her finger at her. "You don't want anyone's help. I could set you up with a great guy right now." She snapped her fingers as if it was going to be that simple.

"Mm-hmm, she getting more stubborn in her old age," Harrison added with a nod of his head. "I have a few homeboys that have some relationship potential."

"I can find my own dates, thank you," Indigo told them.

Saxon shook her head. "That's how you ended up with Corey."

"Which one was Corey?" Harrison tapped his chin with the licked-clean spoon. "The college boyfriend that had the girl back home?"

Saxon shook her head. "That was Darius. Corey's the one she dated in high school; you know . . ." She snapped her fingers at Harrison as if it was going to help him remember. "The one that got her community service."

"Oh!" Harrison threw his head back. "Corey Hall."

"I'm sitting right here." Indigo frowned at them. "So, can we not do this?"

"Maybe we should." Saxon pushed her back against the soft cushion of the cream couch. "Then maybe you'll see that you need to let someone help you find love because your picker is broken."

"Is not." Indigo drummed her manicured nails on the raw wood coffee table. "There's just an abundance of lames out there."

She thought about the gold-toothed father of six who'd asked her out while she was pumping gas last week.

"I mean, maybe she's right because you did pick Ian." Harrison scooted to the end of his chair. "Or should we say Christian Ross or Michael Earnest? What name is he going by now?"

"His government name is Jason Nelson," Saxon said with a sad quirk on her lips.

"A girl dates one con man and she gets branded." Indigo slapped her hand on the table, feeling a little heated. "I don't keep bringing up y'all's tragic little trysts."

Harrison pointed his spoon at himself. "Because we don't let our failed relationships define us, but you—"

"I what, Harris!" Indigo seethed, jumping to her feet. "I ejected myself out of the dating field because I'm tired of getting hurt. You think it's fun to fall in love with a guy, start planning a wedding, only to find out later that he isn't who he says he is? You think that shit's easy to rebound from?"

It wasn't, but it had forced her to subtract her focus on her social life and add to her business endeavors. Twenty-six had been a wild time for her, but it had been lucrative.

"Then what about Tate?" Saxon interjected. "Are we going to talk about that one or—"

"You know what—" Indigo snatched her purse off the armchair and slipped on her shoes. "I'm out!" She marched toward the door and flung it open. A gust of humid air smacked into her face. Out of all her relationships, that was the only one she couldn't handle reliving. "Let the Hamburglar help you organize your baby shit." And with that, she slammed the door behind her.

Chapter 2

"They don't know what they're talkin' about," Indigo mumbled to herself as she steered her dark-green 1951 Chevy pickup down the idyllic neighborhood street. The community of Forestwood claimed its name from the robust pine trees scattered throughout the planned preserve of contemporary homes and manicured lawns.

Sure, her dating history was riddled with mistakes, but every one had also taught her a lesson. Showed her what she didn't want in a relationship. And her picker wasn't broken. She'd picked a good one once. Too bad her younger self hadn't known that at the time.

And yeah, she said no to a lot of the guys who asked her out. Scratch that. She said no to *all* the guys who asked her out.

She was exhausted from the dating game, from picking the wrong guy to give her heart, mind, and sometimes body to. From Corey to Darius to Jason, she'd found that her luck with love sucked. However, she didn't want to be single for the rest of her life, even though she had no problems with singledom; the years of spending time with just herself had been rewarding and beneficial. Besides growing her business, building a strong social media presence, paying off her debts, and blossoming her savings account, she'd formulated a self-care routine to recharge her battery and restore her soul after her busy workweek. The past four years had been productive, but it was time for a change.

She could feel it in her gut. Her heart was ready; the pain of heartache had subsided, and she no longer flinched at the thought of investing time in another guy who wasn't her dad, brother, or best friend. Especially her best friend, Tate, who had become more than a friend when they were eighteen. Maybe it was Usher, Lil Jon, and Ludacris that had convinced them that they could be lovers also. But it had been a mistake that had taken years to correct.

Now she was ready to bid the single stage of her life adieu. It was time for her to get back in the ring. The world was full of men, and they weren't all Coreys, Dariuses, or Jasons.

The loser is probably right, Indigo thought as she eased her pickup into her driveway and shifted the gear from Drive to Park.

The stereo was barely loud enough to pick up the quiet storm mix she had created on her iPhone. She blocked out all the ambiance of suburban life swarming around: the kids running down the street playing soccer, riding bikes, or skateboarding; homemakers gossiping on the sidewalk; and couples walking their dogs at a brisk pace.

The clack of nails and soft paws swishing on the car window pulled Indigo out of her thoughts. She killed the ignition and swung open the door.

"My baby!" she squealed, patting an overexcited cane corso on the head.

"We have a problem," a familiar voice said.

Tate Larsen stood almost a foot taller than Indigo's 5'3" frame, even in all the heels she wore. He was in his usual attire of basketball shorts with a white University of Houston T-shirt that stretched across his lean frame and contrasted with his golden-olive skin.

He flashed her a smile that didn't match his serious words.

Indigo echoed his expression as she stopped petting her baby and stood up straight. "A new one?" She took the leash he handed her.

"Well . . . a new couple moved in two streets down . . ." He combed an ink-stained hand through his wavy chestnut tresses. "And they have a Pomeranian." He twisted his mouth.

Indigo scratched the black-furred head. "Gambit! You made another enemy?" Her tone turned motherly. The dog looked up with big eyes as if he could comprehend every word. "You got to make a friend." She patted his massive head. "Tate's not going to be around forever."

"Hey!" Tate dropped to his haunches and flung his arm around Gambit's thick neck. "Don't tell my homie that." Tate stood before Gambit could drag his pink tongue up his ruggedly handsome face and slobber in his well-groomed beard. "How was the baby shower?"

Indigo folded her arms and tilted her head. "Do you think I'm going to die a spinster?"

Tate's brown eyes went wide. "Huh?"

"I'll tell you over dinner." She strutted to the porch of her modern farmhouse-style abode.

The cool air chilled her cheeks as she stepped inside. Her home could've been mistaken for a Pottery Barn showroom if it hadn't been for the pops of purple accent pillows, Black art on the walls, and lavender lingering in the air. Once she kicked off her heels, she headed straight to the kitchen, in need of nourishment. Tate and Gambit followed close behind. Tate pulled out a ceramic dish of pasta primavera from the fridge and let the door shut behind him. "So . . . did someone call you a spinster?" He set the dish on the island and started fetching other items from the fridge. "I'm lost." He stared at her with a puzzled gaze.

Indigo's chic kitchen was the meeting ground for most of their conversations. Conversations that happened between 6:00 and 10:00 p.m., mostly because Tate loved to eat, and she loved to cook. It was a mutual agreement, and she didn't have to clean out her fridge since he'd feast on most of the leftovers.

"Everyone at that little baby shower was pregnant, married, engaged, or in a committed relationship—except for me." Her face twisted with disdain.

Tate switched the oven on. "Harrison was there. He's not married, engaged, or pregnant." He smiled at his attempt at a joke, but she didn't, so he let his smile fade.

"He's the one who brought it up. Then he enlisted Saxon, so they both let me know . . ." She poured herself a glass of tea from a pitcher, wishing it was something stronger, bourbon perhaps. No, too strong. She did have work tomorrow; sweet tea would have to do the job. "That I'm a loser who doesn't date."

"Wait!" Tate stopped scooping pasta into the pan. "They said that?"

"I know how to use context clues." Her mouth quirked to the side sourly. "This is not how I expected my life to be by twenty-nine."

"I think you have a pretty great life." He leaned on the island countertop pensively. "You're a talented, educated Black woman with the best shoe store in Texas."

Indigo narrowed her eyes at him. "Don't use my words on me."

"All I'm saying is, you shouldn't let a man or the absence of one dictate your success." He tossed a green bean into his mouth, gave it two bites, then swallowed it. "Or anyone else."

"I want to be a mother." She spun the glass in her hands.

He was quiet for a moment as he carefully placed pieces of oven-barbecued chicken into another pan like it was gold. "You could adopt. There are a lot of motherless, family-less children out there."

She gifted him a faint nod, acknowledging he was right about that. "But I want companionship."

"You have a sister, a brother, parents, a niece, a nephew . . . and Gambit." He slid both pans into the oven at the same time.

She propped her chin on top of her fist, looking at her baby lying on the kitchen floor, watching all the food with a string of drool hanging from his mouth.

"True . . ." She moved her gaze back to Tate as he set empty dishes in the sink, wrinkling her nose, and she thought of something that would stump him. "But I need sexual gratification." She smirked at the blood draining from his face. "A mind-numbing, leg-shaking orgasm would be nice." She lifted the glass to her lips with a snicker.

She wasn't the type to go out to the club, strike up a conversation, and bring a guy home, or to swipe left, go out for a coffee date, then burn off all that caffeine with a quickie in the back seat. Long-term commitments were her style, and since she hadn't been in a serious relationship in a while, she'd been in a drought. Her vibrator didn't count.

"You can either read the Bible . . . or . . ." He turned on the faucet and pulled a dishcloth off the counter. "Call me up and put me in the game, coach."

Mischief played on his handsome features, making it hard for her to read. Was he serious or playing around? She assumed the latter and rolled her eyes.

"You're dumb." She let out a sigh then added, "You have an answer for everything, don't you?"

He shrugged. "What can I say . . . I'm a writer. We make shit up on our feet." His mood faltered a little as he folded the cloth.

"You still have writer's block," she intuited.

"Like the freaking Great Wall of China."

She glued the palms of her hands to the cold, pale-gray granite of the kitchen island. "It'll come to you. Don't rush it, Tatie Tate."

The nickname she'd been calling him since elementary school brought a smile to his lips. "Now look who has an answer for everything."

"What can I say . . ." She spun off the stool with the vigor of a child. "I'm Indigo Clark!"

"You don't wait for things to happen; you make things happen!" Tate boasted.

"Right!" She slapped her bare feet on the shiny hardwood floor that they'd buffed last week. "So, this is me getting back out there. I'm back on the market." She danced to the music filling the background.

"Uh-huh." Tate's face scrunched up with disgust. "Don't say market."

"I'm back in the game."

Tate nodded slowly. "Better, but don't do anything you don't want to do. If you want to say no, say no."

"Trust and believe." She slid her hands into the pockets of her romper. "If I'm not feeling the dude, he'll get the boot. You don't have to worry about that."

"I'll always worry about you." He leaned back against the farmhouse sink. The golden sunset seeped through the panoramic windows in the breakfast nook, painting them with warmth. "You're my best girl . . . friend."

"Come on, Tate. Let's be real . . ." She grinned with a tilt of her head. "I'm your *only* best friend."

"Oh! No!" He slapped his palms on the sides of his scruffy face, *Home Alone*-style. "The horror."

Indigo laughed. "You got jokes." She wagged her finger at him as she backed up out of the kitchen. "But if you eat up all that food while I'm in the shower, I'll give you a *Friday the 13th* massacre."

"A man eats the last oxtail once, and he never lives it down." He tossed the dry towel on the counter. "Can you believe that, Gambit?"

"Believe it," she called over her shoulder as she sauntered out of the kitchen.

For a second, her steps slowed as she remembered the look on his face when she'd brought up the notion of her dating again. She had her assumptions about why he felt that way, but he had to know that she wasn't going to be single forever. Right?

Chapter 3

An hour before opening, Adorn, Indigo's upscale boutique, was quiet. The quaint corner shop was like the closet many women fantasized about: walls of shoes, a small rack of dresses, a back corner of high-end handbags, and a display case of sparkling jewelry. Raw oak floors, exposed brick walls, and modern fixtures made up the place Indigo had dubbed her second home.

"What did you say you hit again?" Hazel Rodgers, the shop assistant, asked. She looked away from the shattered windshield on Indigo's truck, visible through the shop's glass front door, and back to Indigo.

Indigo stopped counting her stack of five-dollar bills. "I didn't hit anything." She placed the greenbacks in the cash register. "A crazy bird flew into me." The incident still made her heart beat a little faster. The way the sparrow had crashed into her windshield had startled her and caused her to swerve into another lane as she sped down the busy freeway.

"Is it still alive?" Emery, who was leaning against the checkout counter, asked. Emery Cortez was the owner of Percolate, a coffee shop two stores down, and had been Indigo's friend since their days at Crawford University. Hazel, whom Indigo had hired a few years ago when the shop started turning a profit, was Emery's cousin.

"What?"

"The bird."

Indigo shrugged then closed the cash drawer. "I don't know." She grabbed a pair of orange ballet flats off the counter and advanced to the side wall. "But look at my windshield . . ." She pointed to the vehicle parallel-parked in front of her store. "It looks like someone balled up a piece of paper and then tried to straighten it back out."

Hazel, a caramel-hued twenty-three-year-old, nodded in agreement with her boss. "It looks jacked." She sprayed cleaner onto the glass door.

"Something else I have to add to my to-do list," Indigo breathed out as she slapped the shoes back on the shelf. "Along with finding a man to escort me to my thirtieth birthday party."

Her mom had sent her a voice memo that morning reminding her to send a list of people she wanted invited to the party—an event she'd hoped her mom had forgotten about since she hadn't heard anything about it recently. But apparently Stella had just been waiting until after the baby shower to focus on the next big Clark family shindig.

"Find a man?" Emery asked and pushed away from the counter. The corners of her mouth quirked up. "What are you talking about, Indie?"

"Yeah." Hazel stopped dragging the rag over the glass, making more streaks than wrinkles on a pug's face. "'Cause that's easy." She rested her hand on her narrow waist. "All you have to do is come to the club with me, and I'll have you with a bae in no time."

Indigo's flawlessly made-up face scrunched. "I'm looking for a well-suited suitor."

"Not a hookup." Emery cut in. "And you can't find love in a club."

"That's not what Usher says," Hazel rebutted.

"But didn't he get divorced, though?" Indigo's nude pumps clicked on the hardwood as she crossed the store. "Or are you talking about his second marriage?"

"He didn't meet her at the club," Hazel clarified with a flick of her curly hair.

Emery tsked. "How do you know?"

"Shouldn't you be at work?" Hazel frowned at Emery. Their family resemblance shone through in moments like this, the snark in their tone and the roll of their eyes, even though Hazel was three shades browner than Emery. "Isn't coffee like . . . in demand right now?"

"I have employees for that." Emery gestured to Hazel. "Kinda like you."

Hazel pointed her rag-wielding hand at Emery. "I am a partner." Indigo's forehead crinkled, and her mouth twisted. "I am a coworker of . . ." Hazel rephrased, but Indigo slowly shook her head. "I am a—"

"Em . . . ploy . . . ee," Emery filled in, dragging out every last syllable.

"Argh! I can't stand you." Hazel sprayed glass cleaner at Emery. "I'm just here for the health insurance, anyway."

"Don't do that!" Indigo chimed in. She yanked the rag out of Hazel's hand. "The last thing I need is someone strutting in here and busting their ass on my floor." Her parents were lawyers; she knew people would sue for just about anything.

Emery gasped like a light bulb had flashed on in her head. "We have a cousin!" She gestured to Hazel then grabbed her phone from the back pocket of her jeans. "And he's single . . ."

"No." Hazel spoke up with a crinkle of her wide nose. "I mean, he is single, but she don't want him."

"Why not?" Emery stopped scrolling through her list of contacts. "He's a catch."

Hazel shook her head at Indigo. "She lies. He has a wandering eye."

"He's a cheater?" Indigo waved off the suggestion. She didn't want to put up with that again.

"No. I mean, his eye actually wanders . . . like, literally," Hazel cleared up. "It's glass."

Indigo stopped mopping the glass cleaner off the floor. "What?"

"Not Craig." Emery slapped Hazel's shoulder. "Nathan."

"Oh!" Hazel gasped. "Nathan." She nodded. "He's . . . cool. Plus . . ." She pointed toward the truck. "He can fix your window."

"Umm." Indigo fixed the waistband of her blush floral pleated camisole. "I don't know." Resistance formed in her coffee-filled stomach. She knew nothing about this man. Not his birthday, his sign, his relationship history, political party, favorite movie. Nothing. Hesitation made crinkles form in her eyebrows.

This is how it works. Just say yes, the voice in Indigo's mind told her. *What's the harm?*

She exhaled her doubts. "What's his number?"

Emery resumed scrolling through her phone. "I'll give you the address to his shop."

• • •

Indigo decided her lunch hour was the best time to go to the repair shop. It was only three blocks from her boutique, and she didn't want to drive her truck during rush hour in that calamitous condition.

It took her a while to get there. She had to squint through the cracks and slither like a slug down the road.

She pulled up in front of a fire station. *Wait.* She checked the address Emery had typed into her phone, the one she'd let Siri navigate her to. The number and street name were correct. It was the place: 3915 Paramount. There was no sign hanging on the fire station's brick frame to quell her confusion, but a candy-apple-red Chevy Nova in the parking bay caught her eye, so she pushed her nerves down and climbed out of her truck.

Early 2000s hip-hop boomed from surround sound speakers, and chilled air blasted all the skin the spaghetti straps of her top didn't cover. Her lust was genuine as she held back her curls to lean over and gawk at the 1966 vehicle. She wanted to touch it, glide her hands over its hard, sleek body. Her mouth watered as she bit her bottom lip and stood back up.

"Ma'am, can I help you?" a deep voice asked.

Indigo jumped before turning her head in the direction of the baritone. "Umm . . ." Her words got lost somewhere between her brain and her mouth as she let her eyes roll over the raven-haired, cocoa-eyed man invading her space.

Her brain began to thaw, and she spoke the first words that came to mind. "I'm in love."

The man kicked up his thick eyebrows in confusion.

"With this car," she continued, looking back at the vehicle then back at him before something else caught her attention.

She rushed past him, brushing against his arm in her haste. "Oh my God in heaven!" she squealed. "Is this a 1968 Plymouth Barracuda?" Her excited words rushed out as she quickly looked back and forth between the man and the car.

She saw something else, and her path quickly changed. Indigo almost ran into the man. He quickly used his hands to guide her toward the vehicle and away from his foot. "And a . . ." She stopped with a gasp and held her heart. "A '68 Firebird. I could cry."

He snapped his fingers as a smile grew on his handsome face. "You're Emery's friend." He placed his finger near his supple lips. "She told me you were coming in." His smile dimmed to just a little less than blazing. "And Hazel texted me . . . which is strange 'cause I didn't know she had my number."

Indigo turned to him, not realizing he'd been talking. "Huh?"

"Hazel texted that you needed a tune-up, with a . . . winking emoji." The dress-shirt-and-jeans-clad man shrugged. "I don't know what the faces mean, but . . . I'd be happy to help." He held out his hand. "I'm Nathan."

She placed her hand into his. A spark coursed up her arm as he firmly shook her hand. "Indigo," she softly replied, barely loud enough for him to hear over the music, so he leaned in, and she caught a whiff of the bergamot and lemon notes of his cologne. "Indigo Clark."

He stood back up with a nod. "How can I help you, Indigo?"

Chapter 4

Nathan said it would take roughly thirty minutes for his guy Ivan to fix her windshield, and the bistro nearby had the best matcha lattes that weren't made by Emery's baristas. She thought about gently letting him down and calling an Uber but decided to do something different. The only way Indigo would find her happy ending was by not saying no (unless necessary), right? So, she accepted Nathan's offer. They briskly walked to Monay's across the street.

The lunch rush was dying out as waiters collected plates and bussed tables. Indigo decided they should sit in the middle of the establishment to distance themselves from the raucous kitchen and the urban ambiance that leaked in every time the door opened.

Typically, she would've been staring out the window, eyes trained on the cars flitting by while her mind went over her to-do list for the day, but Nathan occupied the space in front of her, blocking her view of the window. He held her attention as her hand rested at the base of a sweating glass of unsweetened tea.

"Where did this love for retro cars come from?" Nathan asked, moving his hand away from his coffee mug.

Indigo swallowed the brew. "I saw this movie with one of my

parents when I was little. *Super Fly*. And it had this song. I don't know if you know it." She faintly shrugged. "'Diamond in the back, sunroof top—'"

"'Diggin' the scene with a gangsta lean.'" Nathan completed the lyric. He chuckled at her shock. "Yeah. I know it. Why is that surprising? 'Cause I'm Filipino?"

"No." She shook her head, and he cocked his head to the side. "I'm being honest," she assured. "I don't judge a book by its cover."

She knew looks could be deceiving. Her best friend, Tate, had only a tenth of his Afro-Brazilian mom's melanin but 80 percent of her culture, mannerisms, and creativity. Even though he looked more like his Danish-German dad—if the man could tan—they had very little in common, which wasn't surprising to Indigo because Gregory Larsen had worked just as much as Stella Clark before he'd retired earlier that year.

"Cool." He sat back in his chair with a faint smile. "I love the classics. My uncle, Hazel's dad, has this collection of albums, and when I went over to their house for birthdays and barbecues, he'd be playing Curtis Mayfield, Al Green, the Isley Brothers . . ."

"The O'Jays," she added, feeling a little giddy. She didn't know many people who had an attraction to things from the '70s besides Tate.

He nodded. "Man, I can listen to those songs all day." His smile widened, flashing his Chiclet-straight teeth. "So, what kind of name is Indigo?"

She wasn't taken aback by the question. Her peculiar name always amused people. "I'm sad to say, there's no story behind it. My mom had a friend named Indigo when she was in middle school, and I guess the name just stuck."

"Um. Well . . ." His eyes drank her in. "I think it suits you. I like it."

She stopped stirring the straw around in the glass, clinking the ice. "I'm pleased to hear that." She leaned over the table to whisper, "'Cause I'm rather fond of it myself."

"So, is your love for old-school music the reason you love classic cars?" he inquired, getting closer to the table and giving her all his attention.

"Well, not really." She shook her head. "More like old-school movies. I spent one summer watching all the seventies movies in my dad's collection, from *Bucktown* to *Trouble Man*, and fell in love with the cars. The was also the beginning of my bell-bottoms era." She grinned fondly.

"I bet you wore them well."

"Oh. I did."

Nathan's phone chimed, but he didn't look away from her as he pulled the device out of the pocket of his jeans. The phone chimed a little louder, and he quickly shifted his eyes to it. A frown formed on his face.

"Your car's ready." He twisted the phone in his hand.

She quickly crunched the small cube of ice. "I forgot to ask how much it was going to be."

"Well, it depends . . ." He stopped and turned the phone in his hand. "It could be free . . . if you agree to let mc take you out."

"Are you serious?" She used the table to push herself up. "You want me to go out with you for fixin' my windshield?" She narrowed her eyes. "How much does this window cost, exactly?"

"Two-fifty." Nathan slowly rose from the seat. Dishes clattering in the back of the restaurant snatched his attention before he placed it back on her.

"Do you think my time is worth two-fifty?" She grabbed her purse and rested the handles on her forearm.

Nathan swallowed hard. His Adam's apple slowly fell and rose.

"I feel . . . like this is a trick question." He massaged the back of his neck with one hand. "I mean . . . I wouldn't put a monetary value on you . . . unless you want me to. I mean . . ." He stopped jabbering when she started to laugh. "What?"

She rested her hand on her cheek, a smirk growing. "I'm just kidding."

"So . . ." Nathan's nerves seemed to fade as he stopped fidgeting. "You'll let me take you out?"

Her demeanor turned serious. "Are you good at taking quizzes, Nathan?"

"I was the salutatorian of my class." Cockiness dripped from his shoulders. "I can pass any test."

"Good. I'll ask you seven questions, and if you pass . . ." She folded her arms, the purse hanging at her elbow. "I'll go out with you."

Nathan pulled his wallet out of his back pocket. "Sure. Why not?" He set a ten-dollar bill on the table. "I'll pass."

"Cocky." She nodded slightly. "I like it." She clasped her hands together. "Question number one, do you believe in God? Does he impact your character?"

"That's two questions."

"It's two points in one question." She pushed away a twirl of curls that fell in her face. "It's not too hard for you, is it, Nathan?"

"No. It's actually easy." He grinned. "Yes, to your two-pointed question."

"Are you in a committed relationship?"

"No." He chuckled. "Are you?"

"No," she answered quickly. "Do you have a criminal record?"

"No."

"Do you like kids?"

"Sometimes."

Indigo shrugged with a tilt of her head. That was understandable; it depended on whose kids you were around. "Have you ever cheated?"

"No." He gently shook his head. "Been cheated on, though."

"Me too," she said, feeling the pain from the past twinge her heart a little for the both of them. "Do you cohabitate?"

"No," Nathan said. "No one lives with me. No roommates. No parents. I have a loft off Chestnut." He pointed like they could see the street.

"That warehouse that was once a sugar factory." Indigo remembered when the place had been gutted a couple of years back. "I've always wondered how those lofts looked."

"Well . . ." He tapped her shoulder. "You can come by anytime."

"I'm sure."

The waitress came by and settled their bill, placing his change on the table.

"You can keep it," he told the college-aged girl, and she departed with thanks.

He was generous. Indigo liked that.

"Okay, last question." She held out seven fingers. "What is your relationship with your mother?"

"I could tell her anything. She was my number-one fan."

"Was?"

"She died."

"I'm sorry."

He shook his head. "It's not your fault. Life happens." He took a step closer to her. "So, did I pass your quiz?"

"You exceeded my expectations."

He pulled a card out of his wallet. "Here's my card."

She pushed his card-wielding hand back. "I'm old-school." She plucked a lavender card from her purse and handed it to him. "You chase me." She let her fingers graze his hand as he took the card from her. "Call me when you're ready for that date."

"Oh, I don't need to call." He slipped the card into his back pocket. "I'm asking you right now. Let me take you out."

She nodded before she even got the words out. Accepting his offer just felt like the right thing to do. "I can do Thursday."

"Then it's a date." He smiled back at her, and something awakened in her that had been dormant for a while.

She was giddy.

Chapter 5

It was the house across the street. Bigger than hers, more suited to a family of four, maybe five, with a lighter stone exterior and dark-gray shutters. She and Tate hadn't planned on living across from each other, but finding a pair of homes for sale while bike riding with her niece and nephew when they were both looking to move out of apartments had felt like kismet. It also ensured that distance wouldn't be a problem in their relationship again, and the last thing she wanted was a problem in their relationship.

It had been years ago, but she remembered the void she'd felt in her life when she wasn't able to call him up and talk about anything, even mundane things.

Indigo didn't have to knock on the burgundy door. She had a key that rested right next to her own house key. She'd spent numerous days and nights there.

Music met her as she swung the door open.

Gambit greeted her in the foyer, where there was only a small pine table. Stacks of mail and a set of keys sat upon that table. It worried her a little.

She knelt down and patted Gambit's smooth head. "Hey." His

tail wagged more vigorously from the jolliness of her tone. "My little boy." She sighed, standing back up. "Where is he?"

Gambit led the way as if he understood. She followed the pooch down the dim hallway and into the dusky living room.

The blinds were shut, and the curtains were open. An unfolded blanket was draped over the chocolate leather couch. An empty pizza box, half-eaten bag of chips, and three dirty mugs sat on the coffee table. Papers with colorful illustrations, pencil drawings, and twelve-point-font type littered the rug-covered floor. On top of the Persian rug lay Tate in jeans and an unzipped jacket sans T-shirt.

She kicked off her heels and sat down beside him. "You didn't go to sleep last night?" It was less of a question and more of an observation.

"I can't." Tate opened his eyes to reveal red lines riddling them.

She leaned back with a yawn. "If you lay off the caffeine, you could."

"No." He rubbed his face roughly. "I mean, I can't write anything else. Nothing new. I'm going to be stuck in one genre. The Zombie Writer is what's going to be etched on my tombstone."

"This pity party is unnecessary." She looked at the enlarged and framed cover of the first volume of his graphic novel, *Chronicles of the Undead: Zombie High*. "Millions of people love your books. They trek to Comic-Con to see you—"

"But I want to write a novel. Pages full of words . . . like King, Grisham, Hibbert . . ."

"You want to write romance?" Her tone rose in surprise. Tate had never told her he was interested in genres other than thrillers and science fiction.

"I want to write about something other than zombies." Tate scratched at his unruly mane. "Romance could be something I could do."

"And you will." She flipped on her side to face him. "Just give it time." He pouted, twisting his face with a frown. "There's an idea in that head of yours." She tapped his forehead, and he wrapped his hand around her finger. "You got this. It'll come to you." She watched Gambit plop down next to them. "I know it."

Tate exhaled deeply, still holding her finger as he lowered his hand to his chest. "You always know what to say."

"Aren't you glad you met me?" She winked.

"Yeah." He let go of her finger, sitting up. "The girl who gave me a black eye at recess. I'm so lucky."

"You shouldn't have stolen my pencil."

"I didn't steal it." He began to smile, and it made her do the same. "I found it."

"That's what they all say. Now . . ." She pushed herself up. "Are you ready to go to game night? Because we have to be there before Harrison. I don't wanna have to play Scrabble while he makes up words."

Tate lifted himself up off the floor. "In Texas, *fixin'* is a word. Just saying."

• • •

Indigo leaned over and whispered, "I told ya."

"Yep." Tate dropped his back against the tan fabric couch that matched beautifully with the earthy tones in her parents' living room, settling in to watch the drama unfold between Indigo's brother and brother-in-law.

"*Swagtastic* is a word," Harrison professed, slapping the back of one hand in the palm of the other. "Get the dictionary!" He rose from the middle cushion of the couch. "Never mind, I'll get it myself."

"You don't have to get the dictionary!" Xavier protested. He brushed his hands down his crew cut. "'Cause we all know it's not in there. Like all your other made-up words." He pointed sharply at the game board on the coffee table.

"Baby." Saxon patted Xavier's leg with one hand while her other hand rested upon her belly. "It ain't that serious."

"There are rules to the game, Sax. You know what . . ." Her hand slid off his limb as he abruptly stood. "You don't have to get the dictionary." He motioned to Harrison. "I'll get it."

"Stella! Where did we go wrong?" James Clark asked his wife. With gray hair that had more waves than the ocean during a storm and his chunky jade cardigan, he brought images of Mr. Rogers to mind.

"Nowhere," Stella replied. "Spelling just isn't his forte." She finished pouring freshly made carrot juice into two glasses and placed them in the hands of her two grandchildren, River and Adira.

Stella shuffled back into the living room and took a seat on the couch next to her husband, straightening her denim dress as she sat. "So, Tate, how's the new . . ." Indigo frantically waved for her mama to stop, but the woman didn't take the hint. ". . . story going?"

"It's going," Tate answered with a tight smile, his faraway eyes still lingering on the Scrabble board.

"Told you." Xavier walked back into the living room, toting a weathered dictionary in his hands.

Harrison sneered. "It ain't even all that important. It's just a game." He fell back onto the couch and slapped Tate in the chest. "When is volume four coming out? I want to know what happens now that they've left the school. Does Mr. K die?" He pulled his leg under him, watching the writer intently.

Indigo leaned forward. "Tate has writer's block," she whispered as if she was telling her brother Tate had a terminal illness.

"Oh." Harrison nodded. "So, you had to drag him here."

"Is that why his words are all depressing?" Saxon chimed in, fiddling with the lettered squares sitting on her stomach.

Xavier leaned over and peered at the board, reading. *"Gone. Over. Astray. Clog."* His eyebrows drew together. "How'd you get so many vowels?"

"I didn't cheat." Tate plunged his hand into the bowl of chips Harrison was cradling. "I'm not the one who took all the draw fours and skip cards out of the Uno deck."

"I ain't cheat, never cheat," Xavier proclaimed. "Saxon just can't shuffle cards."

"Don't lie about me." Saxon punched him in the shoulder. "You cheated."

Voices mixed, everyone telling their own account of events. The flat-screen television was playing a movie no one was watching.

"Are we going to finish this game?" James asked Stella.

Stella shrugged as she watched River and Adira play with Gambit on the floor. River favored his mom more, with russet eyes, full cheeks, and an expressive face. The nine-year-old was wiser than his age, a side effect of intently listening to the adult conversations around him as he played games on his phone. Adira was three years younger than her brother but gave him a run for his money, always having a slick reply or quick opinion for him, a trait she'd inherited from her dad.

Indigo felt the warmth of her mom's gaze and lifted her attention away from the *How's your night?* text Nathan had just sent her.

"Why are you looking at me like that?" She eyed her mom suspiciously, tapping the phone against the bare skin of her thigh, which her knit shorts didn't cover.

Her mom grinned. "I'm not the one acting suspicious. You're

the one smiling at your phone. Are y'all having one of those private conversations during a conversation?" She gestured to Indigo and Tate.

Tate shook his head. "Nope."

"She's probably on Hinge." Harrison added his two cents. "Because she's dating again."

Indigo tsked. "I'm not online dating."

"You better not be," Saxon quipped. "I don't need you becoming an episode of *Criminal Minds*."

"You mean *Dateline*," Harrison corrected.

"Not everyone who does online dating is a serial killer," Tate said.

Harrison, Saxon, and Indigo all glanced at each other, and then Xavier added, "But they could be."

James chuckled with a shake of his head. "I don't care where you meet any person you're thinking of dating, I'm still running a background check."

"Daddy," Indigo hissed. "You can't just invade someone's privacy like that."

He humphed, taking a long sip of his ginger ale, and Indigo knew that she wouldn't change his mind on anything. He was still going to vet anyone his children dated. Ever since the con artist, being proactive was a must.

"So, is this person going to be your date for your thirtieth?" Stella rested her back against the couch and crossed her legs in one fluid motion. "Or is this something for fun?"

Indigo shrugged. "I don't know. It could be both." She glanced down at her phone, hoping Nathan didn't think her not replying was a sign she'd lost interest. "But having fun is a valid reason to do anything."

"I love fun," Tate stated, gifting her with a smile.

Stella's mouth tipped up, but humor didn't swell in her eyes. "But at y'all's age, it's time to get serious. Don't you think?"

"Stel, they're twenty-nine," James said, angling his body toward his wife. "Let them have some fun. Life tends to happen naturally when you don't try to follow rigorous lists and checkpoints."

"Absolutely." Indigo gave her dad a look of appreciation, and he gave her a subtle nod. "I'm opening myself up to possibilities again. Isn't that enough?"

"As long as you're happy, I'm happy too." Her mom gave her a genuine smile. "Now, can we finish the game?"

"Yeah," Xavier started, "when Harrison learns to spell."

"That's what spell-check is for," Harrison informed them. "Let's play Spades instead."

As Harrison and Tate cleared away the Scrabble board and letters and Xavier went to get a deck of cards, Indigo refocused on her phone to reply to Nathan's text.

Chapter 6

The next day, the crowd inside Adorn made Indigo swell with contentment and pride: the Summer Sandal Sale was always a great day. Customers fawned over shoes, tried on shoes, and modeled shoes as their friends searched for pairs of their own.

Lula, a blue-haired college student who worked afternoon shifts, was trying to pull a shoe off a woman's swollen foot.

Then Indigo noticed the crinkle of Hazel's eyebrows and the frustration of her clenched jaw, probably fighting hard to hold back blunt words from bouncing off her tongue. Hazel quickly gestured for her to come over.

The man standing across from Hazel at the register caused Indigo to pause: a delicious umber man in a navy suit, with a fresh fade and an immaculate beard. She swallowed and walked up to the counter.

"How may I help you, Mr. . . ." She gestured for him to supply her with his name.

"Simpson," he replied with a velvety voice that could give Barry White a run for his money.

"How may I help you, Mr. Simpson?"

Mr. Simpson pushed the signature Adorn bag—lavender with the store's name italicized in gold—over to her. "I need a refund."

"Okay." She held out her hand. "All I need is your receipt."

Hazel took out a shoebox and shook out the paper shopping bag. "He lost it." She set the bag on the counter. "I told him we needed the receipt."

"I didn't lose it," he corrected. "I misplaced it."

Indigo held out her hands. "There's no need to get upset. We can work this out."

"By giving me my money back."

"We don't give refunds without receipts." She settled her hands at the base of the bag. She didn't remember making this sale. She would have especially remembered seeing this Tom Ford–suited man. "I can give you store credit."

"Store credit!" he barked. "What the hell am I going to do with store credit at this fucking store?"

"I don't know, sir." Her skin warmed at all the eyes of other customers swinging her way. "It's not my job to judge the personal lives of my customers."

"Well, I'm not fucking wearing them."

"Can you stop saying *fucking*?" She inwardly groaned since she'd repeated it herself. "There are children here."

He glanced behind him at a toddler on the floor playing with the straps of a gladiator sandal. "I'm sorry. I just don't want 'em. I don't need 'em." He held up his hands in protest. "You can have them. Do whatever you want with them." He backed up. "Burn them for fu—" He caught himself. "I don't care." He turned around and strode out of the store.

Hazel nudged her.

"What?" she asked.

"He forgot his credit card." Hazel handed her the plastic card. "Mr. Diego Simpson."

Indigo took the card. "I'll get it back to him."

• • •

Diego Simpson. She'd googled his name, but she hadn't expected to see his handsome mug on the Stewart & Snyder website. It wasn't just any Houston law firm—it was the winningest law firm in the South. It also happened to be her parents' workplace. It had been her own first job—sorting mail and rolling the cart up and down the hallways, delivering packages and letters to the lawyers. She'd worked at the firm until she went away to college. Then she'd done her internship there and realized she didn't want to be a lawyer.

She stepped out of the elevator, and she didn't have the queasy stomach she'd had every day that summer. This time she wasn't a freshly graduated, no-life-plan twenty-one-year-old.

She stepped up to the reception desk. "Cassie . . ." she called in a whisper so as not to disturb the quiet ambiance in the sleekly modern corporate building.

The woman, who was in her twenties but had already been with the firm for many years, stopped tapping on the wireless keyboard. "Indigo." Cassie beamed with a friendliness that was key in her line of work. "What are you doing here?" She cracked her knuckles. "Helping your mama plan the party?"

"My b-day party?" She flipped the credit card in her hand.

"No. The Oleander Gala." Cassie read the confusion that made Indigo's forehead crease. She waved her caramel hand, and her artfully loose bun bobbed. "It's not until July. But your mama's not here." The phone rang, and Cassie immediately picked up the receiver.

"I'm not looking for my mama. I'm looking for a Diego Simpson," she said as Cassie placed the phone to her ear.

"Hello, thank you for calling Stewart & Snyder," Cassie sang in a flowery tone, "how may I direct your call?" As she listened to the voice on the other end, Cassie jotted down something on the back of a business card. "Well, Mr. Kingston has been in meetings all day, but I can connect you with his secretary." She slid the card over to Indigo with a wink.

"Thanks, Cassie."

Cassie covered the bottom of the receiver with her hand as Indigo began to turn around. "Are you still having that Summer Sandal Sale?"

"All day," she answered. "I'll save you a pair . . . beaded and strappy."

Cassie gave her a thumbs-up.

Indigo read the number on the card. Office 712. Indigo knew it well. It was the corner office with a view of the Bayou City. It had been her daddy's office. This was probably the guy who'd replaced him when he'd retired recently. She smiled and waved at familiar faces, stopped to chat, even said yes to lunch plans she knew would never be fulfilled because court dates and client briefings would always come up.

Though her daddy's name placard had been scraped off the door, Indigo confidently and quietly walked into the office. Even with his broad back turned to her, she knew it was the man from the shop. The same spicy aroma fluttered in the air-conditioned air, and his husky tone vibrated in her eardrum.

"Just tow it!" he barked at the person on the other end of the line. He turned around, and his look of disdain intensified. "What do you want?"

She huffed with a roll of her eyes. "You left this?" She placed the credit card on the fastidiously organized desk. "Didn't want anyone to steal it. You might be in an even shittier mood than you are now."

"How kind." He slapped the phone receiver back down on the base. "Do you need anything else?"

"No. I don't." She glanced around him at the view bathed in the blazing sun. It was a steamy ninety outside, and she knew it was going to be a blistering summer. She padded her way to the floor-to-ceiling windows that wrapped the office.

"What are you doing?" He gawked at her with annoyance.

"Burger. Fries. And a salted caramel milkshake . . ." She pulled in a deep breath, placing her hands on her waist, where she could feel a sliver of skin under her orange crop top. The glass buildings, the murky water resting in the bayou, and the jogging, bicycling people who looked like humanoid fleas reminded her of her youth. "Dawn in this office is the stuff memories are made of."

Diego rolled his shoulders before massaging his neck. "What . . . You used to work here?"

"No." She looked over her shoulder. "My—"

Cassie dashed into the room, frantic and out of breath. "Indigo!" She inhaled deeply. "Your truck is being towed!"

"What?" She ran out after her.

"You're *that* Indigo?" Diego called after her, but the words were lost, because the women were already darting down the hallway . . . in heels, no less.

Chapter 7

Indigo reached the parking garage out of breath and barefoot. She'd taken off her shoes as she got back in the elevator, but it wasn't because of a sore heel or because they hampered her gait. She'd ripped them off her pedicured feet because her ankle had twisted like a corkscrew when she rounded the corner.

"Wait!" she yelled at the man in coveralls, a cigarette dangling casually from his mouth. Her stomach lurched from the sight of her baby hoisted midway in the air. Or was it the throbbing in her ankle? She couldn't decipher between the pains. "That's my truck!"

"Sir, there's been a misunderstanding." Cassie spoke calmly with her sugary, can-convince-a-drug-dealer-to-buy-aspirin-off-her tone. "This is her car. This space used to be her dad's parking spot."

"Yeah," she grunted as she finished crossing the dimly lit parking garage and finally reached them. "His name is still on the sign." She pointed at the blue sign on the concrete wall that read JAMES CLARK.

"I don't care. Once it's hooked, it's mine." The tow truck driver, built like a bamboo tree with the face of a snapping turtle, removed the cigarette from his lips. Smoke wisped from his mouth. "Or you can pay the drop fee."

"How much is the drop fee?" Indigo's voice shook as she tried to balance her body weight on one leg.

"Two-seventy-five," he spat out before sticking the cigarette back in his mouth.

"Two-seventy-five!" the women simultaneously barked.

Indigo groaned and clenched her fist. "You expect me to pay you to get my truck back when it's still in the parking spot?"

"I damn well do." His voice was muffled as he spoke around the dwindling cigarette. "I put in work, and I gets paid for it."

"You put in work." She leaned on Cassie's shoulder. Her healthy leg was getting tired, and the pulsating pain in her wounded ankle was getting to her.

"Sorry, man." There was that deep voice that was becoming the bane of Indigo's existence. She looked over her shoulder as Diego approached. She rolled her eyes as he sidled up to her. "It's my mistake. I didn't know that this car belonged to someone in the Clark family."

"I don't care if it was a misunderstanding or a mistake." The tow truck driver plucked the cigarette away, spraying ash. "This truck is locked and hooked, and if you don't pay the two-seventy-five, it's coming with me."

She peeled back the flap on her clutch. "Do you take debit cards?"

"Hell no!" the tow truck driver responded.

Diego dug for his wallet in his back pocket. "What about credit? Visa?"

"Visa may be everywhere you want to be . . . but not here," the tow truck driver stoically informed Diego. "Not here, bruh." Cassie laughed but killed it when they all looked at her. "Y'all ain't got no cash?" He gestured to them, in their smart wardrobes and precious jewelry.

"Not on me," Indigo replied. "No one carries money on them like that anymore."

"Well . . ." The tow truck driver backed up to his truck door. "They should."

The three of them watched the driver climb into the cab of his truck, start his engine, and roll out of the lot, carrying the green pickup with him.

"I'm sorry." Diego expressed his feelings with clasped hands and a less rigid face. "I didn't know you were Indigo Clark, James Clark's daughter. Plus . . ." He gestured in the direction of the tow truck. "Who'd have guessed you'd be driving that kind of vehicle?"

"What is that supposed to mean?" She looped her arm around Cassie's shoulders. "I should be driving a Toyota Camry because I'm a girl?"

"Hey!" Cassie chirped. "I drive a Toyota Camry."

She quirked her head Cassie's way. "And it is very . . . dependable." She turned back to Diego. "You freak out at my store. You get my truck towed. My ankle is probably sprained." She looked down at the appendage, which was swollen tight like a sausage. "And you insult me. Where the hell did you come from?"

"LA," Cassie answered.

"I'm originally from Dallas," Diego corrected her. "I went to law school in California."

Indigo moaned, the pain intensifying. "Cassie, can you take me to the hospital?"

The receptionist shook her head. "Can't." She pulled Indigo's arm from around her shoulders. "I shouldn't even be away from the phones this long."

"Okay." Indigo exhaled deeply, trying to balance her weight

again. "I'll just wait until my mama gets back. Can you help me to her office?"

"Sure." She reached for Indigo's arm again.

"This is stupid," Diego said. "I'll take you." He took hold of her arm before Cassie could.

Indigo quickly pulled her arm away. "I'm not going anywhere with you!"

"So, you want to sit here and wait till your ankle swells up like an elephant's trunk." Diego peered down at her tender limb.

She shrugged. "I'll take my chances."

"No, you won't." He grabbed her by the waist and hoisted her over his shoulder.

• • •

"You should be next." Diego lifted Indigo's purse out of the chair and sat down. "Unless a woman in labor or gunshot victim comes in." He set the purse in his lap. "Is it still hurting?"

Indigo's ankle was elevated on a chair and covered with a cold pack. She rolled her eyes at his concern then surveyed the faces sprinkled throughout the hospital waiting room. Some had been in there as long as her, which had been—she checked the wall clock by the TV, currently on the Weather Channel—two hours and counting.

Two-plus hours. Indigo was away from her store in the middle of the biggest sale of the season. Granted, she was only a little concerned. She knew Hazel could make a sale, but the girl didn't have the most patience with unruly customers. Then again, Indigo hadn't gotten any calls, so things must've been going smoothly, or Lula was running interference.

She exhaled the tension that was starting to bubble under the surface of her chill exterior.

Diego undid the button of his suit coat. "At least the swelling is going down." He rubbed his hand down his pin-striped tie. "That's a good sign."

"A good sign of what?" she sneered.

"That it's not broken."

"I know it's not broken."

"How?" He twisted his body toward her, placing his arm on their shared armrest. "Are you a doctor?"

"No." She moved her arm off the armrest. "Are you?"

He peered at the arm she'd moved away from his. "Look, I said I was sorry." She kept her eyes trained on the television. "It was a mistake. Your dad's parking spot is mine now, and when Bobby told me someone was parked in it, towing it was the best option."

"Why wasn't your car parked in the spot?"

"Because Bobby took it to the car wash." He confiscated both armrests while widening his manspreading. "Not that you need an explanation."

"I don't."

"'Cause maybe if you were wearing practical shoes, we wouldn't be in this predicament. My ex-girlfriend had poor taste in footwear too."

"Indie!" The calling of her nickname made both of them whip their heads in the same direction—to the hallway next to the nurse's station. "What the hell did you do?" Tate stepped quickly toward her.

"You didn't have to come all the way up here." When she'd texted him that she was on her way to the hospital, she probably should've let him know it wasn't really an emergency. "And I didn't do anything." She pulled herself up in the chair. "It's this jackass's fault." She jabbed her thumb toward Diego.

Tate's look of confusion intensified on his bearded face. "Diego?"

Diego leaped from his chair. "Tate motherfuckin' Larsen!" The men locked hands and embraced each other in a half hug with two pats on the back. "How long has it been?"

"What. The. Hell." Indigo switched her stunned gaze between the two men. "Y'all know each other?"

"Yeah." Tate nodded cheerfully.

"We went to college together," Diego elaborated, then quickly turned back to Tate. "Lived in the same dorm."

Tate went on, "Xavier was our RA. I thought you were never coming back to Texas."

Indigo's gaze ping-ponged between the two of them as they caught up.

"I wasn't, but—" Diego looked at her, and she averted her eyes, prompting him to smirk. "I was hunting for a firm I could advance in, and Xavier told me about Stewart & Snyder."

Indigo toyed with her lotus ring, wondering what qualities Diego shared with her dad that had convinced the hiring board that he was a worthy replacement; he'd have to be hardworking, intelligent, and persistent.

"The way you grind I'm sure you'll be partner in no time," Tate said.

A nurse by the nurse's station shouted, "Indigo Clark!"

"Right here." Indigo waved then grabbed her purse and started limping toward the nurse.

"Let me . . ." Diego hopped up and hustled to her side, "help you."

"I got it." She batted his hand away. "My friend's here. You can go back to my dad's office."

"What did you do?" Tate asked Diego as Indigo let the nurse assist her toward the examination room.

Diego sighed. "Got her truck towed."

• • •

With crutches and a limp, Indigo didn't return home in the same condition as she'd left. The amount of exertion it took to hobble from the driveway to her comfortable couch made her appreciate a best friend with a flexible schedule. Tate not only gave her a ride home, he also got her the crutches, picked up her pain meds from the pharmacy, coordinated a tow truck to deliver her truck to her house, and fed Gambit.

"They ran out of chicken egg rolls," Tate announced, entering the room. He hustled to the coffee table with the grease-stained paper bag. "So, they gave us shrimp and four extra vegetarian."

"Uh-huh." Indigo let out a yawn. She blinked dazedly at him, then dropped her scarf-wrapped head against the pillow, emitting another yawn, this one louder.

"Did you . . ." He eyed her curiously then glanced at the prescription pill bottle on the coffee table. "You can't take those on an empty stomach." His voice took on a parental tone, and she couldn't fight her chuckle. "It won't be funny when your stomach's upset." The paper bag rustled as he opened it, causing Gambit's head to pop up from his lounging spot on the floor next to Indigo.

"My ankle is legit throbbing." Her wounded limb was wrapped tight in a bandage, elevated on several of her decorative pillows and topped with a cold compress. "It was giving me a headache." She pouted.

"Here," Tate said, producing a crispy golden-brown egg roll. "Eat this while I get plates."

Indigo ordered Gambit to his bed before taking the napkin-wrapped egg roll. She crunched into the appetizer while scanning through Netflix for something to watch as they ate. She had Gambit's full attention as the sun cast the living room in a mellow orange. The pooch didn't care that the day was turning into evening, but he did sit up at attention on his fluffy pillow when Tate reappeared in the room as if one of the plates in the man's hands was for him.

"Hell no. Don't put that on," Tate groaned, viewing what was queued up on the flat-screen.

"I thought you liked magic." She flipped away from the series that had brought disgust to his features and settled on a genre that they both enjoyed: thrillers.

"I do." He scooped a generous helping of shrimp fried rice onto the plate. "I just oppose shows without plots. Is that enough?"

"More than enough," she answered, pushing herself up, trying not to disturb her impaired appendage. Between herself and her canine friend, she didn't know whose mouth watered the most as the room filled with aromatic notes of ginger and garlic. The last time she'd eaten was a quick breakfast of an almond butter–slathered bagel.

He sat the plate in her lap, and it took her a moment to decide if she wanted the fried rice, Mongolian beef, or garlic ginger chicken pot stickers first. She chose the fried rice. The soy sauce–coated egg, scallion, shrimp, and rice caressed her tongue as she chewed.

Once she swallowed, she inquired, "You've never talked about a friend from college named Diego. How come?"

"Because," Tate said, mixing the Mongolian beef and jasmine rice, "he's not a friend. Just a guy I went to college with who happened to live in the same dorm as Xavier and me. We were all prelaw and hung out a few times, but nothing special."

"Hmm," she said around a mouthful of pot sticker.

"What does that mean?" he asked, moving the spoon to his mouth. "Indie, don't tell me you like him."

She scoffed. "No. He's an arrogant ass . . . but he is fine, though."

"Indigo." His tone was serious as he trained his attention on her completely. "No."

She chuckled at the definitive way he uttered the two-letter word as if he had a say in who she did and didn't date. He didn't. But besides being delicious in a suit, Diego had nothing that appealed to her.

"You don't have to worry about your not-friend from college," she said, wondering what had gone on between him and Diego.

"I'm not worried," Tate said, flipping the fork in his hands as if he had a hard time deciding what he wanted to eat first.

She could tell he was holding back, but that time period wasn't something they talked about, so there was no way she was going to pry. Thankfully, her phone ringing dragged their attention away from the conversation at hand—a conversation they both avoided for the sake of their relationship.

Tate turned back to the television as Indigo checked her phone. It read *Vintage* on the screen, which brought a faint smile to her lips.

"Hello, Nathan." The sultriness of her tone caused Tate to flash her a questioning glance.

"Hello, how are you?" he asked with a voice that sounded far away.

"Fine." Her eyebrows knitted. "Where are you? In your car? Am I on Speaker?"

"Yes." He was clearer now. "I just got out of the shower. Getting dressed now."

Indigo's cheeks burned as scintillating images of him draped in a towel and sans towel as droplets of warm water trickled down his taut physique fluttered in her psyche. "You . . . called me right out of the shower?"

Tate shot her another glance then shook his head as he turned back to the screen.

"I was thinking about you . . ." His voice dipped again. "Or better yet . . . thinking about our date."

"About that . . ." Indigo cut in, wriggling her manicured toes to make sure circulation was still flowing in her limb. "There's been a complication. I sprained my ankle. It's low-grade, but that kind of limits our date."

"Then . . ." he started. She was preparing to give him another day a couple of weeks away when he said, "Just come over here."

"Here . . . as in your loft?"

Tate's head whipped around, and he mouthed, *No*.

She waved his words off.

"Yes," he uttered with humor hanging in the word. "I want to cook for you."

"Cook for me." She smirked. "Bold move."

"What can I say . . . I'm a bold man."

"Well, *bold man*, is that all?" Her food was getting cold, and she really needed to get to the bottom of why Tate was peering at her the way he was.

"That's all." Nathan's baritone hummed in her ear. "Good night. See you on Thursday."

"Good night, Nathan." She ended the call and then matched eyes with Tate. "What?"

"Going to a strange man's house. Is that safe?" Lines formed in the space between his eyebrows as he pointed to her ankle. "And with a limp."

She sighed. "He's Emery and Hazel's cousin, and I always carry a Taser in my purse. Relax."

"I'm relaxed," he said, sitting back in the chair. He drew in a deep breath then said, "Now, can we watch the show, or will you have any more boyfriends calling?"

"You know . . . I might, so keep the remote handy." She grinned.

"Bullshit," he shot back, then the corner of his wide mouth ticked up. "I'm your only boyfriend."

"Male friend," she clarified, and he shrugged.

Tate bit into an egg roll with his gaze glued to the TV. She released a faint hum as she savored a spoonful of food, knowing it wasn't just from the nourishing grub on her plate but from the comforting way he took care of her without making her feel like a burden. She chewed a pot sticker and focused on the show until the medicine summoned her to sleep.

Chapter 8

It was not how Indigo had planned to spend her Wednesday, but Gambit was ecstatic. He raced ahead of her as she took her time that morning, limping down the stairs. Nonetheless, she tried to find some comfort in not being able to be at work at all today. She sipped Earl Grey out of her *Rise and Shine* mug while watching Gambit wolf down his food and lap up his water.

After a long shower and almost an hour spent moisturizing and detangling her curly locks, she threw on a dress and collapsed back on the couch with a bowl of cereal. Some said Wheaties was the breakfast of champions, but apparently, they hadn't feasted on Froot Loops.

"Which one should we do first, boy? Read *The Other Black Girl* or catch up on *Chicago Med*?" she asked the pooch sitting in front of her as she held a book in one hand and the remote in the other. Gambit stood, went into downward dog, then dropped his butt to the floor. "I know you don't want to be stuck in the house all day, but I'm working with a leg and a half here." She gestured to her bandaged ankle propped up on the pillow. Gambit flipped over on his back, legs kicking in the air. "Okay, *Chicago Med* it is."

She tossed the book on the coffee table and turned on the TV.

Hours later, and Indigo was all caught up on the shows on her DVR; the silence in her house became too loud. She scrolled through her phone in search of someone, anyone, to eradicate her boredom. Saxon and the family were at River's field hockey game, and their plans afterward depended on if the Mighty Armadillos won or not. Harrison was out with Tulip on a date in Old Town Spring, and her parents were entertaining an old friend who was in town.

Her phone vibrated in her hand, and she burst with excitement at the sight of the name. Emery's call asking her to stop by was a happy surprise for the woman who hated being pulled into situations without a couple of hours to plan an outfit.

Indigo got dressed as fast as she could on crutches. She shimmied into some denim shorts, tossed on a yellow tunic, and slipped on a sandal.

She'd vowed to Tate that she wouldn't disrupt his work hours, but who'd turn down free food? She banged her knuckles on his door, the abrupt noise echoing through the dormant neighborhood bathed in springtime sunshine. She dropped her hand, looking over her shoulder to see if Gambit was still in the bed of her truck. Yep, he was still there, eating air (or it could've been a bug). She shrugged just as the door's lock clicked.

The door swung open, blasting her skin with cold air. She turned back to be greeted by a half naked, weary-eyed Tate.

She scrunched her nose as the aroma of day-old cabbage smacked her in the face. "You stink!" She craned her neck to look around him. "And why is it so dark in there?"

"I've been busy." He shifted over, blocking her view. "I thought we had an agreement. Canceled communication for the rest of the week so I could finish."

"I know, but Emery invited us over for dinner." She tightened her hands around the grips of the crutches, redistributing her body weight. It was a lie, but Emery wouldn't mind Tate showing up. "And I've seen so much *Chicago Med* that I can perform surgery."

"Not on me." He chuckled. Gripping the loose pajama pants covering his lower half with one hand, he rubbed the side of his face roughly with the other. The lackluster beard on his chin was a testament to just how deep he was in the writing process— only when he was working did he forgo his usual morning grooming and moisturizing ritual. "What are you up to? No way Emery invited me too." He looked behind her as if she had a camera crew lurking in the bushes.

Indigo rolled her eyes at the extent of how well he knew her. "Fine. I took a pain pill, and I'm too high to drive, but if I stay in my house any longer, I'm going to flip my wig, which is going to be quite difficult 'cause I don't have one." He leaned against the doorframe, and she batted her eyelashes. "Will you drive me to Emery's? I'll make it worth your while."

"I need coffee. Lots of it." He pushed himself off the wall, regaining his height over her.

"You got it," she affirmed with an eager nod.

"Give me ten minutes to unfunk."

"You might need fifteen," she teased, twisting her face and fanning her nose. "Maybe thirty."

"Don't push it."

• • •

Eleven minutes later, they were on the road. Tate guzzled coffee, steering with one hand as Indigo played hit after hit, singing along despite Tate telling her she was tone-deaf.

Emery's barndominium was almost an hour from Houston and more than thirty minutes away from their suburban oasis of Forestwood, depending on the traffic. A massive white barn greeted them at the end of a dirt road, surrounded by oak trees that were saplings when the Karankawas ruled the area.

Emery's invitation to dinner had one limitation—dinner wasn't ready when they arrived. Indigo rolled up her sleeves and began washing vegetables while Tate and Gambit disappeared outside, getting into their own adventure.

White cabinets, silver appliances, granite countertops, and a butcher block island made Emery's open kitchen a cooking delight. Sunlight beamed through the windows, bathing the room in light and nourishing the fresh herbs on the windowsill.

Indigo admired her friend for moving out of the cookie-cutter world of suburban living. Her house was her own design. Months had been spent with contractors, drawing up the right plans and determining how to turn a ninety-year-old barn into a dream home. Hardwood floors, modern lighting, a brick fireplace, rustic charm, and a vegetable garden out back made the property Emery had purchased for seventy-eight thousand now worth more than twice that.

After twenty minutes, pots were smoking, skillets were sizzling, and the dessert was chilling in the fridge.

"He really told you that?" Indigo asked her friend, who'd been entertaining her with stories of men on Hazel's dating app.

"That's what's wrong with the world today: not enough blow jobs." Emery tipped a teakettle over a glass pitcher, steam swelling up around her like a cloud. Today she wore a coral sundress, and her chocolate mane was held back with a brass headband.

"BJs for world peace." Indigo smirked. "But that's why I stopped online dating in 2017."

"I hope you don't believe sucking a guy off on the first date is the reason you're single now." Emery faced her, circling her fingers around the handle of another teakettle—this one steeping hibiscus.

"No." Indigo rolled a plump lemon under her palm.

"Good." Emery's mouth transformed into a grin, as if she was the one who got the last honey bun. "How did things go with you and Nathan?"

"We have a date tomorrow." Indigo stopped playing with the citrus fruit, noting the pang in her chest. "He's the only stallion in the race."

"Competition-free?" Emery asked. "Not even . . . him?" Her brown eyes glided to the side, toward the patio where Tate sat talking to Hiran—Emery's longtime, sometimes long-distance, boyfriend.

Indigo snatched her eyes away from the patio just as Tate's robust, guttural laugh sounded. "Tate and I are friends. Nothing more. Nothing less." She picked up a paring knife and pierced it into the lemon. Juice spilled from the gash into a bowl Emery had given her for that purpose.

"But not always. I mean, I was your college roommate, and I still don't know the whole story there."

"I don't like talking about it, but you know the basics." Indigo shrugged. "We dated the summer after graduating high school. Tried to make long-distance work as freshmen."

A hollowness grew in the pit of Indigo's stomach as she kept her eyes on the lemon she was squeezing. The juice tingled her finger, reminding her of the paper cut she'd gotten the other day.

"It was a teenage dream that we woke up from in the most devastating way." Indigo inhaled deeply. "We're in a good place now. I like us like this."

"I want to remain honest." Emery whisked a long wooden spoon in the pitcher of tea. "So, I'll let you know. I hope Nathan's your guy. I would love it if we were actually family."

"Nathan or no Nathan, we'll always be family." Indigo leaned over the island to hand Emery the lemon juice.

"Good." Emery took the bowl with a smile. "I second that."

• • •

Emery wanted to serve dinner outside since the sun was going down, but everyone else protested. The humidity made the air too thick, and they didn't want to break out in a sweat while they ate, so Tate set the dining table inside.

The dining room showed Emery's love for farmhouse charm with a built-in wooden bench opposite three bone-colored fabric chairs. A black-and-white photo of her parents, smiling in each other's arms in front of the Kawasan Falls, hung on the wall. On another wall was a chalkboard with FOOD, FAMILY & FOREVER MEMORIES ARE MADE in elegant penmanship.

On top of the unstained, thick-cut cedar table sat the entrees Emery and Indigo had worked on all afternoon: cilantro lime rice, baked Parmesan zucchini, and penne with basil pesto. Indigo noted that there was a green theme, including the banana pudding, and then she remembered Emery was going vegetarian for the summer.

"We're thinking about going to Cancun at the end of May." Emery dumped a scoop of pasta onto her plate then handed the bowl to Hiran.

"Cancun," Indigo said with amusement. Hiran didn't seem to go anywhere that didn't include him getting paid for his time. "You plan on sticking around the whole summer this year?"

Emery gave her a pleading look, but Indigo shrugged it off. Hiran was an absentee boyfriend, and she knew her friend deserved better.

"I'm an agent," Hiran proclaimed. "My life shifts with the demands of my clients. She knows that." He stroked Emery's forearm where it was resting on the table, and she flashed a routine smile his way. "Houston is my home, but the bulk of my work is in New York and California."

Emery's in Houston. That should count for something. Right? The words scrolled through Indigo's mind, but she held her tongue. This wasn't the time or the place.

"Texas needs to get in the publishing game," Tate stated, raising an asparagus spear to his mouth with his hand. "Not everyone wants to work in oil, energy, or agriculture."

"Technology is where it's at nowadays," Indigo added, dropping a scoop of rice onto her plate as she eyed the banana pudding. "But who's going to be worrying about Wi-Fi during the apocalypse?"

"What?" Hiran fluttered his eyes to Emery, who just sipped her chilled tea.

"She's joking." Tate laughed at the man's confused face, and Indigo bumped his bicep, happy that someone understood her brand of humor. "Austin is our very own Silicon Valley, so Texas does have a little diversity."

Hiran shook his head. "While we're on the subject of diversifying, there's this producer in LA that's interested in *Chronicles of the Undead.*"

"I'm not interested in film." Tate stabbed his fork into the pasta fiercely. Indigo could tell from the shift in his demeanor that this was a conversation they'd had before.

"You'd turn down a multimillion-dollar deal because you 'don't like film'?" Hiran made air quotes as he said the last three words, as if Tate was being childish.

Tate dropped his fork; the clang of metal against ceramic made Emery cringe. "I don't need the money. My bank account is good."

"Oh, I know it's good." Hiran inched closer to the table. "It's good because you follow my advice."

"Follow," Tate bit out, his tone tinged with irritation.

"I think," Indigo said, putting her hand on Tate's arm, "it might help your block . . . on that particular story. You know, doing something different may spark your creativity."

"I am doing something different," Tate countered, but his voice was no longer marred with ire. "I'm writing a novel."

Hiran opened his mouth to speak, but Emery quickly hushed him with a shake of her head.

"But you're still stuck." Indigo stroked his arm with her thumb. "You know you're stuck, and I know you're stuck. I know you're writing a novel because you think you'll be stuck forever, but you're not, and you need to stop running away from it and work through it. Break that wall. I know you can." She offered him a gentle smile, and he nodded along as if he was replaying her words in his mind and digesting them one at a time. "The *Chronicles* on film . . . I think that'll be a hit."

"A masterpiece," Hiran chirped up with a megawatt grin, already counting his commission.

"You think?" Tate asked.

"I do." Indigo's hand slipped off his arm, and she picked her spoon back up. "Just entertain the thought. You don't have to commit to it yet."

He nodded slowly but kept his eyes connected to hers. For a brief moment, warmth churned in her chest, and it was as if they were in their own world. The sensation reminded her of a time when they were more, so much more, than mere friends.

Chapter 9

Hazel practically pushed the last customer out the door of the boutique at 4:55. Indigo didn't reprimand the less-than-pleasing customer service, since she really needed help picking the right outfit for her date tonight.

While Hazel put back any boxes of shoes lingering on the dark-blue leather benches, Indigo selected some dresses off a rack.

In her small, cluttered office in the rear of the store, Indigo tied her hair to the side and zipped up the first dress she'd swiped from the rack—a simple fit-and-flare black dress.

Back on the shop floor, Hazel was buffing a pair of pumps. Emery had arrived and was standing in front of a floor-length mirror, fiddling with the brim of a hat she had propped on her head.

"Eww!" Hazel's face squished as she furiously waved her hands. "Take it off. Burn it!"

Indigo pushed her curls back over her shoulder. "What's wrong with it?" She gawked down at the simple dress. "It's cute."

"But you need sexy. You look like you just came off the *Mayflower*." Hazel gagged, placing the neon-yellow pump on the glass display. "Why have an ass if you don't flaunt it?"

"She has on a thong." Emery pulled the hat off her head. "You want her to flaunt that too?"

She twisted around toward the other woman. "How do you know I have on a—"

"If it helps," Hazel grunted out, heaving an armful of boxes off the floor. "Then yeah, flaunt that too."

"If it helps," Emery parroted. "What is that supposed to mean?"

"If it helps to get you some." Hazel dropped the boxes on the bench in the middle of the store. "I mean, how long have you gone without quality—"

"Don't say it." Emery gawked at her. "That's our cousin you're talking about."

"And he's a man." Hazel held up her hands in surrender. "All I'm saying is, why be on birth control if all you're doing is reading, working, and watching Netflix?"

"I do more than that," Indigo affirmed, looking at herself in the mirrored wall. It wasn't a lie. She was doing more than reading, working, and watching Netflix. She shopped, hiked, and had started growing vegetables in her backyard. It wasn't bumping and grinding, but it wasn't nothing either. She wasn't twiddling her thumbs, sitting on the couch watching the sun rise and set every day.

Indigo took in the black dress that swallowed her curvy frame. "I thought it looked good."

Hazel snorted as she slapped a pair of wedges in a shoebox. "If you're teaching kindergarten."

"It looks pleasant." Emery offered her opinion with a sincere smile.

"Oh, God." Indigo groaned. "I'm taking it off." She headed to the back of the store.

"And this time, don't look for something that looks good,"

Hazel yelled. "Find something that he'd want to rip off."

Emery threw a balled-up scarf at Hazel. "What is wrong with you? She's looking for a husband. Not a sex buddy."

"Whatever."

Indigo rolled her eyes, but back in her office, she pulled on a dress she thought might actually fit the description.

A bit shyly, Indigo went back to the shop floor. Hazel stood in front of the mirror, holding a sequined, spaghetti strap minidress to her body. "You like?"

"Yeah." Emery's eyebrows rose. "If you're working a corner."

Indigo clicked her shoe against the floor, making her presence known.

A smile formed on Hazel's face. "See, that's what I'm talking about!" She snapped with each word. "Get. It. Girl!"

"Okay." Emery nodded. "I don't agree with her all the time . . . but you look amazing."

• • •

Not usually one to show off all her curves on a first date, Indigo had to admit she loved the formfitting burgundy dress she limped out of the store wearing. Thirty minutes later, she pulled up in front of Nathan's building. She calmed herself as she rode the elevator up to the fourth floor. Door 421 was on the left and three doors down from the elevator bank. After three strong knocks, the lock clicked, and the door swung open.

"You're early." Nathan sounded out of breath. He wafted his eyes slowly down her body. She could feel his gaze sliding down her cleavage and across her hips to take the same route back up. "Damn," he whispered to himself. Indigo cleared her throat, and he shook his head out of the trance. "I—I mean . . . come in." He eagerly waved for her to enter. "Come in."

He glanced down at her ankle, catching a sliver of the KT tape wrapped around her ankle, "Are you sure you're okay?"

"Yes." Her curly ponytail danced as she nodded her head and entered his loft with a slight limp.

Tribal rugs covered buffed concrete floors. Wanderlust-worthy photography hung on brick walls, and floor-to-ceiling windows gave a breathtaking view of the evening sky. A song she hadn't heard since her college days tantalized her eardrums . . . as smoke suddenly clogged her nostrils.

She frantically fanned her hands in front of her face, trying to pull in air, but her lungs were gasping, and her nose burned from the pungent haze. She coughed.

"I'm sorry." Nathan patted her on the back, but it didn't help. "Are you okay?"

"What did you do?" she asked through watery eyes.

His firm pats stopped. "I . . . burned our dinner. And I cut myself."

She heaved in a breath and followed his eyes. The kitchen was a disaster. Used, scarred pots littered the countertop, unprepared vegetables still sat in the produce bags, wilting on the table, and a bloodstained towel was draped over a tall chair at the bar. "I thought you could cook."

Nathan scratched his eyebrow. "I . . . may have exaggerated. A little." She narrowed her eyes at him. "A lot." He dropped his head. "I exaggerated a lot."

"What can you cook?" She held a hand to her chest, taking slow, steady breaths.

"Uh." His hand moved from his face to his neck. "I can make a damn good bowl of oatmeal."

"Well." She threw her hands up. "I don't want oatmeal." She

took small steps toward the bar, getting a better look at the mess. Was that a charred duck in the sink?

He realized what she was looking at. "I had two menus. Just in case one failed."

"So, what's the other menu?" she asked.

He slumped against the fridge. "I burned them both."

She slapped her clutch on the countertop. "If you can't cook, why did you invite me over for dinner? We could've just gone out somewhere."

"But your ankle and . . . I wanted to . . . *impress* you." He combed his hand through his already disheveled raven locks. "Look . . . if you want to call it a night, you can." He gave her big, forlorn puppy dog eyes. "I'd understand."

She pointed to the stove. "Your pot holder is on fire."

"Shit!" Nathan lunged and yanked the burning fabric pad off the scarlet burner and flung it into the sink.

• • •

Indigo sat with her bare feet firmly planted on the rug. She leaned over the coffee table, which had plastic food containers covering every inch of its surface.

Yes, he had lied about not being able to cook. He was also the reason Indigo's voice was raspy from coughing, but after they'd opened every window in the living room and turned the ceiling fan on, the smoke had cleared.

It had taken them a while to agree on what they should eat. They'd studied all the take-out menus in the junk drawer like a midterm review sheet. Indian. Tex-Mex. Soul food. Barbecue. Chinese. Italian. There had been some riveting debates.

She didn't want Tex-Mex, she'd just had Thai a few days ago, and Nathan didn't want barbecue because he didn't want to get his hands messy with sauce. After deciding on Indian, they realized something: they were both foodies.

While waiting on the delivery person, they'd stood elbow to elbow washing and drying all the dishes he had dirtied, which seemed like every dish in the kitchen.

It was not a task she'd wanted to do in the bodycon dress she'd had on so he offered her a T-shirt, and she took it. After all the dishes were clean, dried, and stored in the cabinets, she tended to the gash between his thumb and pointer finger, which had begun to bleed again.

Nathan fetched the first aid kit from the master bathroom, and he grimaced as she dabbed the cut with alcohol. She sealed it with a bandage, puckered her lips, placed a kiss on his booboo, and declared it healed.

Now, with their feast laid out before them, the rich, aromatic spices from the Indian cuisine had her nostrils open. She stood straight up, clenching her fist. "I can't do it." She shook her head with a tight, toothy smile. "I can't. I can't."

Nathan dropped an ice cube from his mouth back into his hand. "Oh no. No. No!" He licked his red lips, which matched his flushed cheeks. "I had the Kashmiri chicken. Now it's your turn." He tossed the ice cube back in his mouth. "Buck up."

She looked at him pitifully. He gestured for her to go on, and now she regretted daring him to a contest of who could eat the spiciest food. She groaned as she leaned over the containers. Her hand floated over the entrees. Although her mouth watered, she wanted to fight the urge, knowing this particular grub would bite back.

"Go on," Nathan insisted, talking around the ice.

She stuck her fork into a chunk of chicken Chettinad and

tossed it into her mouth. Her tongue set off alarms, and her throat burned like concrete on a hundred-degree day.

She collapsed on the sofa. She blew out a huff of air, sure fire should have flared from her mouth.

"Open your mouth," he ordered. Indigo rolled her eyes to the side, viewing what he held, and she followed his instructions.

She slid the ice cube over her tongue, numbing her taste buds.

"What's your middle name?" Nathan scooted closer to her.

She crunched the ice cube in half. "Opal."

"Indigo Opal." Nathan played the name out, seeing how it sounded.

She groaned. "Please, don't repeat it."

"You don't like your middle name, Indigo Opal?" he mocked with a snicker.

She playfully swatted his chest. "What's your middle name?" She faced him and folded her legs under her bottom.

"Patrick." He sloshed the melting ice cubes around in the glass. "Nathan Patrick Cortez . . . but you can call me . . . Mr. Cortez."

Even though her lips were burning, she couldn't help but smile widely. "How 'bout I call you Chef Boyar-don't."

He gasped. "Indigo Opal Clark, that hurt." He placed his hand over his heart. "Right here."

She let out a laugh and rested her head against the couch. Silence took over as a soothing R & B track hummed in the background. Indigo studied the sharpness of his jawline, the steepness of his cheekbones, and the stillness of his eyes as he peered at her.

"Did you always want to be your own boss?" he asked.

"No." She decided to break the intensity with a blink and a faint exhale. "I was supposed to be a lawyer. Like my parents. Since Saxon, my sister, dropped the baton, it was up to me to pick it up."

"But you didn't want to?"

She kicked up an eyebrow. "And that was one of the hardest conversations I've ever had, the 'I'm not going to law school' conversation."

There was another experience in her life that would've been a challenging conversation, but she'd never told her parents about that one. Instead, she'd told only one person. That was Tate.

"How'd they take it?" His voice brought her back.

She twisted the lotus ring around her finger. "I played out this horrible scenario in my head, but . . . they surprised me. They accepted it." She knew her dad was fine with her choice, but she still wondered if her mama resented her for not going to law school.

"I wish I had your parents."

"Why?" She leaned closer to him, listening intently.

His eyes dropped to the glass resting in his lap for a brief moment. "If I disagreed with my dad, there was a bloodbath."

"Did y'all ever disagree?"

"Yes." He slowly nodded. "And I found myself kicked out of the house and staying with my uncle, Emery's dad."

She put her hand on his arm, stroking his skin with her thumb. "I'm sorry."

"It's life. It holds no punches."

"Nonetheless, I'm sorry." Her hand slid from his arm to his hand, which was resting upon her knee.

"Indigo . . ." Nathan gazed at her like she was the last flower in the meadow before winter. "I want to kiss you. May I kiss you?"

Her chest rose with a deep breath she dragged in. "Permission . . ." Her eyes floated over his lips, and she wondered how spicy they would taste. "Granted."

Chapter 10

Sunlight showered Indigo's face as a yawn escaped. She stretched her dormant arms heavenward. Smooth silk slid against her cheek as she pulled the sheet over her cocoa butter–smooth skin.

Wait.

She froze. She didn't own silk sheets. Her bedding was one-hundred-percent Egyptian cotton. All twelve rich-colored sets were cotton from Macy's.

She let her eyelids scroll open, taking in her surroundings. Red brick walls; a large photograph of a boat lolling in a placid lake. French doors sealed her in a room bathed in a mist of bergamot and orange.

She sat up, perplexed. She rubbed the side of her face as another yawn fell out. With her eyes fully open, she knew this was not her bedroom. This room was Nathan's. Indigo groaned. She had slept in the bed of a guy she had just met. Her groan faded as a calm quaked under her skin. Nathan felt like more than just some random guy she had met three days ago. They'd talked like they'd known each other for years, and she'd even told him her middle name. No one besides her family and Tate knew it.

She wanted more of him, which was something she remembered herself saying last night after his hand glided up her plump thigh. Was it an inability to know her limits that got her there? Or had it been the melodic music vibrating around them? She remembered them fawning over his vinyl collection on the floor with the tub of ice cream they'd shared.

She rubbed her eyes, pulling her legs from underneath the blanket and flinging them over the edge of the bed.

Read me. A note with cursive lettering sitting upon the nightstand caught Indigo's attention.

She snatched up the paper and unfolded it. The handwriting on the outside matched the inside, and she grinned. There was something about a man who knew how to wield a pen that made her swoon. Who'd have thought good penmanship could be a turn-on?

She ran her eyes over the words as she softly read them aloud. "Don't panic. We fell asleep on the floor. I didn't want to leave you there. Hence you waking up in my bed. If I didn't need to be at the shop early, I'd be lying next to you." She entertained the thought, which warmed her like a cup of cocoa on a wintry night. "I had a wonderful night. Let's do it again." She agreed. "P.S. You sleep like a dead person."

She knew that. The other men whose beds she had slept in had told her the same thing.

Her ringtone called to her from the nightstand.

"Good morning, Tate." She set the phone in the crook of her neck, hopping out of bed.

"Where are you?" he whispered into the phone.

Indigo gawked at the tangle of her tresses in the mirror of the foreign bathroom. She didn't feel like disclosing her location. "Why?"

"You're late, and Saxon's about to blow a gasket."

"Why? It's Friday!" She frowned. "Damn! *It's Friday*. Career Day." She would've remembered if she'd been in her own bed.

"Sax." Tate's voice went far away. "Told ya. You owe me a twenty."

• • •

Indigo zoomed down the freeway at seventy miles an hour en route to her house. She jumped in the shower, untangled her curls with coconut oil–slathered hands, then slid into a light-blue button-down shirt, burgundy pencil pants, and black heels. She grabbed her purse off the hook, gave Gambit a quick rubdown, and swiped a peach from the kitchen counter. She knew the dog had already been walked and had breakfast. He'd spent the night with Tate.

She was back on the road in forty-five minutes, record time for her. She contemplated speeding, but Henderson Middle School was only two miles away. She decided to play it safe and drive the speed limit. She didn't need a sheriff popping up and pulling her over; that would eat up more time, and Saxon would claim the ticket was her punishment for being late.

She wanted to stop for coffee. Her tired eyes pleaded for java, and her taste buds watered as she passed the Starbucks along her route, but she fought the urge.

She covered her mouth to shield another yawn as she strutted down the empty green locker-lined hallway. Saxon's class was on the second floor at the end of the hall.

Indigo stopped in front of the closed classroom door, smoothed her hands over her tucked-in shirt, and took a deep breath. She let it out and muttered, "I'm taking a nap after this."

As soon as she swung open the door, she inwardly cringed. All eyes were on her: Saxon, the students, visitors, and helicopter parents alike gawked at her.

She smiled awkwardly then tiptoed to the back of the class, where all the other Career Day speakers stood. Tate moved over, and she wedged herself between him and a skirt suit–wearing redhead.

She turned her attention to the shellac-haired man standing in the front of the room droning on about the art of dentistry. Once he began illustrating the characteristics of molars, she couldn't withhold her yawn.

"Humph." Tate peeked over at her. "How'd your date go last night?"

"Fine." Indigo looked at the traveler's coffee mug in his hand, and she fought the urge to snatch it.

"Fine," he countered with a nod. "That's all?"

"Yes." She folded her arms and leaned against the wall, which was covered in laminated sheets of literary terms. "That's all."

Tate pulled the mug away from his lips. "It had to be more than fine since you didn't come home last night."

"Okay, it was good." She rolled her eyes at the scowl Saxon shot her way. "Is that better?"

Tate leaned on the wall next to her. "Aren't good and fine the same thing?"

"No," she sneered, then wondered if he was right.

"I'm pretty sure they are," he taunted. "I minored in English. I know these things."

She glared at him for a second. "Then it was a wondrously fantastic night."

"Whoa!" he teased, pulling away from her and almost knocking his shoulder against the police officer standing next to him. "It was wondrous and fantastic?"

She turned slightly toward him. "What are you getting at?"

He held up his hands. "Nothing. I'm just interested in how my best friend's date went."

"Mm-hmm." She looked back at the dull man at the front of the room, hoping he would have finished by now.

"I just hope you didn't do anything I would do."

A smile crept across her mouth, and she leaned close to his ear so only he could hear. "Like hooking up with a girl and, in the morning, finding out you smashed her roommate too?"

Tate straightened with a look of astonishment. "So . . . you hooked up with him."

"No," she corrected, pushing him back, putting some distance between them. "And I'm not having this conversation with you in a classroom full of thirteen-year-olds."

He nodded. "But you're thinking about it."

The room broke out in polite applause as the drab dentist sat down. Saxon stepped to the front of the class. "Our next speaker is the best-selling graphic novelist and illustrator Tate Larsen!" She beamed with exuberance as she gestured for Tate to join her.

Ferocious applause erupted, and even some cheers broke out.

Tate tugged at the collar of his white polo, which he'd paired with khaki pants, a staple in his no-fuss wardrobe.

"How do I look?" he asked Indigo.

"Like a jack—" She stopped, remembering where she was as the preteens looked their way, and she remembered how much he abhorred speaking in public. "Fine." She gave him a thumbs-up. "Just fine."

Tate spun and made his way to the front of the class.

He combed his hand through his tousled locks as he claimed his position in the front. "I'm Tate Larsen." He smiled, the same smile he'd given her when he got into Stanford. "And before I start,

I'll tell you one thing . . ." He looked at the audience filled with eager and attentive students. "Don't believe the hype. Adulthood sucks."

The redhead in the skirt suit looked her way. She shrugged at the corporate woman. "I can't take him anywhere."

. . .

Indigo was starting to detest Southern hospitality. Family movie night was supposed to be for family, not random college friends of the family.

She stood in the kitchen, chopping jalapeños and growing hotter and hotter with each slice. He was there, sitting on her parents' couch.

An hour ago, halfway through *The Five Heartbeats*, he'd showed up. He'd showed up with popcorn, a movie, and a Hollywood smile that made her spit Sprite on her nephew's back.

Who? *Diego*, that's who.

"Thriller or horror?" Harrison asked, standing in front of the TV with a DVD in each hand.

"We want to watch this, Uncle Harris." Nine-year-old River held out a DVD case.

"We saw *Black Panther* last week." Harrison patted the little boy on the head dismissively. "You can watch that at home."

"Don't be like that." Saxon gestured for River to come to sit next to her on the couch.

Harrison huffed and asked again, "Thriller or horror?"

Tate pulled himself off the couch and treaded to the kitchen. "What do you think?" He set the cup on the countertop and opened the freezer.

"That . . ." Indigo stopped slicing the jalapeño and faced him. "You're an asshole."

"What?" Tate pulled an ice cube tray from the freezer and used his elbow to close the door. "I said I was sorry. One Saturday without habaneros in the salsa won't kill you. And can you hurry? Everyone is eating dry chips out there."

"I'm not talking about that, goofy." She slapped another jalapeño on the cutting board as he twisted the ice tray, popping ice chips on her arm. "Why would you invite him?" She cut her eyes Diego's way.

"Technically, I didn't invite him. Xavier did while playing basketball with us. He's not from here. He only knows us." Ice clacked as Tate dropped cubes into the mason jar he was using as a cup. "What did you want me to do? Kick him out? Send him home, bored and alone?"

"You could have taken him anywhere. This is Houston. There are many things to do. Go to an Astros game. Hit up a club." Indigo shrugged. "I don't know."

"And miss movie night?" Tate tossed an ice cube into his mouth. "I don't miss movie night. Just get over it. It was kind of your fault."

She stopped dropping jalapeños in the food processor to narrow her eyes at him.

"Don't get mad at me because I'm telling the truth. You knew Mr. Clark retired and that wasn't his spot anymore." He held the empty tray under the faucet. "You brought it on yourself."

She grabbed a tomato out of the bowl. "I hate you."

"I love you too." He playfully blew her a kiss and missed the eye roll she shot him while sliding the tray back in the freezer. He grabbed a pitcher of tea out of the fridge. "So, I've found inspiration for my novel."

"Oh, yeah?" She warmed with happiness for him. "From what?"

"From you." He gently shook his cup, sloshing the ice around in the tea.

Her happiness dissipated quickly. "You can't write about me."

"I'm not. You're my inspiration. My character's name is Charisma." He backed out of the kitchen just as Diego entered.

"Play nice" were Tate's parting words, but then Diego smiled at her, and she couldn't help but roll her eyes in agitation.

Diego had traded in his suit for khaki slacks and a green polo shirt. He leaned against the counter.

He rubbed his hand down his bearded mouth while taking a quick look at Indigo's ACE-bandaged limb. "How's the ankle?"

She exhaled deeply, slamming the knife on the cutting board. "What do you want?"

"To . . . know . . . how your ankle is?" He looked at her sideways. "That's why I asked, 'How's your ankle?'"

"Fine." Indigo scooped up a handful of tomatoes and pushed them into the food processor. "You can go now." She set the lid on the machine.

"Do you always make your own sal—" The loud whirring of the machine drowned out Diego's voice. He laughed to himself, watching the tomatoes, cilantro, bell peppers, and hot peppers mix into a chunky red concoction.

"If you want a bowl, I'll bring you some." She pulled the top off the machine and let the spices unclog her sinuses. "You don't have to lurk in the kitchen."

"I'm not lurking." He grabbed the tray filled with small bowls on the back counter and sidled next to her. "And I don't like being served."

His arm brushed against hers, and she moved away. "I don't need assistance. I got this."

"Of course." He propped his elbow on the counter and set his chin on his fist. "Then get it."

"I will." She twisted the container off the machine. "Bye." She tipped the container over, letting the chunky salsa slide into the first bowl.

"You spilled some." He pointed to the red line snaking its way down the side of the bowl.

"I'll take care of it." She went to the next bowl, making another mess in the process.

Diego tsked. "I'll do it." He grabbed a dry towel from the counter.

"I got it." She swatted his hand away from the messy bowl. "Go away."

"I'm just trying to help." He pushed her hand out of the way and quickly snatched up the bowl. He rubbed the red trail off the side and wiped the bottom. "See, did that kill you?"

Indigo let the last of the salsa glide into the last bowl. She had a system for things, including the way she prepared the salsa. She cleaned up messes when she was finished and not anywhere in between. He was messing up her system and her method of doing things, which made her burn with indignation. "Fuck you."

The words flew out of her mouth. Granted, they had been sitting on her tongue since Diego had gotten her car towed. But the suave way he spoke and the smug grin on his face just brought out her inner bitch, and she couldn't hold back any longer.

His first laugh was soft and light, but his second was a little louder. His laugh died as he set the towel on the counter and stepped into Indigo's space. He peered into her eyes like he could read her life story. She wanted to look away but couldn't convince her brain to initiate the order.

Diego leaned toward her ear. "When and where?" His voice

sent an electric current through her body that heated the pit of her stomach. He stepped back with the same grin that had made her curse him to begin with. He held up the bowl he'd cleaned. "This one's mine."

Diego dipped a chip in the salsa then brought it to his plump lips. He emitted a slight moan at the taste of the rich, fiery concoction then swallowed. "Mmm, just how I like my women: thick and spicy." He gave her a wink before leaving.

Her face twisted at his flirtatious gesture. Harrison, entering the kitchen, chuckled at her expression.

"Aww, damn!" Harrison mocked as he watched Diego walk back to the living room. "Does Nathan have competition?" He dipped his finger in a bowl, and Indigo slapped it. Harrison flexed out the sting. "Just to be clear . . . I'm team Diego." He sucked the salsa from his finger.

She scoffed at him. "You're nasty, and that's yours. Take it with you." She fanned him away. "And take your little comments with you too."

She didn't care what team he was on. This wasn't a game, and she wasn't interested in Diego.

Chapter 11

"How much longer do I have?" Indigo asked huffily with her eyes closed, visualizing the moment when she could call it quits.

The weeks had flown by; April was gone, May had begun, and her ankle was better, so when Harrison had invited her to work out with him on Friday afternoon, she'd thought it was a great idea before her date with Nathan.

Wrong.

Her biceps were trembling from holding up her torso. Her calves were throbbing from keeping her bottom half elevated over the yellow yoga mat blanketing the grass. Her stomach muscles were screaming and pleading to be lowered to the ground. "Ten seconds?"

"Ha!" Harrison croaked, standing in front of Indigo with his eyes intently on the stopwatch ticking seconds away on his wrist. "Wishful thinking. Try forty more seconds."

"Nuh-uh, that can't be right," she whined with a shake of her head, sweat dripping from her temples onto the mat. "You just can't count."

"Stop talking and concentrate," he instructed. "Thirty-five more seconds."

She heaved out a breath. "You mean to tell me just five seconds passed after I told you you couldn't count?"

"Believe it." He patted her damp shoulder. "Thirty seconds."

She shifted her shoulder. "Don't touch me. It's already hot enough out here as is . . . I don't need your body heat too."

"Oh, she's feisty when she's exercising." He stepped back, peeling his drenched red shirt off his taut stomach, and wiped the sweat from his face. "You should've joined a gym if you couldn't handle working out outside."

"Then I could've gotten a real trainer," she whimpered. Her muscles were starting to weaken, and her back began to dip.

"Straighten up!" he ordered, and she corrected her plank posture with a grunt. "You don't need to pay money to have some thick-neck, swole-back trainer when you got me. I eat cookies, cakes, and cupcakes every day, and look at me." He flexed his arm, showing off his bulging bicep. "Locked and loaded."

"You're stupid." She started to laugh, but the burning from her abdominals quickly put a stop to it. "Ugh."

His watch beeped. "Time."

Indigo collapsed on the mat, feeling sweet relief. She'd been at the park with him for a little over an hour. They'd started with a brisk jog around a trail that cut through a small thicket, continued past a lake where a couple of retirees were trying to catch some bass, and then returned to the manicured lawn.

The cardio emptied Gambit's tank. He plummeted on the warm grass and watched Harrison call out drills for her to do until his eyes closed.

She went over the regimen she'd finished as she lay on the yoga mat, watching some teenagers play football on the other end of the field. Forty Russian twists. Forty squats. Twenty lunges—each leg. Thirty push-ups. Ten burpees. Twenty-five high-knees, and a minute plank to round it off. She didn't know if she'd be able to walk into work tomorrow or, more importantly, how she'd get herself off the ground.

"Here." Harrison tapped her shoulder with a perspiring bottle of water. "Drink up."

She sat up with a grunt, twisted the top off the bottle, and downed half the contents in three big gulps.

"Thirsty much," he teased, sitting next to her on the yoga mat, still nursing his bottle of water. He was a Vitaminwater guy, so it was no surprise to her.

She wiped her mouth with the back of her hand. "I sweated a pint. So, yeah. I'm thirsty." She twisted the cap back on the bottle, watching Gambit roll in the grass. "But if I keep this up, I'll be able to get the dress I wanted."

"Mama still wants your party to be formal?"

She didn't mind celebrating her birthday with just the family she saw every week, but her mom insisted the entire family, even the relatives from Louisiana, wanted to celebrate her three decades of living.

Indigo nodded. "I don't know why she's so adamant about it being fancy. I don't particularly feel like celebrating anyway."

"Why?" His eyebrows knitted. "'Cause you're turning thirty?"

"Just tell the whole world, Harrison." She fanned her arm out, gesturing.

"Turning thirty is a good thing," Harrison stated. "It's either that or death. Do you want to die?" He pensively looked at her as if she would say, *Yes, I'd rather die than get older.*

"Ugh." She playfully nudged her elbow into the fleshy portion of his bicep. "I'm older than you, remember."

"Don't let it go to your head." He capped his bottle and dropped it on the mat. "Saxophone's upset you won't give her teacher friend a shot."

She kept her eyes ahead on the football game just as one of the guys got tackled, and she made a face.

"She'll get over it. Plus, she's terrible as a matchmaker." She patted her thigh, and Gambit immediately knew the gesture meant she wanted him to come to her. He picked his body up and lay by her side. "And she needs to learn not to meddle in things."

"Saxon, our older sister, learning not to meddle." He shook his head. "That shit ain't happening, but if you want to get a good man, you should come to me because I'm the reason Saxon and Xavier started dating."

"You're not responsible for them. That was Tate. Stop spreading lies."

"Lies!" He abruptly sat up. "He might have brought him home for Thanksgiving, but I was the one that got them talking."

She burst out laughing at the seriousness plastered on his face. "Sure, at the ripe age of thirteen, you were playing Cupid. I—" Her phone started singing Curtis Mayfield's "Diamond in the Back" in the grass next to her. "Hold on." She reached for the still ringing phone.

"Come on, X-Man . . ." Harrison clapped his hands, getting Gambit's attention. "Let's go see a squirrel about a tree."

Indigo watched Gambit trot behind Harrison as they made their way to the tree line. She accepted the call and set the phone up to her ear. "Ready for that second date?"

"Yes and no," Nathan blurted out. "I'm in Nashville; my sister was in a wreck."

"Is she okay?"

"She will be."

She sighed in relief. "That's good to hear."

"I'll be back tomorrow," he said as if he was expecting her to say something, but she didn't, so he continued. "Can we do something then?"

"Yeah. Of course." She toyed with the strap of her racerback shirt. "But my weekend is pretty jam-packed." She had to look for venues with her mom on Saturday, and Sunday was her self-care day. "I'll be going to the mall to get some things I need . . . if you don't mind joining me—"

"I don't mind," he eagerly chimed in. She heard the glee in his tone, which made her smile. "I'll meet you at the mall. In the parking lot. Just give me the location."

"Good." She chuckled, watching one of the teenage boys pat Gambit while Harrison chatted with another one. "I'll see you tomorrow."

He ended the call by telling her that a doctor needed to speak to him, and he'd call her back later.

She tapped the palm of her hand with her phone while Gambit and Harrison made their way back to her.

Harrison shielded his eyes from the sun and told her, "That little boy wants to buy Gambit." He pointed to the kid, who seemed to be about seventeen. "He said name your price."

"He's priceless." She patted Gambit's sturdy back as he panted. "It's time to go. He needs the AC."

• • •

"The wall of windows provides an abundance of natural light," the party planner told Indigo and her mother. In a cream pantsuit and with Senegalese twists hanging down her back, the young woman was as elegant as the venue. She gestured to the glorious view of the lawn. "And once the sun recedes, the gold chandeliers will turn on automatically." She motioned to the light fixtures overhead.

Indigo gifted the party planner with a tight-lipped smile then said, "Sounds nice."

"What's the occupancy? How many guests can fit in this hall with the tables, waitstaff . . ." Stella Clark started to list questions as she scrolled her eyes over the white walls, massive windows, and maple floor. "The dance floor . . . Where do you put the band?"

"Band?" she quipped before the planner could answer her mom's question. "Mama, are you serious? I don't want a band. Technically speaking, I don't want all this." She fanned her arms out, taking in the expansive room that was the size of two basketball courts placed side by side. "Why are we even at the Wyndemere?" She enunciated the country club's name in her best posh accent.

"And where do you suppose we should have such an elegant function, Indigo?" Stella twisted her neck to peer at her child, but Indigo was reading a text that had just appeared on her phone from Emery.

Hazel and I are going rock climbing. You in?

She quickly typed, *Can't. With Mom. Then a date with Nate. Rain check?* She tapped Send, feeling her mother's disapproving eyes on her.

She caught the uptick of her mama's eyebrow, which meant the woman who'd reared her wasn't too happy. Maybe it was the texting or the fact that she was critiquing the venue. Most likely the latter since it was her mama who'd asked—well, told—her to come to check out this venue for her birthday party to see if she'd like it.

"This is for my birthday, right?" she asked slowly with her hand on her chest, making sure her voice was void of any sarcasm.

"Your point . . ." Stella glanced over at the party planner only to see the young lady tapping on the iPad, acting like she wasn't listening. "Make it."

"Mama, we decided that it'd be simple and elegant." She started motioning. "Harlem Renaissance glamour, that's what we agreed on."

"Yes, that's still the theme, sweetie."

"But this isn't simple." Her hand fell to her side with a sour taste on her tongue. "Why can't we just have it at the house . . . throw up some canopies and get a deejay?"

Stella scoffed slightly, leaning back. "You want a barbecue too?"

"I mean," Indigo said, smirking, "who doesn't love ribs and potato salad?"

"As long as it doesn't have onions," the planner added. Indigo chuckled, but her mama glared at her. The young woman cleared her throat, holding the iPad to her chest. "What I mean is . . . no matter which venue y'all choose, I'll make it work. It'll be a magical event, regardless."

"You hear that, Mama?" Indigo eagerly rubbed her hands together. "She can do magic!"

"Magic," Stella grumbled with disdain. "I don't need magic. I need you to be able to turn my backyard into the Savoy. Can you do that, Tulip?"

Indigo muttered low enough so her mama couldn't hear, "It's not a shack."

"Yes, ma'am," Tulip confidently affirmed with a nod of her head. "It'll be the talk of the town."

The statement created a gratifying grin on Stella's face, but Indigo frowned. She didn't want to be the talk of the town, at least not for a birthday bash. She could tell her mama had ideas swirling in her head of news reporters, photographers, and magazine editors.

"Let's keep it down to chatter, and we'll be good," Indigo proclaimed, digging in her shoulder bag for her phone as it rang the familiar tune. "Wait!" She pointed to the planner, finally registering her name. "Your name's Tulip?"

"Yes."

"Tulip on Tinder?"

"Um . . ." Tulip drummed her nails on the back of the tablet. "I don't talk about my private business with my clients."

"And you shouldn't," Stella said, unzipping the Dooney & Bourke satchel hanging from the crook of her elbow. "Keep it professional."

"True." Indigo shrugged. She didn't need the twentysomething to confirm it. There weren't that many Tulips roaming around Houston. "Is that all, Mama? Because I have to get going." She clung to her phone and car keys, inching toward the door.

Stella nodded politely at Tulip then took hold of Indigo's arm and walked her out of the party planner's earshot.

"Where are you off to?" Stella whispered with concern flooding her bronze features.

She pouted. "Mama." The moniker came out as a plea. "I'm just running errands."

"Mm-hmm," Stella said. "While you're running these errands, make sure you keep your cookie in the cookie jar."

"Mama!" she squawked. "What are you talking about?"

"I know you're around here dating." Stella pointed at her sternly. "Make sure you're safe."

"Safe?"

Stella tilted her head to the side with a "don't play me" expression. "Your daddy and I didn't raise you to go around bed-hopping and sleeping with every Tom, Dick, and Harry. Be wise."

"Mama," she whined, hoping she'd stop. If she were three

shades brighter, she'd be beet red for sure. "I'm not having . . ." She paused and lowered her voice further. ". . . sex with anyone."

Not yet anyway; she decided against telling her mama that part.

"Don't worry about me." She patted her mama's shoulder. "I'm a grown woman. I got this."

Stella exhaled a deep breath through her nostrils. "Okay. Go ahead and run your little errands." She flicked her hand toward the door. "And I'll take care of this."

"Thank you." She gave her mama a quick hug then padded away, thinking one thing—Saxon was being ejected from her circle of trust.

• • •

If Indigo had to pick one word to describe her date with Nathan, it would be *casual*. They met at the mall. Emery had told her it was a bit teenager-ish, and Hazel had gagged, but it was Saturday—a day designated for the chores she didn't have time to do during the week.

Besides, Nathan had fit himself into her schedule, and since her bottle of Estée Lauder's Beautiful was on the slim side and she'd sat on her sunglasses, they started at Macy's.

After two hours and having visited four stores, they entered Sugarplum's, a candy shop that was a child's delight and a sweet tooth's paradise. Nineties pop tunes pumped through the saccharine air as droves of people gushed about Gushers and cooed over the multitude of lollipop flavors.

"Thanks again." She held up a small shopping bag that held her bottle of perfume.

After the saleswoman had rung up her bottle of Beautiful,

Nathan had surprised her by handing over his debit card before she could pull hers out of her wallet. She'd told him he didn't have to, but he'd insisted.

Nathan was examining a giant KitKat. "No problem." He waggled his thick eyebrows. "I just hope you think of me when you spray it on."

"Oh, really?" She nudged his arm, "Well . . . maybe I will, maybe I won't."

He leaned over, his lip almost grazing her diamond-studded ear. "You will."

His warm breath tickled, and the gruffness that dripped from his words sent a chill down her body that made her flex her shoulders.

"So . . ." She stepped away with the hope that space would dampen the heat in her core. "What's your favorite candy?" She glanced over her shoulder at him, claiming the space behind her in the small, crowded store. "I love Now and Laters."

"Warheads and Atomic Fireballs were my go-to as a kid." Nathan sidestepped a rack of multicolored lollipops and a gummy bear that came up to his knee. The petulant wail of a small child broke out from the front of the store.

Indigo stopped in a corner. "And what about this?" She held her arms out grandly. "Chocolate! Do you like chocolate, Nathan?" She peered at the clear plastic canisters lining the wall, filled with all types and variations of chocolate treats.

"Yes." He laughed at the way she beelined to one of the canisters and grabbed a chunk with the tongs. "Apparently, you're a fan."

"Mmm," she hummed, savoring the chocolate square drizzled with caramel, peanut shavings, and sea salt. "Delicious! Try one."

"I'd love to, but . . ." He held up his hands—copious shopping bags hung from his appendages.

"Let me help you out." She turned back to the canister and dug out another piece of candy. "Okay, get ready for your taste buds to do the Electric Slide." He laughed then opened his mouth while closing his eyes.

She placed the chocolate treat between his teeth. As he took a bite, she scraped her incisors over her plump bottom lip, wishing she were the treat he was tasting.

"Mmm, you're right." He opened his eyes. "I feel electric."

Me too, she thought to herself. "Whoa, boy! Just don't break out into dance."

"We should get a pound," Nathan said, nodding to the canister.

"Oh, no!" She quickly shot him down, turning her attention to the table covered with chocolate bars from around the world. "Not me. I'm working hard enough to get my last sugar trip off my hips."

"Why?" he asked. Indigo could feel the heat of his eyes scanning down her frame. "Your hips look good to me. Your everything looks good to me."

She peeked up at him. "What are you up to?"

"I'm up to nothing." His brown eyes dipped to her lips then lifted back to her eyes. "Just being honest."

"Uh-huh." She drummed her fingers on the candy bar. "So . . . how's your sister . . . um, Brynn, right?"

"Oh . . . yeah." He blinked as if his mind was a million miles away. "Brynn's doing better. She's up and walking, but I'm going back out there to help her get situated."

"She's not out of the hospital yet?"

"Nope." He flipped over a candy bar with Cyrillic letters sprawled across it. "Not yet. The doctors wanted to keep an eye on her after the spleen removal."

Her mouth dropped at the ease with which he spoke about his

sister's serious procedure. "Then what are you doing here, man? I thought she was out of the hospital."

"Calm down. I'm going back tomorrow." He set the bags at their feet and rested his hands on her waist. "I came back to see you."

"You didn't have to." She inched her hand up his arm until she reached the crook of his elbow. "A call would have been fine."

"No, it wouldn't," he assured her, dipping his head until it rested against hers. "I wanted to spend the day with you . . . in person."

She breathed in as her heart thudded. He smelled of bergamot. "Then that's what we'll do."

Chapter 12

"Where's your tie?" Indigo heard Hiran ask Tate as she walked up to them in the graphic novel section of Barnes & Noble.

Tate rolled his brown eyes at the man who had been his agent for more than seven years. "I don't wear ties. You know that. He knows that." He shot the latter statement over Hiran's shoulder toward Indigo.

Hiran twisted around, agitated, and she promptly asserted, "He doesn't wear ties. I think he had a dream or something where someone used one to choke him." She sighed with a shrug.

"Correction." Tate held up his finger. "It wasn't a dream. It was a nightmare."

Indigo laughed, and Tate's mouth kicked up in a handsome yet playful quirk.

Hiran, unlike them, didn't see the humor and sneered. "I don't care what it was. Dream. Nightmare. Daymare." He turned back to his client. "You are a professional."

"Writer," Tate added.

"A professional writer." Hiran slipped his hand inside his navy suit jacket. "Which means you have to look professional and not as if you rolled out of bed at four in the morning."

"I don't look like I rolled out of bed." Tate looked down at his attire—black slacks and a white dress shirt—and then he looked directly at Indigo. "Do I?"

"Uh." Indigo gave him a once-over, starting at his oxfords and moving up to his tousled tresses. "You could use five more strokes of a brush and some argan oil."

"Here." Hiran pulled a black tie out of his coat pocket and pushed it into Tate's hand. "Put this on." He surveyed the crowd of people sitting in chairs chatting as a store employee tested the microphone at the podium, and then he looked down at his watch. "You've got ten minutes. Get it together." He turned to Indigo for backup. "Help him get it together." He placed his palms together. "Please."

"I'll try." Indigo grinned, highly amused at Hiran's flustered state. "You'd think this was his first Q&A/book signing." She refocused on Tate as Hiran wandered off to pester someone else. Tate fumbled with the tie as he fitted it around his neck, but his attention was on the rows of energetic people in their seats. "It's not your first time either, big fella." She tapped his forearm with her lilac clutch, which matched her A-line dress and pumps.

"It's not." Tate placed his dazed eyes on her, his hands still on the tie.

"Hold this." She set her clutch against his chest. "Let me do it."

Their hands traded objects, his grabbing her clutch and hers moving to his shirt collar.

She knew he was a closet introvert. He hated hanging in crowds or talking in public; she was there to be a friendly face amongst the masses.

"They're just people, Tate." Her hands fussed with the black tie, looping it around. She was thankful that she'd worn heels so she wouldn't have to stand on her tiptoes to be in the range of his broad shoulders. "Take a breath and relax."

Tate tapped the side of his leg with her clutch as he peered at the seated crowd. "They're not just people. They're people who are going to ask me questions. If they were questions about my book and its structure, that'd be fine, but it won't just be those questions . . . it's going to be personal questions too. You know how I hate that. My private life is just that . . . private."

"You don't have to get personal if you don't want to." Indigo smoothed her hand down the tie, feeling the hard plane of his chest under her fingertips. She cleared her throat, taking a step back. "It's your prerogative. Answer the questions you want and say 'no comment' to the ones you don't."

Tate gave her a wry smile. "You make it seem so easy. I want to be likable and not rude."

"It is." She held her hand out for her clutch. "You can be likable and have boundaries."

He moved to place it in her hand then stopped. "You're staying, aren't you?"

"Just for a little bit." She reached for her clutch, and he pulled it back, not all that happy with her answer. "I have an appointment with my mama to get flowers for my b-day shindig, and I have to get back to the store; fifteen minutes is all I can afford." She snatched her clutch from him with a little effort.

He smirked, finger-combing his shoulder-length hair. "That's all I need."

Tate stayed true to his words, wrapping the Q&A portion of his public appearance at fifteen minutes, but Indigo wished she'd left at the thirteenth minute. The last question, which a twentysomething book blogger had asked Tate, had Indigo sitting straight up in her front-row seat.

"I heard you were single," the admiring fan, decked out in a *Chronicles of the Undead* T-shirt, started as she stood. "Which leads me to ask if you've ever had a serious relationship, or are you a playboy?"

"I'm single." Tate abandoned his slouch against the podium. His eyes sought out Indigo's, then he let out a faint breath. His answer garnered smiles from some of the ladies in the audience. "I'm not a player either. I've had one real girlfriend . . . fell in love once." He cleared his throat. "But right now . . ." He snaked his hand down his tie, focusing back on the blogger. "I'm just focusing on my writing. That's all."

Indigo peered down at her hands, studying her nails with an uptick of her heartbeat—she knew who that person was. Tate's first love was incredibly familiar to her.

· · ·

Indigo ducked out of the bookstore after Hiran barged to the podium and closed the Q&A portion of the event. She hopped into her truck and sped to the flower shop, and within a couple minutes she wanted to dip out of there also.

"I don't even need to be here," Indigo scoffed around the straw in her mouth. She took a long pull of her smoothie as her mama discussed delivery schedules and blooming times with the florist.

She had learned about the florist appointment weeks ago and had pushed it to the furthest, deepest corner of her mind. She'd wanted to conveniently ignore it, but after her mama had sent her a text reminder that morning, there was no way of feigning forgetfulness. She could have gone with, "The store is so busy; I couldn't step away"—a line that had worked oh so many times before. However, that excuse wouldn't fly since she wasn't even at the store, and her family knew all about Tate's bookstore appearance because he told them things like that.

"I think she wants you to be a part of . . ." Her dad gestured to the metal buckets of colorful flowers on top of crate-like tables. ". . . all this."

Her dad was an easygoing, low-key man, probably where she got those traits. He always tried to see the bright side and the good in every situation, even the terribly gloomy and depressing ones. This time wasn't an exception.

"Are you sure, Daddy? Mama wants me to be 'a part of' the planning." She air-quoted with her smoothie-free hand. "She didn't get my opinion on the floral arrangements." She stole a peek at the arrangement of light-pink roses, carnations, and orchids her mama was fawning over and had insisted the florist replicate twelve more times for all the tables. "I don't even like pink. I detest pink. Pink makes me puke. Purple's my color."

Her dad chuckled lightly at her intense feelings for the mixture of red and white. "If you hate pink so grandly then why didn't you tell her?" His dark eyes went to his wife, and his smile deepened.

Indigo's phone chirped and vibrated in her hand. The text, from an unknown number, made her pause with confusion.

This is Diego. You probably don't have my number. I thought you should, though. Just at work and thinking about you.

Indigo tsked as she quickly shot a text back, asking how he'd gotten her number. "You're never going to take my side," she said to her dad over the pert stems of calla lilies.

"I always take your side." Her dad sniffed a lively bouquet of zinnias. "When you didn't want to go to Tulane, I debated your mama. I reminded her of the pros of a state school . . . having you closer to home. I defended you when you didn't want to be a lawyer."

"Of course, you did." Indigo felt a bit childish at the way she was speaking. She didn't know why she'd lashed out the way she had. Or maybe she did, but she didn't want to admit it to her dad. "This just isn't me, Dad. You know I don't like public displays of . . . well, anything."

Indigo's phone chirped again.

Saxon gave it to me. That's not important. What is important is when are you going to let me take you out?

"You're a private person, like me. I know." Her dad inspected the snapdragons to check that each flower was standing at the same height. Indigo smirked, realizing she'd gotten something else from her dad—his need to have everything precisely in its correct spot. "But your mama likes to—"

"Have all eyes on her," Indigo interrupted, "and bask in the glow." She flexed her shoulders, getting a little annoyed with trying to have two conversations at once; she quickly texted Diego, *Delete my number*, and dropped her cell in her satchel.

Indigo's snide remark made her dad shake his head even though a knowing grin made its way onto his face. "She likes showing you kids off. When Harrison opened his bakery, she raved all around the office, brought his Danishes to the firm every morning, and when you—"

"'Shoes are an accessory that will never earn you a living,'" Indigo said, regurgitating the statement her mama had spewed at her the day she'd told her about her idea to open her own boutique.

"And since the day she said that, she's been looking for a way to show you she's sorry." Her dad let his gaze drift to his wife as she handed over a credit card to the florist. "I think this party is her way of saying it."

"She could just . . . say it," Indigo retorted before sticking the straw back into her mouth.

"You know your mama's not good with apologies. The words get stuck in her windpipe." He snickered as he inched to the end of the table. "Debating is her talent, as well as procuring information, like how my middle child is dating someone named Nathan whom I've never met."

Indigo spit her straw out of her mouth with a groan. She hated when her life became pillow talk for her parents and knew this was Saxon's doing. "It's very new, and we're nowhere near the meeting-the-parents stage of our relationship."

"Relationship." Her dad's hand went to his chin, and she didn't at all like the way he slowly articulated the word. "The use of that word makes it more pertinent that I meet this gentleman."

"So, you're saying if Harrison were dating someone, you'd have to meet the girl too."

"No."

Indigo's jaw dropped, and dismay clouded her eyes.

"Don't look at me like that." Her dad wagged his finger at her. "It's not because he's a man but because he's not serious about any of these young women. But you're looking for a husband, and I just don't want you to get hurt again."

"Me neither." The words slipped from her mouth before she even knew it, maybe because they were true and a fear she'd been grappling with since she'd started dating again. "I'm just not ready yet. I want to be sure before I take that step. I don't want to waste anyone's time and get everyone's hopes up." She pulled on the straw. All this emotional spewing made her thirsty. "I'm just dating, Daddy, chill."

"Okay. I'll give you time, and maybe you'll see what I've always known." Her dad plucked a pale-purple ranunculus from one of the bouquets and made his way back to her.

"What?" she asked, taking her favorite flower from her dad.

Her dad spoke warmly. "Sometimes the thing we need, what's best for us, is right in front of our eyes, but the simpleness of it bewilders our complex minds." He tapped her chin. "Now, let me go get your mama before she buys this entire store."

Indigo stroked her thumb over the ranunculus's crepe-like petals, pondering her dad's words, knowing who and what he was referring to. The twist of her gut brought a name to mind, but the fear prevented her from even traveling down that road. It was a no-go, that person . . . he was not an option. Not anymore.

• • •

Adorn was busy when she arrived, and she was thankful for the distraction. Time flew by, and before she knew it, the store was closed, the sun was sinking, and she'd swapped her fashionable outfit for some yoga pants and a Texas Southern University shirt.

Just as Indigo was inserting her Fire Stick into the docked flat-screen TV that usually supplied Adorn with soundscapes and music, knuckles rapped against the glass door.

She started but relaxed when she saw who was there.

Indigo unlocked the door and swung it open. "Baby!" She dropped to her haunches and hugged an excited Gambit.

"He grew tired of waiting for you," Tate said as he closed the door and locked it, "while you set up your little kids' corner." He gestured to the metallic gold miniature picnic table in the far corner of the store and the box propped up against the wall that held a bookshelf she still had to put together.

"I missed you, baby boy," Indigo cooed, bending down to ruffle Gambit's ears. "I just have one more thing to do." She sighed.

"What about me?" Tate sauntered away from the door en route to the checkout counter. "Did you miss me too?"

"Meh. I already saw you today," Indigo teased as she rose back to her full height. She pointed to the paper bag that he'd set on the counter that was filling her store with a delicious scent. "What's that?"

"Dinner." Tate pulled out a black Styrofoam container. "I stopped by Shay's and picked us up something."

Indigo eyed the two containers on the counter. "Us?"

"Yes, us." His eyebrows furrowed. "I'm not letting you hang out at this store by yourself."

"I don't need protection." Indigo peeked inside the paper bag and was filled with happiness at the sight of the massive slice of red velvet cake. "I took tae kwon do."

Tate guffawed.

"I can fight." She punched his rigid bicep with her small fist. "Ow." She flexed her hand, spreading out her fingers, trying to work out the throbbing ache.

Tate's laugh gave way to a smile. "As I said . . . us." He opened the lid to the first box. "'Cause you know Mr. Clark would slaughter me if I didn't."

"True," she uttered, not able to say much as her mouth was watering at the sight of the smothered chicken and rice with slow-cooked mustard greens and yams on the side. "Hey, you know, I was thinking of trying something new . . ."

"What?" Tate looked up from his meal, which was different from hers. He had fried chicken with homemade macaroni and cheese and mustard greens on the side. "Taking karate?"

"No." She chuckled, grabbing the remote and selecting the first show on Netflix. Just as the intro to *Stranger Things* started to play, she said, "Getting a bob. What do you think?"

Tate lowered the fried drumstick from his mouth, and his eyes wrinkled. "You mean cut your hair?"

"Yeah." Indigo stabbed her fork into her greens. "I'm not talkin' about a person."

Tate nodded. "I like your hair like that." His eyes trailed over her hairline then glided down her massive curly ponytail. "It's . . ." He swallowed, pulling his gaze back to his food. "It's beautiful the way it is."

"I just want to try something new." She half shrugged, bringing a chunk of yams to her hungry mouth. "You know? Something big for year thirty."

He nodded again, spooning up his mac and cheese. "All change isn't good change, though."

"Change is inevitable, Tate." She tried to read his face. "It's a part of life. Sometimes you can't always prepare for it or plan for it. You just have to adapt."

"You not caring about plans." He turned to her with faraway eyes as if he was holding years of secrets. "That's new."

She glared at him.

"I didn't mean it like that." He held up his hand as if it was an offering of peace. "You know I didn't mean it like that." His tone went soft. "I just meant . . . I love the way we're growing and maturing . . . together."

She peered at her lotus ring then displayed it so he could see. "Isn't that why you gave me this? A promise to always grow together and never apart."

"Yes."

"And always be friends."

He humphed. "Something like that."

They refocused back on their food, and she said, "Maybe you're right." She shrugged. "I should just get a wig."

Chapter 13

"Are you done yet?" Indigo asked as she walked into the bakery. The aroma of freshly baked rye and sourdough bread lingered in the air, mingling with the scrumptious Danishes and syrupy glaze drowning pound cakes.

Harrison's bakery, Decadent Delights, sat in the middle of the shopping district of a sprawling suburban locale. The premier bakery was known for its vegan and gluten-free selection but renowned for its mouth-watering chocolate cakes and the delirium-inducing assortment of seasonal pies.

"I guess people stopped saying 'good morning' and whatnot," Harrison chided after handing a middle-aged woman a yellow cake box.

Indigo sauntered over to the dessert display. The diminished selection of muffins, bagels, cookies, and pastries revealed how the bakery had performed that morning. That was why she usually frequented it between the hours of four and five, when there was a lull.

"Good morning, Harrison," she greeted sweetly, leaning on the display window. "How is your day?" She spoke as if she was a preschool teacher and he was one of her runny-nosed pupils.

"Ugh." He left the checkout counter; the sprinkle of customers who remained were sitting at the canary yellow tables, tuned into their own worlds.

"Is my cake ready?"

"It's cooling in the back." He pulled his apron off the hook on the wall. "What's this cake for, anyway?"

"Nathan's coming home tonight." She followed him, rushing through the swinging doors before they slammed closed. "Well, actually tomorrow." She scuttled around the racks of cooling loaves in her rose gold patent leather Ralph & Russo pumps. "His flight lands at midnight."

"Midnight." He marched over to a twentysomething man dusting powdered sugar over a lemon sponge cake. "Peter, I need you to watch the front."

"Cool," Peter quipped, setting the duster down, flashing Indigo a welcoming smile, and strolling out of the kitchen.

"Peter." She sang the young man's name as she opened the dishwasher—steam blew over her arm as she grabbed a dessert plate, fork, and knife. "You fired Kenny, I see."

"I can deal with a lot of things," Harrison said as he started mixing smooth melted milk chocolate into a silver mixing bowl of buttercream frosting. "But being late isn't one of them. I'm running a bakery. Punctuality is a necessity."

"Mm-hmm." She carved into an apricot-almond tart. "I had to cut some losses last year."

Harrison nodded as he watched her lift a paltry slice of tart. "That'll be $5.50." He held out his palm. "Pay up."

"You still owe me for that time I didn't snitch on you for flattening Daddy's tire," she chortled, piercing the fork into her slice of tart. "You're still blaming it on that raccoon."

"Raccoons have sharp nails. It's very plausible."

"Yeah," Indigo teased. "Whatever."

"You still not talking to Saxon?" Harrison scraped frosting out of the bowl and onto the top of a three-layer chocolate cake resting on the metal table in the middle of the room.

She scrunched her face with disgust. "Ugh. I didn't tell her I wasn't talking to her. I told her she can't hold water and her ass ain't Cupid."

"Same difference." He smirked. "You know Sax is sensitive, and these hormones have just turned her into Jell-O. Plus, she's trying to help."

"I don't want to like Diego." She twirled the fork.

"What about cake-boy? You seem to like him a lot. Or are you jumping in headfirst?"

"Yes. I like Nathan, and we've had plenty of conversations." She stood up straight. "We want the same things. He's thirty-three, and marriage is something he's looking for."

Harrison's icing hand stalled. "Are you glowing?"

She couldn't hide her smile. She clutched her gold link necklace as she peered at the oven, baking more cakes. Maybe one day Harrison would be making a cake for her. Not one for a birthday, a homecoming, or a sweet tooth craving but an actual wedding.

"Indigo." He sang her name in the same chiding tone as their dad whenever she divulged a misstep. "Please, don't tell me you're falling for this guy."

Was she falling for Nathan? She couldn't be sure. All she knew was how he made her feel. They hadn't shared the same space in weeks, but he still made an effort to communicate with her. He texted her good morning and good night regularly. She could talk to him about anything, everything. Text about anything, anytime. He didn't try to solve her problems but listened to her, acting as a sounding board. They wanted the same things in life, and he didn't rush her to do anything that she wasn't ready for. And then there was that smile—the cheeks pushing up into her eyes, jaw muscles tight kind of smile. The smile she had right now.

"Dammit, Indigo!" He stabbed the icing spatula at her. "Stop it!"

She shoved a bite of warm, juicy tart into her mouth. "Stop what?" she muttered around the flaky crust.

"Falling too fast."

She minced the dough down in two bites then swallowed. "What do you know about falling? You've never dated anyone longer than a month."

"Because I knew they weren't what I was looking for." He spun the cake around to ice the last side. "You're in the getting-to-know-you stage, and you're already in your feels. This is how you get your heart broken."

"I like the guy. Is that so bad?"

"No." Harrison dropped the icing knife in the empty mixing bowl. "Just don't get too attached."

"I guess . . ." she whispered.

Her phone lit up. A slight frown dipped her mouth low as she read the text that came in. "Mama's hounding me to make a playlist for the deejay." She smirked. "I'm putting Juvenile's 'Back That Azz Up' on it."

"That's it." Harrison slapped the island.

"Juvenile?"

"No," he said. "Your birthday."

"What?"

"June twenty-third's your birthday." He glanced at the calendar on the wall filled with orders he had to fulfill. "It's May eighth, which would make it around a month since you and Nathan started dating." Harrison held up a finger. "By then you can determine if he's the guy worthy of investing your heart in."

"So, you're saying by my birthday, I'll know if Nathan is the one," she surmised, not fully buying Harrison's theory. Knowing if someone was right for you didn't have a time limit. It could take a day or years.

"'The one' is a bad term, but . . ." Harrison read the apprehension on her face. "I'm telling you what works for me, but you can do what you want." He waved his sticky hands around the cake. "Does it pass the test?"

She grew hungry just looking at the delightful, gooey frosting, knowing the cake underneath would be moist, rich, and delectable. "It's perfect, as always." She spun the cake around on the pedestal. "Duff Goldman, eat your heart out."

Their laughs filled the kitchen, but in the back of Indigo's mind, she wondered if Harrison was right. Should she lock her heart up until her birthday to be sure Nathan was the guy for her? Or should she just go with the flow?

• • •

At the stroke of midnight, Nathan's plane was landing. Indigo, however, wasn't at the airport. She was at his loft. Emery had let her use the spare key that Nathan had given her. It was a risky move being in a guy's home when you'd only been on two dates with him, but she had woken up in his bed after their first date, so she took the gamble.

Unfortunately, his homecoming wasn't heart-pounding or butterfly-inducing. Through a sleepy haze, Indigo caught the shadow of a form passing through the partially lit living room. Indigo rubbed the confusion from her eyes as she tried to remember where she was. Then, once she realized, she belted out a yawn trying to remember why she was in the minimalist loft. As soon as she remembered why she was in the cozy bachelor pad, she peeled herself off the leather couch and stretched.

The gentle patter of the shower was all that could be heard as coffee began to percolate, pumping out the rich aroma of Colombian java. She started pulling containers out of the refrigerator, spices off the rack, and pots from the cabinet, and minutes later, a garlic-rosemary diffusion filtered through the air as sizzling filled her eardrums.

"It smells good in here." Nathan's low voice broke her determined focus. "What is it?"

"Salmon." She flipped the searing fish over. Nathan pulled a black T-shirt down his dewy torso. She quickly picked up the other piece of turmeric-coriander-crusted fish, checking it was properly coated, just as strong arms wrapped around her waist. "Pan-seared salmon." Her voice died, giving way to an inaudible moan as the skin that her backless dress didn't cover met the soft cotton of his shirt.

Nathan set his head in the crook of her neck, inhaling deeply of her rich vanilla-and-jasmine scent. "Well, you didn't have to . . . pan-sear salmon or . . ." He looked at the other skillet on the stove. "Fix green beans."

"Garlic butter green beans," she clarified, feeling the subtle tickles of his stubble as he placed a soft kiss on her neck.

"Green beans. Brussels sprouts. I don't care." He spun her to face him and wrapped his arms back around her. "The only thing I want is you."

"Same." She rubbed her hands over his arms, letting his chocolate-and-evergreen redolence linger in her nose. "But I thought someone ought to get some use out of this kitchen." She smirked to herself, remembering the fiasco on their first date.

"I missed you." He tightened his hold.

Her arms settled around his neck. "We talked every day."

"No." He pulled her closer, chest against chest. "I missed this." He caressed her jawline with his rugged hand. "Touching you. Smelling you." He placed his hand under her chin, lifting it. "Kissing you." He placed his pursed lips against hers, and the French onion risotto was the last thing on her mind.

• • •

With a full belly and tired eyes, Indigo lay fully clothed in bed next to Nathan. The moon painted a glow over their bodies in the quiet comfort of the night. She stared longingly out the massive, blindless window. Doubts and worries illuminated Indigo's mind like the stars dangling in the dark sky. She thought she should get up, go home. This was too much, too fast—too intense, too early. Maybe she was investing her heart into this man too soon.

Along with doubt came something akin to it that had made her turn down a lot of men in the past: fear. It coursed its hand up Indigo's spine, raising goose bumps on her skin, reminding her of all those who had mistaken her heart for a basketball, playing games with her emotions and taking her love for granted.

"What are you thinking about?" Nathan's voice was low but still able to pull Indigo from the world of past loves.

She flipped over, facing him as he was splayed out flat. "Life stuff. What about you?" She knew he hadn't been sleeping since he'd changed positions every minute or so. "You seem restless."

He inhaled deeply then let out a yawn. "Nothing."

"You don't have to 'nothing' me . . ." Indigo slipped her hand under the pillow, letting the cold fabric chill her skin. "You can be real with me."

"Be real." He finally opened his eyes but fixed his sights on the ceiling above. "You want me to be real?"

"Yes." The word came out as a whisper, although she didn't mean for it to. "We've talked about things but not about life . . . not since the first time I was here." She pulled her legs into her body, feeling the breeze from the air-conditioning that had kicked on five minutes ago. "Did something happen while you were away?"

Nathan roughly rubbed his hand down his face, and when he moved it, his eyes were closed once more. "My dad showed up—at the hospital. No one called him, but since Brynn is still on his insurance, he received a notification." He exhaled heavily. "I hadn't seen the man since my mom's funeral . . . where we got into a fight."

Indigo kept quiet.

He sat up and pushed his back against the black tufted leather headboard. Silence claimed the room, holding it in a firm embrace.

She decided to sit up too, but she settled for the opposite end of the bed. She wanted to see his face. She pulled her navy dress back down and set the pillow on her lap.

"He's remarried," Nathan said. "The bastard's remarried." The heat that laced his words stopped Indigo's finger from inspecting the intricate stitching of the gray pillowcase. "After all the issues he saddled us with. He gets to move on. Unscathed."

Indigo didn't know what to say. She wasn't new to family problems, but she didn't know the full story. So, instead of putting in her two cents, she went for a generic response. "I'm sorry."

"No, I'm sorry, " he said as his hand discovered the hem of her dress and brushed his thumb over the stitchwork. "For this woman he married. Richard Cortez isn't a good man. Not even close to being a decent person." He looked at her candidly, eyes brimming with pain. "He seems it from the outside. Put together and successful . . . but he's not. The night I was kicked out, I broke his cardinal rule."

"What rule?"

"I bucked the system. Wanted to be my own man. Go to college and not the Marines. We weren't people but characters in his perfect family, and when we weren't perfect, there were . . . consequences."

"What kind of consequences?" she asked slowly, leaning forward. The movement caused the hem of her dress to slip from his grasp.

Nathan looked at her with pink-stained eyes illuminated by the moonlight, and she knew.

"He hit you." Her brows drew together, as the question sounded more like a statement.

"Until I hit puberty. Then his assaults turned more verbal."

"I'm so sorry," she said, gently patting his stiff knee.

"Ah." Nathan dropped his head in his hands. "I don't want to talk about this anymore."

A few seconds of silence cloaked them, then she thought of a way to change the topic to something lighter. "I played volleyball in middle school."

"Really?" He peeked through the cracks of his fingers, and she nodded. His hands fell from his face. "Do you still play?"

"Only when I'm at the beach." She couldn't stop the yawn that escaped her mouth. "I have a new hobby now."

Nathan grabbed the pillow behind his back and flipped to the end where Indigo was sitting. "Which is?"

"Cooking," she said. "And beautifying people and places."

"Well, I do love the way you cook." He yawned. "And everything about you is beautiful." He yawned again.

"Aww." She rubbed his head, feeling his hair slip through the creases of her fingers. "Is the baby sleepy?"

"Yes." He peeled her hand from his hair and tried to coax her over to his side. "So, stop talking and sleep with me."

"Well . . ." She smirked at Nathan's big brown eyes. "I should be going."

"Please."

"Uhh," she hummed. There was a war raging within her. She wanted to stay with Nathan, make up for all the time they'd missed, but she didn't want to rush. She needed to get to know him more before giving in to him emotionally and sexually. "I've got to get back to Gambit."

"Your dog?"

"Yes," she said, sitting on her haunches, widening the space between them so her hormones wouldn't persuade her to stay. "He's been home for hours."

"I'm pretty sure he's fine." Nathan nodded as if he knew for sure. "Probably sleeping good or chasing his tail."

"True, but I still need to check on him." She climbed out of bed and smoothed her hands down the skirt of her dress. "If these dates keep happening, y'all will have to meet soon."

"Oh," Nathan uttered dryly, his face going slack. "Meet your dog." The way he spoke the three-letter word as if it wasn't a canine but a villainous mythical creature threw her for a loop.

"Don't tell me you don't like dogs?"

"I'm . . . not fond of them." He read the twist of her face and the knit of her eyebrows and quickly quipped, "But I'm sure I'll love your dog." He nodded.

"I hope." She warily fiddled with the strap of her dress. "I really, really hope so."

"Let me walk you to your car." He reluctantly slid out of bed. "And you can tell me all about this little *perro* of yours."

"First of all, he's not little," Indigo started as she rounded the bed. Seeing the caution in Nathan's eyes, she hooked her arm with his and added, "But he's a teddy bear, and he's supercute."

Chapter 14

Five hours later, hard, police-like knocks pounded on Indigo's front door. She wrestled the covers that snuggled her in her comfortable bed. She decided to ignore it and slip back into her slumber. There was no way the police were looking for her—she'd paid her speeding ticket months ago. She clenched her eyes and held a pillow over her head, and the knocking stopped for a bit, but Gambit's bark still boomed.

"Simmer down, boy," Indigo murmured, flipping over in the bed, lying flat on her back and trying to cling to sleep. "It's probably just Jehovah's Witnesses."

"I'm not a Jehovah's Witness," a snarky male voice quipped from the door of her bedroom.

"What the—" Indigo sprung up. "Tate! Really, dude!" She frowned at him and the other noisemaker sitting at the end of her bed. "I had a late night. You better have a good reason for using your Gambit key to stroll up into my house."

He leaned against the doorframe, the aforementioned key on a ring hanging on his finger. "You're gonna thank me when I tell you."

She folded her arms sternly and hardened her eyes; there was no chance of that happening.

"Saxon's in labor." He pointed to her nightstand. "That thing's called a phone. Turn it on."

"It's on." She threw back the covers and slithered out of the bed. "Where is she?"

"The hospital."

"But it's not time yet." She stroked her temple, worry causing her nerves to churn. "Where are the kids?"

"Downstairs." He pushed his shoulder off the door, watching her rummage through the drawers of her dresser. "They want pancakes."

"What?" She tossed a red lace bralette on the bed. "They asked for that?"

"No." He rubbed the back of his neck. "I suggested it as a technique to ease their stress, but I'll help."

Before his hand shifted to his heart, she already knew his intentions were purely sincere.

"Oh, you're helping." She shuffled to the bathroom with the claws of sleep still embedded in her body.

• • •

The hot water and lemongrass shower gel Indigo bathed in did wonders for waking her, but the robust aroma of coffee quickened her steps down the stairs to her kitchen, where she found Tate with her sister's kids.

"How are my babies?" she asked, going straight to the coffeepot; a cup was already sitting out for her.

"They're worried," Tate said, lowering his mug from his mouth from the other side of the island. "I had to take this away." He held up an iPhone. "Too much WebMD."

"I just needed to research the labor process," River affirmed, and the boy's midnight eyes immediately went to his aunt. "Isn't education important to you people?"

"Yes. It is." Indigo stirred the creamer into the still steaming coffee. "But that's not the best source to be on right now."

River frowned, not happy with her explanation. "I just need to check some things out because Mama's eight months, and pregnancy is supposed to last nine, right?"

Adira stopped stroking Gambit's back and asked from her spot on the floor, "Mama's going to be all right, right? And the baby?"

Worry was written all over her niece's and nephew's faces. She was also anxious about her sister; she couldn't let them know that, but she also wanted to be honest with them.

"Bringing a baby into the world is a big job." She put down her mug and went to her nephew's side. Taking him in an embrace, she gestured for Adira to join her. The little girl bolted over and glued her body against her aunt.

Indigo held them tightly. "But your mama's strong, and your daddy's taking care of her along with doctors and nurses. And while we wait for news, we're going to celebrate."

"Celebrate what?" Adira asked, peering up at her with big brown eyes.

"Your little sister's birthday," Tate exclaimed and tapped her nose, making the girl giggle. "Are you ready to be a big sister?"

"Another sister." River sighed. "I want someone to skateboard with."

"Girls can skateboard," Indigo said, tickling him. He claimed he was too old for that but still laughed. "I taught you, remember?"

"Auntie Indie . . ." Adira started before emitting a yawn. "Can we have pancakes? Uncle Tate said we could."

"*Uncle Tate* can't cook, so he shouldn't be promising things." Indigo shot him a look then turned back to her niece. "But yes, I'll make y'all pancakes." She brushed her hand over Adira's pink scarf–covered head, knowing she'd have to do her hair later. "Now, go play with Gambit outside, and I'll call you when breakfast is done."

"Yes, ma'am," the kids said in unison and led Gambit to the backyard.

Tate handed her her mug and said, "Put me to work, chef."

"Oh, your ass is working." She accepted her mug from him with a smile.

He went to the cabinet above the stove and opened the doors. "Which cookbook are we using?"

"I don't need one." She went to the fridge. "I'm a pro." She winked at him then asked, "Can you get the flour?"

Her phone vibrated on the counter. She thought it might be her parents or Harrison, but it was a text from Nathan.

Good morning, gorgeous. How are you?

Tate looked at her coyly. "How are you doing, *gorgeous*?"

She pointed to the labeled ceramic canister of the thing she'd asked him for. "Flour, please. Thank you."

She shook her head at his nosiness and quickly replied, *Fine. My sister's having the baby. Aunt duty has been activated.*

Tate did as he was asked, and they got to work making a breakfast that would have the kids begging for an extra helping.

Chapter 15

"How do you think the baby will look?" Adira asked, circling her arms around her aunt's waist.

"Wrinkly," River uttered, watching the floor numbers above the elevator door light up. "And bald," he added as the nurse in the corner chuckled as she stared at her iPad screen.

The elevator dinged, coming to a slow stop, and then the door opened.

Indigo kept one arm around Adira and placed her other arm around River. "She'll be precious just like the both of you were."

"I thought Adira looked like a gremlin," River teased.

Adira swung her hand toward him. "And you look like Gollum's long-lost twin."

Tate chortled, and Indigo glared at him.

"Stop," Indigo deepened her voice and ordered. "We . . . are . . . in public," she bit out, then smiled widely at the medical professionals and visitors roaming the hall.

"Nana! Granddad!" the kids called. They pulled away from Indigo's hold and ran to the elders.

They bombarded Indigo's parents with questions, and Indigo

sighed with relief because she didn't have to play twenty-one questions.

She took the chance to slip into her sister's room with Tate in tow. The massive windows gave a view of Houston's busy skyline littered with medical towers and corporate offices. But Saxon was lost in the eyes of her newborn. Xavier was fast asleep on the sky blue love seat next to the bed.

"Where are the kids?" Saxon asked without looking up.

Indigo leaned on the plastic bed rail. "They're outside with Mama and Daddy." She absorbed the presence of the new life resting on Saxon's chest, the chubby cheeks, the twirls of curls, the big auburn eyes, and the blue blanket. Wait.

"I thought you were having a girl," Indigo muttered.

Saxon caressed her finger along the baby's cheek as his eyes scrolled closed. "I did too."

"River's going to be happy," Tate said.

"Mm-hmm," Indigo agreed, rubbing her hand over Saxon's tousled hair. "How is Mama doing?"

Saxon dropped her head back on the pillow. "Tired."

"I'll take him." Indigo had the baby firmly in her embrace before Saxon nodded. "What's his name?"

"Baby Shaw for now." Saxon yawned. "We'll think of something."

Indigo swayed with the infant. "Little one, it's so nice to meet you."

Love teemed through every nerve in her body, though a bittersweet ache throbbed in her chest—she just wished one day she'd be holding her own baby and not someone else's.

"What are you looking at, little one?" she asked.

She realized Tate was at her side with zoned-out eyes. She knew that look. It was the look he got when his mind highjacked his body. He wasn't in the present anymore but in a distant place she called Tate-land.

She waved a hand in front of his face, knowing what he was thinking about. He blinked at her, and she whispered, "Come back."

"Sorry," he said quietly then reached out and caressed the baby's cheek with the back of his finger. "Just remembering."

Tears pricked her eyes, and she blinked them back. "I know." She claimed his other hand and squeezed it. "You'll be a great dad one day."

"You don't have to say that."

"I just . . ." She paused, emotions clogging her throat. "I feel like I should say something."

"You don't have to say anything." His voice was mellow as he held her gaze.

"Am I interrupting?" an extremely deep voice questioned. Diego stood in the doorway with two bouquets of roses and a stuffed teddy bear.

He was, but Indigo didn't want to be rude, so she waved for him to enter before placing the baby in the mobile cradle. Tate rolled his shoulders, clearly annoyed, as Diego closed the distance between them.

"Eventful day." Diego's eyes went to the new parents, who were both asleep. "Congrats on being an aunt again." He handed her one of the bouquets.

"Thanks," Indigo said. "That's thoughtful."

Diego beamed.

Tate rolled his eyes. "She hates roses."

She watched Tate's retreating form, wishing there was more she could do.

Diego asked, "Do you like tulips?"

She inhaled the sweet scent of the flowers and told him, "I do like the red of these roses, though. And I like tulips, too, and peonies, but ranunculus are my favorite."

Diego nodded. "I'll remember that for next time."

• • •

Indigo stood on the curb in front of Concord Memorial Hospital. The thick, humid night air had her flimsy dress sticking to her back and gripping at her thighs. After the fourth pair of headlights drove up the hospital ramp, she stopped looking for the Uber car. Apparently, the app had lied.

The cold air from the hospital sliding doors did nothing to cool her heated temper. A car honked at her.

"What are you still doing here?" Diego asked, leaning over the steering wheel of a shiny black Mercedes SUV.

"My Uber should be here any moment." Indigo approached the car and leaned against the open window.

"Uber?" Diego dropped his hand from the steering wheel. "Let me take you home?"

"No, I'm good," Indigo informed him, pointedly looking down the ramp for her ride.

Her parents had offered to take her home, but they lived in the opposite direction, and she'd told Tate she was getting a ride from Harrison. It was a lie. But she didn't want to tell him the real reason she didn't want to be in the car with him at the moment. She just wanted to sit quietly and think, sort out some things in her mind. And probably cry.

The corner of Diego's mouth quirked up. "I promise I won't bite." He shifted in his seat, closer to the passenger side. "Can you please get in so I can take you home?"

Indigo studied his face to see if he was sincere. He'd been pleasant all day, not at all the arrogant jerk who'd berated her shop assistant for a refund and towed her car.

"Whatever." She spewed one of her overused teenaged words as she pulled back the door handle.

The dome light glared on as she climbed in.

"Buckle up," Diego said as he shifted out of Park.

Indigo pulled at the tan seat belt on the side. "Don't tell me what to do." She slid the belt over her waist and clicked it into place as Diego eased the SUV into traffic.

After Indigo gave him her address, Diego turned up the music to cover the silence. He glided down side streets by parking garages, corporate businesses, and busy restaurants before getting onto I-45.

Indigo stared out the window, watching the buildings, cars, lights, and trees zip by as he drove. As soon as Joe's "I Wanna Know" coursed through the speakers, she let out a sigh and dropped her back against the velvety beige leather seat.

"I assume you like this song." Diego's baritone cut through the song's chorus.

"You would assume correctly." She shifted her eyes to him as he switched his gaze to the side mirror, checking if the next lane was clear. "This song was on heavy rotation when I was in elementary school."

"Were you planning your wedding in your head too?" He rested one hand at the bottom of the steering wheel while the other rested on his thigh.

"It wasn't a Meghan Markle–type wedding," she clarified.

"So, you mean you didn't want to be a princess?" He glanced at her then put his eyes back on the clear road.

"Never." She dropped her hands from the seat belt and focused on the taillights drifting farther ahead of them. "I always thought it was more fun to be the gunslinger than the damsel in distress."

"Gunslinger," Diego huffed. "Don't tell me you're a western-loving girl?"

"Woman," she corrected, slowly turning her body toward him. "And yes."

"What's your favorite western then?" Diego sat up in the seat, abandoning his slouch.

She enjoyed his excitement. "Tell me yours first."

"My favorite . . ." He pursed his lips as he scratched at his beard. "I'ma have to say *Gunfight at the O.K. Corral.*" He snapped his fingers.

Indigo pushed his fingers out of the way. "That's a good one . . . but it's not better than mine."

"What's yours?" He eased the car down the off-ramp.

"*Thomasine & Bushrod.*" Indigo held on to the door handle as Diego jumped two lanes on the frontage road and took a right on the yellow light.

"That doesn't have gunslingers. That doesn't count." Diego slowed the car as they approached the corner and a sign that read ORCHARD MEADOW.

"Yes, it does count." Indigo watched the familiar brick two-story homes glide past the window. "It has everything . . . romance, action, comedy, and drama. It's a cinematic delight."

"A cinematic delight." He mocked Indigo, sliding up to the driveway of her house and easing the SUV to a stop. He killed the engine. "Can I come in? We can finish talking."

Indigo read the illuminated time on the dashboard. "It's late. I've got work tomorrow, and so do you."

Diego tsked as he dropped his head to the side. "Okay." He cranked the car back up. "If that's what you want."

"Thanks again." Indigo's hand stilled on the door handle as darkness and silence enveloped them. "Do you want me to reimburse you for the gas?"

"I don't need your money." He returned his sights to her. "I'd rather you gave me a chance."

"You're not my type." The words slid out of her mouth before she could evaluate them.

Diego's mouth twisted. "You and I both know that's a lie."

"I have a guy."

"Do you? Because Xavier told me you're dating some dude named Nathan, but it isn't that serious."

"Xavier said." Indigo made a mental note to give her brother-in-law a verbal lashing. "It's actually serious . . . four weeks of seriousness."

"Four weeks," he snorted. "Then give me four weeks, and I'll show you serious."

Indigo swallowed hard then flung the door open, casting them in the light. "I doubt it." She climbed out and shut the door, the abrupt noise bringing barks from the yard next door to hers. She leaned down to the open window. "Good night, Diego."

"Night." Diego smirked. "I'll get in touch with you later."

Indigo turned on her heel, heading for her door, wondering what he meant. She shook the nagging question out of her head as she unlocked her front door; she had a missed call from Nathan to return, and the last person she needed to think about was Diego.

Chapter 16

"So, what kind of rotation are we thinking about for next week?" Hazel asked, standing behind the checkout counter with her eyes fixed on the laptop. "Some Cardi and Meg?"

Indigo lifted her fingers from her own keyboard. "I want a break from hip-hop." She pulled her black-rimmed glasses from her face and rubbed her eyes. "R & B, please."

"R & B it is." Hazel searched through Apple Music's limitless catalog.

Indigo fitted her reading glasses back on her face. Out the storefront windows, rain battered the concrete, and dark, heavy clouds blackened the sky. She had a love-hate relationship with stormy days. She loved them when she was at home and able to snuggle on the couch with a good book or movie then drift off into a cozy nap. But rainy days at Adorn were the complete opposite; they were a horror—a dull, monotonous horror. Customers were rare, like a spotted llama in the desert, and if someone stopped by, they were only seeking shelter until the rain let up. Cracks of thunder and bright flashes of lightning illuminated the bleakness outside. Nothing had changed since opening, and at a quarter to two, Indigo had had enough of it.

She scanned the laptop screen, where she was preparing a blog post. The three paragraphs she'd written were about picking the perfect summer dress for your body type. She said, "I can do this at home."

"Huh?" Hazel asked.

Indigo shut her laptop. "I can do this work at my house." She massaged her neck, trying to ease muscles stiff from being stooped over the keyboard too long. "And save on the energy bill."

"Are you sure?" Hazel drummed her fingers on the countertop. "Is that, like . . . allowed?" she whispered as if her supervisor were listening around the corner.

Indigo's glossed lips kicked up. "I'm the boss. If I want to close early, I can close early. Plus . . ." She gestured to the pounding bands of rain and the merciless gusts of wind battering the baby trees planted by the curb. "We need to get home before these streets start flooding. You know Houston can't hold a thimble of water."

"Right." Hazel nodded curtly, shutting her laptop. She brushed her hand down the buttons of her black shirt then typed her employee ID into the register, intending to start the closeout. "'Cause my Fusion can't wade through water." The cash drawer slid out, and just then, the door swung open.

The lash of rain intensified as Emery strode into the store. "I'm surprised to see you," she chided. Her blue jeans, pastel blouse, and ankle boots had gotten soaked on the short walk up from her coffee shop.

The door eased closed, cloaking the store in the strumming of soft, melodic tones.

"What's that supposed to mean?" Indigo questioned. "It's a weekday. Where else am I supposed to be?"

Hazel sighed as she counted the tens, which were the exact amount she'd put in the drawer that morning.

"What?" Indigo asked again, glancing between the two. "Am I missing something?"

"Lately," Emery said, brushing her hand down her sleek, damp ponytail, "a lot."

"Is this about the rock climbing?" Indigo hooked her fingers in the belt loops of her jeans and shimmied them up. "'Cause I was on a date with Nathan. There's no way I could have made it. He flew back to see me." She straightened her blouse back out.

"Oh my gosh." Emery held the side of her face, and Indigo couldn't tell if her friend was upset or angry. Maybe it was both. "You legitimately forgot."

"What?" Indigo asked.

"This chick." Emery's hand dropped from her face and slapped her hip. She shook her head, settling her eyes on Hazel.

"What?" Indigo repeated. "What'd I miss?"

Hazel shut the cash drawer with a click. "You missed two girls' nights in a row, and she's pissed about it."

Indigo knitted her eyebrows into a "That's all?" expression.

"Are you serious?" Emery fumed. "You're copping an attitude when you're the one who's been MIA. Oh, I forgot!" She tapped her temple. "Indigo's got a man now. That's much more important than her friends."

"You know what, Emery, I don't like the way you're coming for me." Indigo took a step toward her friend with the palms of her hands glued together. "I would never cause a scene in your place of work."

Emery gestured around at the empty store, but to Indigo, it

wasn't about the occupancy of the establishment but the principle.

"The door is unlocked. We're open. Anyone could walk in."

"Sorry." Emery brushed her hand over her head. "I just saw you and flipped." She shrugged listlessly.

"Aww, she misses you," Hazel teased, twirling her hair into a bun. "Go on, hug it out."

Emery shook her head. "I don't want a hug. I just wish you wouldn't flake on us."

"Not me, I'm not made of flour," Indigo joked, closing the space between them and wrapping her arms around Emery even though she mock-protested. "No more flaking. I promise. You know time management is not my strongest skill."

Emery hugged her back, her resolve breaking. "Yes, I know that. This is why we carved out a girls' day, or else you'd drift into your own world."

"True," Indigo agreed, pulling out of Emery's embrace. "How about this? We're closing early." She motioned to Hazel and herself. "Why don't you come over to my place? I'll pick up a pizza and some buffalo wings, and we can eat like we're eighteen until we get heartburn."

"Shit." Hazel snapped her fingers as she pranced from behind the checkout counter. "I still look eighteen."

They all broke out in laughter, but in the depths of Indigo's mind, she wondered how she was going to juggle it all: work, family, friends, and dating. Would she still have time to herself, or would her energy be allocated to everything and everyone else?

• • •

Indigo was in her favorite spot in her living room, curled up in the corner of the couch with a fleece throw draped over her legs and a slice of pizza in her hand. The rain had slacked up long enough for her to go to Firerock Pizza and get back home.

Emery had arrived just as the second wave of rain moved in, and Hazel had made it just as the downpour began to pummel. She'd gotten so drenched while running from her car to Indigo's front door that Indigo sent her to the bathroom with a change of clothes.

"What took you so long?" Indigo inquired, lifting the spinach-herb-feta pizza to her salivating mouth.

With her wet hair wrapped in one of Indigo's big lavender towels, Hazel skirted the question. "Nothing." She shook her head dismissively while avoiding their curious eyes. "Traffic," she added, rolling the waistband of the shorts Indigo had lent her.

"Hmm." Emery eyed her cousin from the comfort of the other end of the couch. She stirred the bowl of salad cradled in her lap, which she'd mixed using produce in Indigo's fridge. "'Cause we all left at the same time . . . even merged on the freeway at the same time."

Indigo nodded as she chewed. "So, at some point between there and the off-ramp . . ." She snapped her fingers at Gambit to draw his nose away from the food spread on her Ikea coffee table. The pooch scampered away from the table and dropped his body next to his owner with a huff.

"I had something to take care of," Hazel said, dropping a fiery red buffalo wing on her plate. She sucked the sauce from her fingertips. "I know people y'all don't. I have business to take care of that doesn't involve y'all."

Indigo held the thick crust down so Gambit could take it. "Like what?"

Emery stabbed her fork into the mass of greens. "What's his name?"

Hazel glared at Emery. "I resent that."

"Yeah, Em." Indigo playfully slapped Emery's thigh. "She's not man crazy one hundred percent of the time."

"Just, like . . . ninety-eight," Emery added.

Emery and Indigo both laughed. Hazel rolled her cognac-colored eyes at them, balled up a napkin, and threw it at the person that annoyed her the most. The paper ball dropped into Emery's bowl.

"Three points!" Hazel raised her arms over her head in celebration.

"Stop playing!" Emery plucked the paper, now soaked in olive oil and balsamic vinegar, out of her bowl.

"You were done anyway." Hazel gave her a dismissive wave as she danced along with the song. Emery's lips stayed pressed together as her frown lessened, knowing the words were true. "But for real, I had to go take care of some business with Harrison."

"My brother, Harrison?"

"Yeah."

"I didn't know you two talked."

"We didn't." Hazel swirled her hips to the hypnotic, up-tempo beat. "But he stopped by the shop looking for you while you were out on a supply run, and we got to talking. He told me he was looking for an artist, and I do art sometimes, so we linked up."

Indigo slowly nodded. "Mm-hmm."

"Since we're on the topic of dating," Emery said, setting her soggy salad on the coffee table. "How are things between you and Nate?"

"They're good," Indigo said, pushing the remaining three wings on her plate around, no longer feeling the hollow emptiness of hunger in her stomach.

"Just good?" Hazel stopped dancing. "Oh, shit! What did he do?"

"Nothing." Indigo's nostrils flared as she pulled in a breath, and her chest deflated as she exhaled it. Feeling the heat of her friends' curious eyes, she decided to elaborate. "He's easy to talk to. I love how he takes care of his sister. I miss him when we're apart, and I feel myself falling for him. It's just . . ." She abruptly stopped midsentence to bite on her bottom lip as if the next thing she was about to say was top secret.

"What?" Hazel hung on to Indigo's words, her face marred with a twinge of dismay.

Emery was the complete opposite. Her mouth lifted in an understanding quirk. "Scary."

"Petrifying." Indigo slumped back against the arm of the couch. "Especially to invest so much of myself into someone, to start visualizing a future, only to have the other shoe drop. I'm hesitant to let him into my life just in case he's not right for me."

Hazel dropped to her haunches on the floor. "It's always good to go slow."

"When do you take things slow?" Emery asked with a teasing smirk.

"I always take things slow when I'm searching for a relationship. Now . . ." Hazel perused the two boxes of barely touched pizza, trying to decide if she wanted pepperoni or veggie. "If I'm looking for a quickie, all I need to know is if he passed your test and got all his shots."

Indigo couldn't hold her laugh. "I can't take you seriously sometimes."

"Me neither." Emery shook her head at her cousin then turned back to Indigo. "I can't speak for Nate . . . all I know is that he's a quality guy, and when you're dating, it's a gamble. Sometimes you go bankrupt, or you hit the jackpot, but if you cash out, you'll never find what you're looking for."

Hazel clapped, causing Gambit to raise his head. "Look at Socrates. That's my cousin."

"Sound words, Em, very sound." Indigo settled her gaze out the window, with a prime view of the street and the house across from hers.

Indigo's thoughts drowned out Emery and Hazel's conversation as her gaze lingered on Tate's house.

Chapter 17

Timberwood Park was Indigo's favorite stretch of lush green meadow to immerse herself in during the weekend. Not only was the canal long enough to kayak, but there were woodsy nature trails that snaked around primordial oak trees and berry bushes that invited picking. Indigo usually hiked the trail with a leash in hand as Tate jogged ahead. He was a runner. She was a walker. The stroll eased her overthinking as she inhaled the sharp earthiness of grass and mineral-rich dirt with birdsong as her soundtrack.

But today they didn't hit the trail. The Frisbee Tate toted from the car captivated Gambit, and there was no way he was going to strut alongside her with the red disc at Tate's side singing his name. They played Frisbee until Gambit stopped galloping after it like a cheetah in need of a meal.

"Here." Indigo's sandal-clad feet stopped at the edge of their yellow polka-dotted picnic blanket. She held a waffle cone in each hand with two scoops of ice cream apiece; in her right hand she had mango-blueberry and in her left was brown sugar cinnamon.

Tate pulled the baseball cap off his face and looked up at her.

"No, thanks." He propped his body up on his elbows, abandoning his relaxed horizontal position.

"What, are you watching your figure?" She didn't need him to remove his baby blue T-shirt to know beneath the fabric were a pack of tight abs and a broad chest to match. "You're hot."

Tate squinted up at her as the evening sun beamed down. "You think I'm hot?" He smirked then took the cone from her left hand.

She tsked. "It's ninety-eight with a heat index of one hundred and one." She plopped down on the blanket beside him. He'd left her the side that was in the shade, and she was grateful. "It's Texas in the summer. We're all hot."

"True," he said, then quickly licked the melting ice cream that was dripping down the golden waffle cone. Gambit propped his head on her leg.

Tate stopped, probably feeling her eyes upon his perspiring face. "What?"

With a flush of heat, Indigo shook her head. "Nothing." As she peered out at the park's green grass sprinkled with pine trees, she hoped her body's reaction was due to the sun's glow.

These momentary slips, seeing Tate as the man he was and not just her best friend, had been happening more frequently since she'd started dating again. Maybe it was because of the memories she had of when they were more than friends. Opening her heart back up to the possibility of love had reminded her of those moments of affection with him. She swallowed, pushing those thoughts back down where they belonged, then grinned.

"You know, it's not every day you meet a man who eats ice cream like a two-year old."

She handed him a napkin, and he slipped it from her hand.

"You're the one who gave me a cone." He cleaned the ice cream from his beard. She knew it was soft from the almond and jojoba oil he massaged onto his face every morning, and it smelled of spicy cinnamon and vanilla. "Don't critique me on how I eat it."

"Whatever you say, Tattie Tate."

. . .

Once her ice cream was eaten down to the edges of the cone, Indigo said, "You know, my birthday is getting close, and you haven't asked me yet."

Tate stopped biting his cone. "Asked you what?"

Her mouth opened abruptly, then a corner quirked up. "What I want? What present you should surprise me with?"

She wasn't keen on surprises because most people gifted what they wanted a person to have and not the things that person actually wanted. Providing a list of about twenty things that she'd love to receive was the best plan of action for all parties.

Tate humphed. "I'm not Nathan or Diego. I don't need a list." He gave her a look. "I know you."

A phantom breeze toyed with the short caramel tendrils not long enough to stay in his loose bun. She didn't know how long he was going to let his hair grow out; during his periods of writing, he let it grow, and she wondered if it helped him morph words into worlds.

He continued, "You're a social butterfly who loves staying home. You're a shoe aficionado but take yours off any chance you get. You cook for people you care about, and you have strong emotions. Nurturing is your love language, and you want to be nurtured in return, but you don't tell anyone that because you don't want to come off as needy. You swear you love Now and Laters, but you only eat the apple flavor. I know you. Very well. But . . ." He shrugged. "I love learning . . ." He paused. "New things."

Indigo's lips parted with instinctual words: *I love sharing new things with you.* It was the truth. He was the first person she told things to: the big things, the little things, the things that kept her up at night. It was important that she talked to him and that she was in the same room as him when those conversations happened.

His gaze dipped to her open mouth, and she wondered if he was thinking about the same thing she was. Or was he remembering something? A moment in their past when they were something more than *just friends*. A portion of her hoped he was, knew he was. But people don't rebound from the thing that broke them up, let alone become close friends again, so she wasn't going to push her luck.

Being Tate's friend was better than being nothing to him at all. It was what they'd both agreed on years ago. She ignored the way his eyes lingered on her lips and the hunger she felt to know what he'd do if they didn't care about consequences.

The corner of his jaw threatened to tick up in a grin, and she narrowed her eyes at him.

"You're a smart-ass, and I can't stand you." She stood up, tired of sitting on the ground and wanting to relax on something with a cushion. The leather seats of his Denali would do since he was the one who'd driven them to the park. He always drove whenever they went anywhere, insisting that since he had two cars it was his duty.

It was lame logic, but she loved when he drove.

"I need a shower." She tugged at her neon-orange shirt, feeling sweaty although the fabric was dry. "And sustenance."

"Let's get food after we shower." He stood, stirring Gambit as he tugged at the blanket. The sun still burned bright even though the time had ticked past seven. With the rolled-up blanket under his arm and his keys in his hand, he led the way back to the car. "What don't you want to eat?"

"Sandwiches." She walked beside him, giving Gambit's leash some slack to walk a couple of paces in front of them. "I want food and fun."

He nodded. "Then I know where we should go."

She didn't need to ask because she was keenly aware that he knew what she wanted. With Tate, she didn't have to be in control all the time, and she liked that. Being taken care of was splendid.

• • •

Indigo tossed and turned through the night. Her mattress wasn't as comfy as it had been before she and Tate had filled their stomachs with tender oxtails, cabbage, and rice and peas then danced to reggae until they were hungry again.

Her conversation with her dad at the flower shop and Tate's words at the park had sent her down a spiral she didn't want to journey on. She didn't want to think about the first real relationship she'd ever had, how she'd been in love—real love—for the first time and then lost it all because of her decision.

Indigo's groans of restlessness urged Gambit to plant his head at the end of the bed and nudge her with his snout. A couple of strokes of his smooth, wide ears vanquished her nagging thoughts and soothed her to sleep.

An hour and forty-five minutes later, she woke to the sound of hard knocks against her front door. Unlike last time, she didn't try to sleep through the raucous knuckles tapping against wood or Gambit's boisterous barking. She flung the covers off her nestled body and reluctantly scraped herself out of bed.

"I'm coming! I'm coming!" she shouted, tying her robe over the

Sleeping Is My Hobby nightshirt. "It's . . ." She peeked at the clock in her foyer as she sluggishly stepped off the last step. "Too early in the morning for this." She blinked away the grogginess as streaks of light sank through the cracks of the blinds in the living room.

More knocks rattled the door. The person on her porch must've heard. "Who is it?" she yelled over her Gambit defense system. "Shh," she hushed him as they both stood in front of the door.

"It's me," a male voice on the other side of the door called, then sighed. "Open up!"

Indigo growled, twisting the lock. She whipped open the door, and the sunlight that flooded over her made her grimace and shield her face. "Tate, it's too early in the morning for this."

"Too early?" He smirked, looking down at his silver watch. "It's 8:18."

"In. The. Morning."

He gave the frisky pooch an energetic pat.

"Seems like your mommy's a little grumpy." Tate gave the dog one more rub then stood up. His grin displayed the one slightly crooked bottom tooth that the dentist had said wasn't enough for him to get braces. "I came by early to say bye."

Indigo pushed her shoulder off the door. "Where are you going?"

"The cabin." Distant traffic noises and birds chirping filled the moment. "I finished the outline for Charisma the other day, and I need to go up to the woods to put some words on a page."

"What? You finished the outline!" She beamed, and he matched her happiness. "Congrats! I knew you could do it." She leaned out the door to watch Gambit emptying his bladder on the only tree in her front yard. "Do you have to go to the woods, though? It's not like there's a lot of disruption around here." She indicated the barren street and silent houses.

"Nah, it's not that." Tate combed his hair back just as another warm breeze swept over them. "I just think better out there." He waved his hands around his temples. "In nature. The words flow easier."

Indigo nodded slowly as if she understood, but she really didn't. "Well, you gotta do what you gotta do to get your work done."

"That's right."

"Just remember to shoot me a text so I know you're still alive." She leaned against the doorframe. "And not axe murdered."

"Yes, Mom."

"And remember to get some food." She pointed at him, and he nodded with a cheeky grin. "I'm serious, Tate. Humans need more than cereal, chips, and coffee." She snapped her fingers enthusiastically as she heard another dog barking in the distance. "Gambit, come."

The dog lifted his nose from the grass and stared at her. Just as Indigo moved to repeat his name, he trotted to the porch, darted through the space between her and Tate, and plopped down in the foyer.

"I'll get some apples," Tate said.

"And something green and leafy."

Tate huffed with a shake of his head. "I don't have time to make salads." He opened his arms. "Now, give me a hug bye."

"Pfft. Get back." She pushed him away. "I'm not hugging you."

She didn't need that type of temptation right now. Mornings were when she was horniest, and the last thing she needed was her body flush against his, braless no less. They were friends, that was certain, but she was still human. He was Tate, and she was Indigo, and that spark was always there, waiting to be ignited.

Tate dropped his arms, and she balled up her hand, holding it out. "Fist bump."

"Sure. As always." He bumped her fist with a smile that wasn't as bright as the one before. "I ought to get a move on so I can stop by the store and get on the road." He backed away from the door. "Be safe, Indie."

"Same to you, Tattie Tate."

His smile widened at the nickname. She watched him cross the street and hop into his sleek Denali. A faint twinge nicked her chest, and before it could grow stronger, she closed the door and locked it.

"I almost slipped, boy," Indigo breathlessly confessed to Gambit. He lifted his head and tilted it. "Almost."

She marched away from the door, pulling her hair down. "Let's go fill our bellies before Nathan gets here."

Chapter 18

Indigo's early morning wake-up call didn't disrupt her plans for the day. In fact, it helped her out. Nathan was coming over, and the last thing she'd wanted was to oversleep and be caught off guard.

After caffeinating and getting dressed, she took Gambit for a walk around the neighborhood. Back home, she dropped two cups of food in Gambit's bowl and warmed up some of last night's oxtails and cabbage for herself. Full and fueled, she tidied up her abode, which wasn't that disorderly since she was a stickler for putting things back into their rightful places—a trait from her dad, no doubt.

It had been hours since Tate had pulled out of her driveway, and she'd be lying if she said she wasn't a little concerned. He hadn't sent her a text letting her know that he had made it to the cabin.

With a clean, cinnamon-and-vanilla-scented house, Indigo knew she was making good time before Nathan came over at twelve. Once the brisket she'd been marinating all night was roasting in the oven, she set off to the garden.

Normani's "Motivation" interrupted her playlist, and she reached for the back pocket of her jean shorts to accept the call.

"Hmm, risen from the dead, have you?" Indigo joked with sweat sliding down the small of her back. With her earbuds in, she pushed a mulch-filled wheelbarrow out of her garage. She was ready to get her hands dirty beautifying her front yard.

"Not gon' lie, I feel like a zombie." Saxon's voice was raspy as if she'd just woken up from a long slumber.

"How are things at the Shaw house?" It wasn't really a question Indigo had to ask. She knew the state of things at her sister's house. Ever since Saxon and Xavier had brought home the baby, whom they'd named Frost, the world had revolved around him. It was an occurrence for which Indigo had been prepared; she'd been through it two times before. So, when Saxon didn't return her phone calls or reply to her texts, she didn't fret. Indigo didn't expect the Shaw crew to show up to family movie night or game night, especially after Frost arrived.

Saxon's weak laugh seeped through the earbuds. "Things are beginning to settle down over here. I got my first night of uninterrupted sleep. Just four hours, but it's better than thirty-minute spurts."

"Sounds rough." Indigo cringed, parking the wheelbarrow on the lawn. She'd gotten a total of five hours of sleep last night off and on, and she'd needed an extra cup of coffee to get going. Indigo wiped beads of sweat from her forehead. "But things are better now?"

"Yes," Saxon sighed with relief. "Being a mom of three is more taxing than being a mom of two, but Xavier and I are figuring it out." Her voice lowered as if she was passing by a quiet zone, most likely near the nursery. "And thanks again for letting River and Addie sleep over the other day."

"No problem," Indigo affirmed, dropping to her knees in front of her flower bed of purple angelonias. She'd played the dutiful aunt two days that week when the kids had needed refuge from a crying baby, a cranky mama, and a stressed and overworked dad. "I love the little stinkers." She also liked getting the practice because maybe one day she'd have her own. Hopefully.

"What are you getting up to today?" Saxon asked.

"Nothing much." Indigo grabbed a handful of mulch and deposited it around the newly planted flowers, not bothering with the garden shovel. Getting her hands in the dirt relaxed and eased her mind, grounding her. "Just spending the day with Nathan."

"Oooh." Saxon sang the word, making her sister laugh lightly. "*Nathan*. When are we going to meet this guy? Bring him to family game night."

"Not yet." Indigo shook her head, patting the mulch delicately around the flower stems. It was too soon for him to meet her family. She wasn't ready for her mom to cross-examine him during a game of Uno. "He's meeting Gambit today, though."

"I guess meeting the cuddle baby," Saxon said, "is the first stage of seeing if he's a good partner for you."

"Right." She glanced over toward the house, where Gambit was napping. He was her fur baby, and the man in her life had to get along with him also. "Hopefully, it all goes well."

She liked Nathan and felt that he had the potential to be something more than just a guy she was dating.

"It will," Saxon affirmed. "It's time you have someone who loves you the way you love everyone in your life."

"Thanks, big sis." She smiled to herself. "I raised you well."

Saxon laughed. "We're seven years apart. Stop lying to yourself."

A vehicle inched up to the curb in front of Indigo's house. She knew immediately who was in the black '65 Buick Riviera.

"I'm gonna have to call you back." Indigo pushed herself off the ground.

"Don't call. Text," Saxon said before Indigo pulled the earbuds out and ended the call.

Get it together, Indigo, she thought to herself. *Some curveballs came for you this week, but you gotta stop living in the past. That chapter is closed.*

"Morning, gorgeous." Nathan strolled up to her with an easy smile lighting up his face.

His pleasant and casual demeanor made it simple for Indigo to utter a response. "Aww, thanks, handsome. But it's . . ." She stole a peek at her watch. "It's no longer morning."

"I know what time it is." Nathan latched his hand around her wrist, covering up her watch. "I may have gotten directionally challenged . . . but I was in the area this morning."

"What?" Indigo puffed out a chuckle as she easily worked her wrist out of his grasp and interlocked their fingers. "You should've just called me, and I would've helped you get un-lost."

"I wasn't lost. Directionally challenged," he reiterated, sliding his free hand over the intricate working of one of her goddess braids. "There's like four subdivisions in one over here."

"Okay, Magellan, but . . ." She pulled away from him, checking out his ensemble: white polo shirt, navy shorts, and gray sneakers. "Is this what you always wear to change oil?"

He'd offered to change the oil in her truck yesterday so she wouldn't have to postpone their date to take it to her usual dealership.

Nathan took a quick look down. "Don't worry about the shirt. I'm a professional. I just get my hands dirty." He winked.

Indigo guffawed. "Is that supposed to be a line?" She laughed louder.

"Don't tease my game." He matched her laughter, wrapping his arms around her waist and pulling her into his body. "I'm trying to give you witty banter."

"Oh!" Indigo threw her arms up; her excited laugh boomed in the quiet neighborhood. Barking erupted in her house, and she turned around to see Gambit in the living room window. "Aww, we woke the baby."

"Baby?" Nathan's arms went slack around her waist. "What the fuck? That's not a dog. That's a beast!"

Indigo whipped her head back toward him, pulling her torso away from his. "Don't call him that!" She broke free of his embrace, taking a step back. "He's a gentle giant."

"More like a man-eater." Nathan's wide, shocked eyes were trained on Gambit as his fearsome barks pounded against the window, drawing the attention of other local dogs, starting a canine symphony. "That's not the dog in the picture you showed me." He pointed to Gambit. "That's not the dog!" He ripped his gaze from the window and aimed it at Indigo.

"I . . . might have shown you a picture of him when he was a puppy. He's hard to get photos of." She rushed out the last part since it was only half the truth. Yes, Gambit turned away whenever someone pointed a phone at him, but his current intimidating girth and muscular build were the main reason she'd gone with a three-year-old picture.

Nathan's arm dropped and went limp by his side as mortification clouded his eyes.

"But he's a good boy." She nodded in assurance. "He loves people." She started taking steps back toward her porch. "He'll just sniff you, and then y'all will be the best of friends." She stood on the top porch step with crossed fingers. "I promise."

"I'm . . . not sure about this, Indigo," Nathan nervously muttered as he watched the dog's form scurry away from the window.

"Trust me. The only creatures he doesn't love are small dogs, and you're not a Chihuahua."

Indigo swung open the door, and before she could call his name, Gambit stampeded out the house, shot past her, and pounced on Nathan, sending him tumbling to the ground.

"Gambit! No!" She fled from the porch. "Stop! Down, boy!" Her commands went unfollowed as Gambit fiercely wagged his tail, giving Nathan's face a generous lick-down.

"Get him off me!" Nathan shouted, kicking his legs as he tried to shield his face from Gambit's kisses. "Get him off me!"

"Gambit! No, boy." Indigo grabbed Gambit's collar with her heart in her chest, hoping the pooch's nails didn't draw blood from Nathan. "No!" she commanded once more as she pulled her over-sized baby away from Nathan.

Nathan slowly pulled his arms down as horror painted his face. "Good boy, my ass!"

"I told you . . ." Indigo gently rubbed Gambit's chin as he calmly sat by her leg, emitting a low whine. "He loves people."

• • •

Indigo ended the rowdy meet and greet, pulling Gambit by his collar into the house and into her study. She closed the French doors just in time as Nathan scurried by, and Gambit erupted into an eager, energetic barking fit. The full-body tail wagging cued Indigo to Gambit's state of mind. He was ready to play and roughhouse, but seeing how Nathan had panicked and tensed up outside, she could tell the man was not down for that.

The air in the light-gray room was much different than it was outside. Indigo hoped the cool temperature would calm Gambit's friskiness. He didn't hustle over to the rug and curl up in a ball for a nap, so she could tell he was well rested.

She felt it in the pit of her stomach. Gambit and Nathan weren't going to be fast friends, which was a setback. Her mind went to Tate; his relationship with Gambit was a unique circumstance since he'd known the pooch as a puppy.

"Hey, bud." Indigo patted his back as he panted, still overly excited about meeting the stranger. "Relax. Sit." The obedient dog sat on his haunches, trying to peek around her frame as she stood in front of him. She held his neck still, stroking his smooth fur with her thumb. "I don't think he's a dog person."

Gambit whimpered.

"But I like him, Gammy," Indigo whispered as she scratched the side of his neck. "He could be a good one. So, you know what we're going to do . . . we're going to win him over." Gambit's dark-brown, marble-sized eyes rolled to her, and his butt started to wiggle as he faintly wagged his tail. "That's my boy."

Indigo flipped his floppy ear around her fingers. "Good Gam-Gam." His ear slid from her fingers as she stood, and so did he. "And you have to remember you're a big boy, and you can't body-slam everybody." He took a step as she did.

"Now, stay." The command halted his steps, but his tail still wagged. She exhaled a heavy breath, torn about making her baby stay shut up in a room by himself so she could hang out with a guy she really, really liked. "I'll be back . . ." She twisted the doorknob. "With a juicy piece of brisket, okay?" She pushed the door shut behind her. "I'll be back," she repeated, then scurried away before she lost the nerve to leave him in the room by himself.

Indigo didn't know what to expect when she walked into the kitchen: an angry Nathan, a scared Nathan, or a frantic Nathan. The sight before her was surprisingly welcome. Nathan was sitting at the island, hunched over his phone, scrolling through whatever app.

"I'm so, so sorry," Indigo apologized, placing the first aid kit on the countertop. "Very sorry," she added, seeing the dirt on his shirt and the grass in his messy black mane.

"You don't have to apologize. It wasn't your fault." Nathan locked his phone and placed it down. "It's not like you wanted him to attack me." He twisted his body in her direction with knitted eyebrows. "Did you?"

"No." Indigo quickly shook her head. His chuckle let her know he was just teasing, and the strain in her shoulders relaxed. "But I wouldn't call it an attack. More like an intense dog hug." She opened the first aid kit. "He usually just sniffs people and goes on his way." She twisted the cap off the Neosporin then rounded the island.

"A dog hug." Nathan held out his arm and looked at the scratch that ran down his forearm. "I probably should have warned you that I'm not really into dogs."

"Is that so." Indigo dabbed the greasy ointment along his bruised skin.

"Yeah." Nathan flinched when her finger touched the tender flesh. "Actually, never have been. A dachshund attacked me when I was four."

"Four?"

"Four." He nodded. "I was pedaling my tricycle down the sidewalk, and it sprung from the driveway and chased me. I had to ditch my tricycle and run home."

"Aww, poor baby." Indigo gave him a quick peck on the cheek.

"A kiss for a scratch." He smirked as she washed her hands. "What do I get for being knocked the ground?"

"Let me brainstorm. I'll come up with something." She winked.

"I like the sound of that." His nose lifted in the air, picking up the robust notes of cumin, paprika, and mesquite floating out of the oven. "So, what's for lunch? Smells good."

Indigo decided not to press further about her dog. Nathan swiftly changing the subject was a sign that he wasn't ready to talk about it. "Brisket tacos." She hopped off the barstool and went to the sink to wash her hands. "I just have to make the salsa, and we should be eating in no time."

"You need me to help with anything?" he asked, watching her pull bowls out of the cabinet and a knife from the storage block.

"Nah." Indigo placed two avocados and tomatoes on the cutting board on the island. "I've made this a million times. Just sit there and heal up." She tossed him a grin before opening the fridge. "You want something to drink? Water, tea, lemonade? I have wine if you like." She held up the bottle of merlot. "I usually sip some before bed, but—"

"No." Nathan cut her off. His lips twisted sourly as he shook his head. "Can't have that. I'll take some lemonade."

"Cool," she slowly said, sliding the wine bottle back by the door as she grabbed the half-filled pitcher of lemonade. "Not a wine guy."

"Not a wine guy. Not a beer guy. Most definitely not a tequila man." He shuddered as she brought two glasses to the island. "Alcohol and I don't have a good relationship."

"Oh?" She turned back to the fridge, this time flinging open the freezer door. "Bad hangovers?" She grabbed the ice tray, remembering the last time she'd had a hangover—in college when she had that one and only night of being a party girl.

"Something like that." Nathan blew out a deep breath before she turned back to him, and he was sitting up rigidly straight. "I'm . . . an alcoholic."

Indigo's mind went blank, and the ice tray slipped from her hand, crashing to the ground. "Shit! I mean . . ." She covered her mouth. "Sorry." She dropped down to a squat, trying to quickly grab the chunks and shards of ice before they melted against the hardwood floor. "How long . . . have you been in remission?" She shook her head—wrong word. Her brain was stalling due to the surprising confession and his rough and rowdy meeting with Gambit. "I mean sober."

"Three years," Nathan calmly informed her, no longer sitting at the island but kneeling in front of her, helping in her cleaning efforts. "Three years without a sip of anything stronger than coffee."

"That's good." Indigo stood, dropping the trayful of dirty ice in the sink. "Very good."

Nathan tossed three big cubes into the sink with a clink. "Is this a deal breaker for you, because I get—"

"No," she said quickly, turning on the faucet.

Nathan studied the side of her face. "Are you sure?"

"Sure." She watched the room-temperature water melt the ice and push it down the drain.

"Indigo." His cold fingertips took hold of her chin, and she willingly let him turn her face toward him. "You won't hurt me if you're up-front. You can tell me how you really feel."

"I've never been in a relationship with someone who . . ." She pulled his hand from her chin and set her palm against his. "Has an addiction. I mean . . . I have a few family members who struggle with it. And . . ." She let out a deep breath. "I want to make sure I'm not a hindrance."

"You're not a hindrance." Nathan's mouth twisted grimly as if he was thinking over what details he wanted to share with her. "My therapist says that my upbringing is a factor: having a verbally abusive, authoritative father who also happens to be an alcoholic. The triggers are . . ." He started to gesture with his free hand. "The usual. Stress. Drama. My dad."

Indigo nodded along with his words as if she understood, but could she really? This was serious. Alcoholism was a beast she'd seen before.

"I've relapsed four times before being sober these last three years." He smiled confidently, proud of his success, then his lips sank. "But you should be adamantly sure if this is what you want because I can't promise that I'm going to be sober forever. I hope I am, but I can't promise it."

"I'm sure." Indigo squeezed his hand tighter even though fragments of doubt swam in her mind.

"I need you to be absolutely certain." Nathan took a step back. "You should take some time. Process it, let it sink in, and see if this is something you want to deal with."

Indigo blinked. "Are you breaking—" She stopped because they hadn't really determined if they were at boyfriend/girlfriend status yet. "What are you saying?"

"I'm saying . . ." He paused, taking a breath as he took another step back, his hand slipping from hers in the process. "You should do you for a while and see if dating an alcoholic is something you want to do."

"Do me." Indigo repeated the words, trying to understand what precisely they meant.

"Two weeks." Nathan rubbed his hand down his stubbled chin. "And if you still want to continue with this . . . with us . . . call me." He nodded as if his word was all that was needed to put the agreement into effect. "I'm going to go change your oil." He jutted his thumb at the front door. "Call me when the salsa's ready."

"Yeah." She barely got the word out before he shuffled out of the kitchen. "What the hell just happened?" she muttered to herself as the melted ice and water slid down the drain.

Chapter 19

Indigo happily welcomed the workweek after her awkward weekend. Nathan's confession Saturday had dampened their gardening date and spoiled her Sunday. The uncertainty of her relationship hung over her as Indigo trotted down the stairs on Monday. Her appetite was still on the sluggish side, and all she craved was coffee, but once she got to work, all the tension that riddled her mind fell away. The only thing of importance was the day's sales goal, something she could attain without complication.

"I'm telling you," Hazel started as she sliced through the clear tape that sealed one of the many boxes in the storage room around them, "you need to hire some more associates."

Indigo kicked off her heels in the room she'd dubbed "the closet." It held all of Adorn's inventory; shoes of every color and size were stored in their own cubicles along three walls. The last wall was fitted with hooks where the season's coveted handbags and gowns hung, and in the middle of the room was a rectangular glass island that held sunglasses, accessories, and the small supply of jewelry sold at the store.

"I've been thinking about it." Indigo shimmied out of her black blazer and dropped it over the glass island. "You, Lula, and I have a good rhythm and routine here, and I don't want to have it thrown off by adding a new person."

"We'll just learn a new routine," Hazel grunted as she leaned over the box, heaving up a stack of Manolo Blahnik pumps. "I hope your reluctance isn't because of Amanda, 'cause everybody ain't like her." She shoved the shoeboxes into the almost empty cubby.

Indigo snarled at the sound of the girl's name—the one who had stolen eleven thousand dollars' worth of merchandise. She was the reason Indigo had put up cameras in the inventory closet and the hallway, also adding a numerical code that needed to be punched in to gain entry to the room.

"I know." Indigo opened a box filled with Saint Laurent handbags. "Everyone isn't a thief."

"Yes." Hazel pondered which of the eight remaining boxes she wanted to open next. "That's the spirit, and with another associate, there'll be more time for you to do you."

Indigo groaned. "Argh, not with that again." She chucked the bags on the wall hook.

"What?" Hazel slid more shoeboxes into another cubby. "You don't want spare time?"

"It's not about the spare time." Indigo turned away from the wall on her bare heels, the squeaking of Gambit's chew toy coming from the baby monitor hooked to her back pocket. He was in her office since Tate wasn't around to watch him. "Nathan said the same thing Saturday. For me to do me, like what the hell is that supposed to mean?" She threw up her arms. "We're dating. We're supposed to be dating, and now he wants me to . . . what?"

What did he want her to do? The question plagued her.

Saturday, as she'd watched him eat, they'd carried on a trivial conversation when all she wanted to do was talk about the deeper subject at hand.

What was she supposed to be doing? Did he mean he wanted her to date someone else or search her soul? She didn't know, and more importantly, she didn't know what she wanted to do.

"Hold on. Back up." Hazel blinked at her with confusion. "I thought y'all were good. He's feeling you. You're into him. So . . ."

Indigo let out an audible breath that couldn't be drowned out by the music in the background. "He told me about his alcoholism."

"Oh." Hazel's hands went to her waist. "I see."

Indigo's mouth gaped, remembering Nathan and Hazel's familial ties. "You knew, and you didn't tell me."

"Don't look at me like that." Hazel pointed at Indigo's furrowed brow and tilted head. "You're my girl, but he's my cousin, and I can't share what he doesn't want me to share."

"Right." Indigo nodded, knowing she'd never spill the affairs of Saxon and Harrison to anyone without them giving her the clearance to do so. "You're right."

A moment of silence fell as they went back to unpacking merchandise. "He caught me off guard." Indigo's words brought Hazel's eyes to her. "I wasn't expecting that kind of skeleton in his closet."

"Alcoholism strikes all types of people. You of all people know that."

Indigo toyed with her earring. "It runs in my mama's family, and that's why I was stressed all of yesterday." Her hand fell from her earlobe, and she grabbed the last purse out of the box. "It's an unpredictable beast, and I don't know if I want to—"

"Sign up for that," Hazel interjected, breaking down the box she had finally emptied.

Indigo walked to the wall of hooks with a burgundy satchel. "Doesn't that make me selfish? Judgmental?"

"More like responsible." Hazel cut open another box. "He has a serious condition, and . . ." She stopped, her fingers going to her lips as if she was deciding if she should say more. "Don't take it lightly. You need to be really sure."

The seriousness of Hazel's features gave Indigo even more pause. "Why?"

Hazel quickly shook her head. "He's still navigating his sober life, but that's all I'm going to say about it." She waved her hands as if she was uncomfortable discussing the subject of Nathan's illness.

"I think I'm going to be responsible." Indigo stabbed the sharp tip of the box cutter into the box's tape. "I should take some time."

• • •

It had been three and a half days since she'd spoken to Nathan. Not his choice, hers. She thought it would be easier to make a thorough decision about continuing their relationship if she halted communication for a while. It was a difficult tactic, since they'd been talking every morning and night, with random texting throughout the day. That was why she was more eager than usual for work in the morning and welcomed the next task her mama sent her on the Birthday Preparation List—her mama's title, not hers. It was a list sent to her in an email last month, which she had deleted "by accident."

"I hope you wore your sweatpants," Harrison exclaimed, advancing toward her little table in the back of Decadent Delights with a ceramic platter balanced on one hand up above his shoulder. "Because I have six options."

Her birthday was just over a month away, and it was time for her to pick one of the most important things other than her shoes.

"Six." Indigo set her phone on the table faceup, not paying attention to the eyes of customers on them because of Harrison's booming voice. "I thought there were four choices. I gave you a list of four. Forget it. I know who added them." She rubbed her hand down the front of her black dress with a white Peter Pan collar. She sucked in her stomach as Harrison set the platter down, deeply inhaling the addictively saccharine scent of the cakes cakes in front of her. The sun pouring in the windows shone on the colorful frosting. It was going to be nearly impossible for her to have just one bite of each, especially since it was almost lunch and her tuna wrap was back in her office at Adorn. "These all look good, though. Good job, Harris."

"Hmm." He handed her a fork. "Did you doubt my skills?"

"No. Never." She twirled her fork, trying to decide which mini cake she was going to devour first. "Decisions, decisions." Well, at least this one was going to be a tasty one, she thought to herself, doing a happy dance in her seat.

Harrison flipped a chair around to sit backward. "It's summer, so I wanted everything to be light and bright. That's the lemon poppy seed raspberry layer cake." He pointed to a circular faintly red cake at the corner of the platter. "Blueberry lavender, 'cause you love blueberry and lavender."

Indigo nodded with excitement in her eyes. "Does it smell like lavender?" She moved her fork to the dessert, but he waved it away.

"Wait until I'm finished." He halted her fork with a cake knife.

Indigo frowned with a roll of her eyes. "Continue." She'd forgotten how serious he was about his presentations.

"Caramel cake. Your favorite." He pointed to the third, lightly brown dessert with caramel frosting sheathing the small square cake. "Triple chocolate cake: chocolate buttercream, bittersweet chocolate ganache filling, and of course chocolate cake. Mmm." He fawned over the dessert. Indigo didn't have to guess which one he was lobbying for. "And the last two, mint chocolate chip and dulce de leche, Mama's choices."

"Bypass those." She flicked her fork at the cakes.

Harrison snapped his fingers. "Those were difficult to make. You're going to eat them."

"Good grief, little Harry." Indigo stabbed her fork into the cake that whetted her appetite the most: the caramel cake. "Dial it back. I'm tasting everything, just not picking them." She popped the cake into her mouth. Her eyes rolled back, and her taste buds did the shuffle. "Mmm."

"Good." Harrison's smile rivaled the glee of the little boy behind him getting a cookie from his dad.

Indigo reluctantly swallowed the scrumptious confection. "Fantastic." She hovered her fork over the next cake, chocolate. "They say diamonds are a girl's best friend, but since I'm on my cycle, this chocolate and I are about to be best buds."

"Eww." Harrison gagged. "I don't need to know when you're on your . . ." He gagged again.

"Grow up. It's a part of nature." She cut a generous forkful of cake. Her phone chirped, halting the flight of the fork to her mouth. Her heart began to leap as she shifted her eyes to the phone. She read the name of the text's sender, and her nose scrunched.

Harrison's eyes quickly scrolled across her phone. "Diego. Art gallery. Y'all going on a date?"

"Nosy much." Indigo flipped her phone over before trying the chocolate cake.

"How'd he get your number?"

"Your sister," she muttered through the creamy chocolate frosting blanketing her tongue and the moist cake sticking to the roof of her mouth.

Harrison glanced over his shoulder. "Can you bring over a cup of hot tea?" he asked one of the servers behind the counter, then turned back to Indigo. "So, you and Nathan are still going strong?"

Indigo started to nod but decided against it. This was her brother, and unlike Saxon, he could keep a secret. She shook her head.

A curly-haired teenage girl brought over a dainty cup of tea, and Indigo graciously welcomed it. She took a generous sip of the warm hibiscus tea, loving how it mingled with the traces of chocolate that lingered on her tongue. Over the cup, her eyes found an inquisitive Harrison, so she swallowed.

"It's complicated." She half shrugged, setting the teacup gently on the saucer. "He's an alcoholic, and he wants me to take some time to decide if I want to be in a relationship with an alcoholic."

"Whoa." Harrison scooted closer to the table, leaning over the back of the chair. "That's—"

"Intense."

"Very." He trailed his finger along the edge of the platter. "So, have you decided?"

"No." Indigo dropped her back against the chair, slouching. "Alcoholism, Harris, alcoholism." She took a breath as he nodded. "We haven't spoken since Saturday, and I'd be lying if I said I didn't miss him . . . 'cause I do. A lot." She pulled her braids over one shoulder and began toying with the blunt ends. "But you know what Uncle Ruben went through with Aunt Cora." She neared the table. "He had to raise Cairo by himself 'cause she couldn't . . . the disease got the best of her. Hell, we don't even know where she is to this day."

Harrison rubbed his jawline, peering at her intently. "You know every alcoholic isn't like Aunt Cora, right? He might be coping well."

"He sees a therapist and has a sponsor, so . . ." She exhaled deeply then dropped her face in her hand. "It's not supposed to be like this. I'm supposed to find the right guy, one I click with, and everything is supposed to click." She groaned, lifting her head back up.

Harrison tsked. "Life ain't Legos. Shit doesn't just click into place."

"That I know." She let out a heavy sigh.

Dating someone with an addiction had been one of her deal breakers, but she was starting to care for a man who suffered from the illness, and now she was unsure if it was to remain a deal breaker.

"Let me share this." Harrison glanced over his shoulder at the line that was starting to grow. "I'm dating someone Mama probably won't like, but things don't always come the way or in the package you want them to."

"Tulip?" Indigo tilted her head. "Mama likes her."

"Someone else." He waved off her curious look. "Not important. This isn't about me. It's about you." His eyes went to her phone, then back to her. "Maybe you should go out with Diego. Maybe it'll help you with your decision."

"As what?" She drummed her fingers on the phone. "A distraction?"

Harrison smirked. "Call it what you want." He stood up as the chatter of the line swarmed around them. "Pick a cake. Make a decision. Do something." He walked away from her.

Make a decision, she repeated to herself, reading Diego's text inviting her to go with him to an art exhibit. "Hmm." Her thumbs hovered over the screen's keyboard. She liked art. Correction, she loved art, and Diego wasn't all that bad. She could tolerate him for a night, dress up, and partake of some beautiful artwork.

Indigo quickly typed, *You remember my address. Pick me up, and don't be late.* She tapped Send before she could talk herself out of it.

"Just a distraction," she told herself, picking her fork back up.

Chapter 20

Diego wasn't going to be late. As a matter of fact, he wasn't even going to pick her up. Indigo was busy helping out with the noonday rush when she received a text from him letting her know that a problem with a client had come up and he had to stay at the office. At first, she was upset. She had been looking forward to spending time with him, which surprised her, but they had had a good conversation when he'd driven her home from the hospital, and she wanted to continue it. Then she got an idea. Granted, it was bold.

The afternoon sun quickly faded as she finished tending to her last customer of the day. She took Gambit home and read Diego's text one last time before hopping into the warm shower. She slipped on a racerback blouse, jeans that hugged her curvaceous figure, and a pair of Ralph & Russo pumps, spritzed two sprays of Versace Bright Crystal Absolu on her neck, and kissed Gambit on the head before heading out the door. The last thing her brain wanted her to do was think about what she was about to do. She just acted.

The hallways of Stewart & Snyder were as quiet as a cemetery. After going to Diego's office and finding no one, she was about to head to the elevator until she bumped into his secretary, Vanessa, who informed her that he was in the place most junior partners sent their paralegals—the Law Library.

A couple of baby-faced interns were whispering about torts when she spotted Diego in the corner conference room. Indigo stopped in the doorway, taking in the sight of him huddled over a stack of books. There was something about a man reading that made her heart do cartwheels.

He had had a long day, she could tell from the absence of a tie that had no doubt matched the gray suit he had on. The top two buttons of his white dress shirt were undone, giving her a full view of his Adam's apple. His full lips moved gingerly as he ran his eyes, covered with black-rimmed glasses, over the text.

"So, you begged me for a chance and then stood me up." Indigo broke the silence, and Diego's head popped up.

"What are you doing here?" He tried to hide the smile that had started to form on his face by pulling off his glasses. "I thought you were ghosting me when you didn't text back."

"I'm a grown woman. I don't ghost." Indigo pushed herself off the doorframe. "I'll just tell you to go to hell and not come back." She set a box of burgers and fries on the long table.

Diego unknowingly licked his lips as he took in the spread, prompting Indigo to bite her lip. "So, you brought me food for my trip to hell." He looked back at her.

"Um . . ." Indigo blinked away her carnal thoughts. "No." She cleared her throat, pulling out one of the chairs. "It's your lucky day, Mr. Simpson."

"And how did I get so lucky?" He didn't try to hide the smile that beamed on his face.

"My parents are . . . well, you know, so I know how time-consuming being a lawyer is." She set her tote bag on the table.

"Which is why I brought dinner and a movie to you." She pulled the box of food to the middle of the table. "I didn't know what you liked, so . . ."

"You got four burgers."

"One's for me." She smirked. "Don't be greedy." She grabbed the cheddar jalapeño burger out of the box along with a side of fries. "But the shake is yours." She slid the green cup over to him. "It's a salted caramel milkshake from the place next door. I swear once you taste it, it'll be the only milkshake you'll ever want."

Diego wrapped his hand around the cup. "Where's yours?"

"Oh, God no." Indigo's eyes widened as she unwrapped the green paper from the burger. "I'm trying to get ready for Hot Girl Summer."

Diego smirked as he watched Indigo dump the fries next to her burger. "You're already ready."

"Mr. Simpson!" she said with mock surprise. "Are you checking me out?"

"Every damn time you're around." He placed his lips around the straw. "Damn, this is good."

"Told you." She bit into a fry.

Diego grabbed a neatly wrapped burger from the box. "So, since this is my lucky day, what else do I get?"

"A movie." Indigo reached for her tote bag. "It's my second-favorite western." She produced an iPad.

"And what's that." He blessed her with his deep, throaty chuckle. "*American Outlaws*?"

"Yes," she said with shock.

"With Colin Farrell?"

"Yes."

He narrowed his eyes on her. "Is that why you watched it?"

"No." She rolled her eyes at him. "Yes," she corrected. "But that's not why I kept watching. It was a pretty good movie."

"But not a great one." He plucked the onions off the double cheeseburger. "No western made in the 2000s is."

She pushed her back against the chair, twisting her mouth. "Does that stand for the *Magnificent Seven* remake too?"

"I'm sorry, Denzel." He held up his hands, holding the half-eaten burger firmly. "But the original is still the best."

Indigo tapped the screen of the iPad. "Well, you're in luck, 'cause the movie I downloaded is *American Outlaws*."

Diego stopped chewing as his face went blank, and all the glimmer drained from his eyes.

She busted out laughing. "Gotcha."

"You're a bad girl." He wagged his finger at her as he regained his chew. "Are you going to come over here?" He patted the chair next to him. "Or stay over there?"

"It's my iPad, bruh." She propped the iPad up as the movie began to play. "You can come over here." She sat back in the chair and slipped off her sandals.

Diego pushed back his chair. "You don't have to tell me twice."

• • •

"This is stupid." Indigo turned away from the stairwell. "I'm not doing it." She marched toward the elevators.

Diego ran to catch up with her quick strides. "No. No. No." He jumped in front of her. "You said you wanted to work your food down." He took hold of her hand and led her back to the stairs. "And have fun." He gestured toward the double-wide stairs that led to the lobby of Stewart & Snyder.

"It's not enough that you made me sprain my ankle." Indigo's voice echoed in the empty corporate building. "You want me to end up in traction too." She looked down at the lobby, shrouded in shadows from the welcome desk in the moonlight coming through the glass exterior.

"Traction." He laughed. "Look, I'll go first if you're too scared."

"Don't try to use reverse psychology on me." She flipped her hair back over her shoulder. "'Cause it won't work."

"I'm not." He kicked off his black oxfords then untucked his dress shirt. "I'm going to have fun with or without you." He lifted his body to sit on the stair rail. "See you at the bottom." He gave her a wink before lifting his legs and sliding down the rail like a child, hooting as he descended.

Indigo laughed as he tumbled to the ground. He popped to his feet with his arms up like he had scored the winning touchdown.

"Come on!" He waved for her to join him. Indigo shook her head. "Don't be a chicken."

"I'm not." Indigo flashed him her middle finger.

"That finger's going to get you in trouble." He pointed at her with a glint in his eye.

"Whatever," she said, waving off his comment and hating the fact that she wondered what type of trouble she could get into with him.

He smiled up at her as she pulled off her sandals. She slowly climbed onto the stair rail, inhaling a deep, nervous breath.

"Come on." Diego fixed the roll of his sleeve. "I won't let you fall." He moved to the end of the stairs.

Indigo took another breath and lifted her bare feet into the air. She slid down the rail, picking up speed like a snowball rolling down a hill. She closed her eyes, letting out a squeal.

Indigo's squeal gave way to a squeak as she opened her eyes and crashed into Diego's chest. The impact sent him stumbling back. Their laughter echoed through the lobby as they regained their footing.

Indigo clung to Diego's waist. "That was fun."

"See." He pushed her hair from her face. "I told you I wouldn't let you fall." He lifted her chin as he leaned closer to her. Indigo pulled in a breath as he lowered his lips toward hers.

"What's going on here?" The resonant voice made Indigo feel like a teenager again.

Indigo ripped herself out of Diego's arms and turned in the direction of the voice. "Mama!" She fixed her blouse with frantic fingers. "What are you doing here?"

"I work here." Mrs. Clark, in a taupe suit and cream blouse, strutted out of the dimness. "What are you doing here?" She tightened her grip on her tan briefcase.

"I . . . um . . . brought Mr. Simpson some dinner," Indigo muttered then cleared her throat.

Diego tucked his shirt back into his pants. "Burgers and fries." He nodded and smiled at the older woman, who remained still as concrete.

"Very nice of her." Mrs. Clark shot her eyes over to Indigo then put them back on Diego. "Shouldn't you be working on the Sullivan case?"

"Yes." He scratched his eyebrow. "Yes, I should." He leaned in to kiss Indigo on the cheek then pulled back, patting her on the shoulder instead. "Thanks for dinner."

"You're welcome," Indigo quipped as she watched him jog up the stairs.

"What are you doing?" her mom barked, focusing back on her middle child.

Indigo chuckled at Diego almost tripping on the top stair. "Nothing."

"Nothing." Mrs. Clark's gold bracelets jingled as she crossed her arms.

Her mother's tone vanquished the humor in the atmosphere. "Are you okay?" Indigo studied her mama's knitted eyebrows and tight lips. "Did Daddy do something? Are y'all feuding over the color of throw pillows again?" She smiled, but since her mama didn't, the corners of Indigo's mouth fell.

"He is a lawyer at this firm." Mrs. Clark tilted her head, narrowing her eyes at Indigo. "You cannot carry on with him like that."

Indigo took a step back, taking in her mama's agitated state.

"I'm not following. What's the problem with me hanging out with Diego?"

"So, he's Diego now? Because a couple of minutes ago, he was Mr. Simpson."

"Yes, Mama, he's Diego, and tomorrow I might call him D."

Mrs. Clark's eyebrow rose. "Watch your tone."

"Tone watched," Indigo said, taking a deep breath. "Xavier's a lawyer at this firm, and I don't recall you telling Saxon not to carry on in a particular way."

"It's not the same."

"How is it not?"

"Xavier is a family lawyer, and they were already married before he started working here." Mrs. Clark switched her briefcase to her other arm as she crossed the lobby to stand next to Indigo. "But his profession is not the issue. I don't need my daughter tying her sail to a boat that isn't about to slow down."

Indigo bit down on her lip with furrowed brows. "What are you saying?"

"I'm saying . . ." She took a breath as her features softened. "I know things you don't. His ambitions are not the same as yours, and you need to pump the brakes before you get hurt."

"Are you saying I'm not ambitious?" Indigo leaned back as if her mama's words had physically hit her.

Mrs. Clark shook her head. "I didn't say that."

"Mama, I'm not a teenager anymore." Indigo slipped her hands into the back pockets of her jeans. "If he's wrong for me, then I'll cut him loose."

"Okay." Mrs. Clark gave her daughter a lopsided smile then kissed her on the cheek. "Just know you've been warned."

Indigo nodded as her mama pulled back. She watched the woman whose advice she always cherished climb up the stairs, wondering one thing: What was the reason her mama didn't want her with Diego?

Chapter 21

"Can you not look constipated," Indigo called from behind the camera lens.

Hazel glared back at her, looking flawless in white shorts, a neon-orange top, and beaded leather sandals. "I'm not constipated. I'm hot as hell." She fanned herself, but the flick of her appendage wasn't creating enough air to combat the unrelenting sun. "I hate summer shoots." She stomped her foot like a child on the cusp of throwing a tantrum.

"This is the last shot." Indigo moved the camera away from her perspiring face. "Now, if you stop griping and stand there and look pretty, we can be finished."

Hazel tsked, then turned her snarl to the snickering coming from the shade. "Shut up, Emery! Before you choke on a cucumber."

"Don't hate me because I finished before the crack of hell o'clock," Emery said, lounging on a gingham blanket in the grass with a cup of iced tea in hand. "Get back to work, little one."

"Asshole," Hazel spewed, then turned back to Indigo.

"Okay." Indigo laughed, fixing the camera back in front of her face as Hazel posed like it was a cool spring day.

Someone had once told her that working with friends was a bad idea—her mama, to be precise—but even though it had its cons, the pros were much more rewarding. Also, rule number one of being a successful business owner was to keep costs down. By using Hazel as her model and Emery's spacious acreage as her location, her only cost was a tank of gas and lunch. Plus, where else could you get funny, bickering friends with hearts of gold and the ability to bring along Gambit, who was lying belly-up beside Emery?

"Done!" Indigo held her arms up triumphantly.

"Thank God, 'cause I'm melting." Hazel walked away from the gravel driveway to the blanket, collapsing on her belly beside Emery. "Tea me." She held out her hand.

Emery gave Hazel a sweating glass of tea as Indigo joined them on the blanket. "A little birdie told me you went on a date yesterday, and it wasn't with Nathan."

"I don't have to guess who that little birdie is." Indigo rolled her eyes over to Hazel.

Hazel stopped sucking on her straw, seemingly feeling renewed under the shade of the weeping willow. "There are no secrets between friends." She started swinging her legs. "So, how was it? Is fine-ass Diego a keeper, or do you need to throw his ass back in the water?"

"Ah." Indigo stopped scanning through the pictures she'd taken earlier that day, realizing picking the best frames would be as tricky as her dating choices. "Em, weren't you supposed to be going to Cancun with Hiran?"

"He had a work obligation, but don't switch the subject."

"I'm not." Indigo sat back, propping her head on Gambit's sturdy body. "I'm just asking my friend about her life."

"Mmm," Hazel said, tucking the wisps of her hair that were too short to reach her ponytail behind her ear. "It was good."

"Wrong," Indigo blurted out. "It was great." She pushed herself back up. "I was hoping he would be a total jackass, you know, like the day he came into the store, but he was funny and spontaneous and . . ."

Emery's cheeks were flushed, and Indigo didn't know if it was from the heat or Indigo's confession. "Are you feeling him? More than . . ." Emery's words trailed off as she glanced over at Hazel, then she shook her head. "I just think this is bad all around. You shouldn't be dating him while you're already dating Nathan."

"It was just one date," Indigo declared. "One—"

"Great date," Hazel interjected, wafting her eyes over Indigo's face. "He has you glowing. Y'all didn't do anything R-rated, did you?"

Indigo shook her head quickly, even though what her thoughts had drifted to last night was at least double-X worthy. "Strictly PG."

"I don't like him." Emery plucked a cucumber-tomato sandwich from the platter. "Diego is a heartbreaker, and I don't like him for you."

"Well, this isn't about you, Em," Indigo tossed back. "I'm testing the waters. Seeing if I'm sure about what I want, no matter the repercussions."

"And what're the repercussions?"

"Relationships are unpredictable, but a relationship with someone that has an addiction intensifies things." Indigo's voice carried over the clearing as Emery's eyes widened and Hazel's chewing on ice pellets stopped. "Which you should have told me about before you set me up with him. Both of y'all should have given me all the facts. Let me know what I was signing up for." She pushed herself up off the ground. "But now I'm here. Running all these scenarios and what-ifs in my head, but on the other hand . . ." She held up her palms at her sides as if they were scales. "There's Diego . . . who's the complete package with everything I ever dreamed of.

He's intelligent, successful, adventurous, and fine as hell."

"But he's a lawyer." Hazel spoke up, pouring more tea in her cup. "And doesn't Nathan check all those boxes?"

"That's what I'm saying," Emery added.

Indigo whipped her head toward Emery. "Now do you see my dilemma?"

Both Emery and Hazel went silent, but their faces gave their answer away. They understood that Indigo was in a predicament.

"I say date them both," Hazel proclaimed, only to get a dirty look from Emery and confusion from Indigo.

"I'm not a player." Indigo took a sip from her cup. "Nor do I want to be."

"I'm not saying do it for long, just for a trial period, like one of those . . ." Hazel snapped her white-painted fingertips. "Amazon free trial subscriptions, you know."

"No. We don't." Emery picked up Indigo's camera to peruse the footage from the day.

"I get what you mean, but I don't know." Indigo massaged the back of her neck. "I don't want to string anyone along, but . . ." She let it hang there for a moment as she thought. "I do want to make the right choice."

"Then date them both and be up-front about it." Hazel stood up, feeling antsy. "Let them know, and may the best man win."

"The heart of Indigo." Emery harrumphed. "You've got to be kidding."

Indigo's hand went slack around her neck. "You might be onto something."

"I know I am." Hazel put her hands on her hips confidently. "I'm a genius."

· · ·

Was Hazel a genius? Indigo was still trying to decide, but it was Friday, which meant she was busy and had little time to ponder affairs of the heart. Lucky her.

After work and meeting with Tulip about party planning, Indigo stopped by the grocery store. She was famished from running around all day and desired something home-cooked but had no clue what she wanted to eat.

She rolled the shopping cart down the grocery store's aisles, mentally going through meal options. Lasagna sounded good, but it was too much prep, more work than she wanted to do. A turkey sandwich was low in the preparation department, but she was more in the mood for a hot meal than a cold one. She settled for spaghetti and tossed a bag of tortilla chips in the basket for the ride to Tate's lake house, which was an hour and a half from her house.

Indigo slid her truck into her driveway, grabbed the grocery bags, and bumped the truck door closed with her hip. The bags were heavy, and her biceps were burning, but there was no way she was going back for another trip.

"Baby, I'm home!" she shouted, but her high register wasn't needed. Gambit was already in the foyer doing his happy dance. "Hey, boy!" She set the bags on the bench by the stairwell. "Have you been good?" She rubbed Gambit's back as he sniffed her pant legs, trying to decipher where she'd been and who she'd been in contact with.

Indigo knelt next to her furry friend. She was happy to be back home; she hated leaving him all alone. The canine tried hard to give his human friend a sloppy kiss, but Indigo dodged his pink tongue with giggles and a frisky rub. "Okay, boy, we got to get a move on." She stood, pulling up her waistband along the way. "I don't wanna be driving in the dark."

She strutted to the kitchen, dropped some food in Gambit's

bowl, and ran up the stairs to take a quick shower.

Refreshed and renewed, Indigo twisted her wet tresses into a messy bun. As she massaged her dewy skin with cocoa butter, her mind briefly wandered to the other night, thinking about how much fun she had had with Diego and how much she'd wanted to kiss him. Even now, her thoughts were on his lips and wondering how they'd feel against hers. Soft and luscious, probably.

She snapped her emerald studs onto her earlobes, and another thought invaded her mind—her mama. She knew her mama. She wasn't the most down-to-earth and warm woman. However, she'd never disliked anyone without just cause.

Indigo backed away from the mirror. There was no need to apply makeup for the person she was about to see—he'd seen her through her awkward phase.

In her bedroom, she was greeted by Gambit lying on the black-and-cream rug chomping on his battered Kong bone.

"Dang!" She gaped at the alarm clock on her nightstand: 5:45. She let out an annoyed breath. She had to hurry if she wanted to get to her destination before the sun went down. "Spent too much time in the shower, boy."

She bustled to her dresser for something comfortable to wear. She settled for a lime T-shirt and yoga pants then quickly packed an overnight bag. With swift hands, she rolled up some clothes, tossed in some underwear, grabbed two pairs of flip-flops and her toiletry bag, and threw it all into a striped canvas duffel bag. Seven minutes later, she and Gambit were out of the house.

• • •

The warm, brisk wind brushed across Indigo's face as she steadily pressed her foot on the gas pedal. Out of Houston's city limits and free of bumper-to-bumper traffic, she was able to enjoy the drive.

Indigo lounged in the driver's seat with one hand gently holding the bottom of the steering wheel and the other gliding a tortilla chip toward her mouth. Her mind was free of all the worries and doubts that wore her down during the week. The view was all green sprawling land scattered with livestock. She wasn't thinking about Nathan's alcoholism or Diego's appeal, nor was she ruminating over the remaining details that had to be ironed out for her birthday soiree or over which one of the three interviewees she was going to hire come Monday morning. The only thought in her mind was, *Damn, I should've bought salsa.*

Her cell began ringing, interrupting her music and disrupting her chill. The Texas Trooper driving at her side prevented her from taking her eyes off the road to see who was calling, so she just tapped the green icon on the phone's screen.

"What's up?" she shouted over the loud air whipping in the windows.

"Nothing much. Just getting home." Diego's voice boomed through her speakers, and Gambit stopped sniffing the air to bark. Indigo quickly shushed the pooch and turned the volume down. "What are you up to?"

"Going to visit a friend." Indigo eased her foot off the gas as she rolled down the four-lane highway. "Why?"

"I just wrapped up a class action suit and was wondering if you'd like to meet up."

"And . . ." Indigo lifted her foot off the accelerator as an eighteen-wheeler merged into her lane. She didn't blame them; the state trooper had exited, and the sedan in front was driving slower than a sloth. "You want me to—what? Drop what I'm doing and come celebrate with you?" Indigo smirked to herself. He was fine but not that fine. "That was a onetime thing."

"I'm cool with that." She could hear the smile in his voice. "But when you get back, can I take you out . . . for real this time."

Indigo sighed contently as she caught sight of the sign for her exit, only a few miles away. "I don't know about all that . . . I'm a dog mom." She glanced at Gambit staring out the front window like he was a person. "I can't be dipping in and out." Since Tate had been gone, Gambit had had to be stuck in the house for more than eight hours a day, and the last thing she wanted was to come home and leave again.

"Again. That ain't a problem. Hell, bring him."

"You want me to bring Gambit on a date?" Hearing his name made the dog swivel his neck and peer at her. "Seriously?" Sure, Gambit was her homie, but was he a dating companion? She wasn't sure about that.

"Yeah, as long as I get to see you, I don't care who you bring." He chuckled. "Bring your dog, your brother, and your granny. Just come."

She laughed, and he matched her. "Tuesday'll work for me." Her pitch went higher unexpectedly. The minivan in front of her slowed down, and she hit the brakes. Her stomach lurched just a little as her reflexive arm held Gambit back, even though he was snug in his seat belt. She fixed the aviator sunglasses on her face. "When and where?"

"I'll text you when I have it all planned out," he assured her. She could hear music in the background. Was that the Spinners? She grinned, giving him extra points for his taste in music. "No later than Sunday."

Indigo looked at the orange sky above the highway with a sprinkle of cars. "Cool." She flicked on the turn signal. Her exit was coming up.

"Are you driving?"

"Yeah." She sailed off the highway, converging on the frontage road.

"I'll let you go so you can focus." His tone turned serious. "I don't need my girl wrapped around a pole just because I wanted to hear her voice."

His concern warmed her heart, but was she really his girl? "It's hands-free, and I'm an excellent driver, might I add. I passed driver's ed on the first try."

"That may be so, but it's the other jackasses that you need to watch out for," he explained. "Let me know when you get there safe."

"Sure."

"See you Tuesday?" he said as if he was asking.

"Certainly."

"Bye." His baritone was laced with cheerfulness.

"Bye," Indigo echoed, then the line died. Her music turned back on, but now she was in the mood for something else. "Hey, Siri, play Anita Baker."

Siri did as it was told, and the song that streamed out of her speakers made her smile.

"Gambit . . ." She looked over at the canine leering out the window as "Caught Up in the Rapture" crooned from her speakers. "I think Siri may be reading my mind."

• • •

"Turkey." Tate glanced over his shoulder as she entered the kitchen. He turned back to the small round balls sizzling in the iron skillet. "Really?"

Indigo yawned loudly, leaning on the kitchen island. The dark granite was cool on her forearms, and the oregano and basil floating through the air brought a smile to her face. There was almost nothing better than waking up to the smell of a home-cooked meal.

"The only thing you had here was Funyuns and Coca-Cola.

So, don't start." Her voice was still raspy from the thirty-minute nap, but her eyes were no longer foggy with sleep. "You ought to be happy someone cares about your little heart."

Tate humphed, flipping over the meatballs with tongs while his sous-chef, Gambit, leered up at the stove from a safe distance.

A contented warmth washed over Indigo as she watched Tate. He tipped the lid to the stockpot next to the skillet, flooding the air with more earthy herbs, making Indigo's mouth water. She hadn't expected the food to be simmering when she woke up. At the most, she'd hoped he would unpack the bags.

"Where'd you learn to cook?" she asked, reaching for the garlic bread still wrapped in its paper sack.

"YouTube, Pinterest, and . . ." Tate fixed the lid back on the pot then faced her. "Years of watching you, but the jury's still out on taste."

Indigo swiped a serrated knife from the wooden block. "Did you oversalt it?"

"Just added a little salt." He shook his head, defying the odds—the bun twisted on his head with a chewed-on pencil in it didn't come undone. "But the top to the black pepper did fall off."

Indigo laughed. "Hey, pepper never killed anybody. The hotter, the better. Can you turn the oven on Broil?" She delicately peeled the paper away from the garlic bread while he hit a button on the stove. "How's the book coming along?"

"It's coming," he sighed, moving to the fridge. "Twenty chapters deep." He opened the door and studied the meager selection of beverages on the top shelf: wine, water, and kombucha. He chose the wine. "My editor loves the idea, but Hiran isn't a fan of contemporary romance."

That didn't surprise Indigo. Hiran was lobbying Tate to sign on to the *Chronicles of the Undead* film project and not spend any more time crafting a manuscript in a new literary genre.

"I think the most important thing is . . ." She grunted, kneeling in front of the stove and the storage drawer stocked with pans of all shapes and sizes. "Do you love what you're writing? 'Cause you're the one who'll have to spend months on it." She grabbed the pan she wanted—a cookie sheet—hopped up, and closed the drawer with her foot.

"It captivates me. I think it's going to be a hit."

"Great." Indigo set the halves of the garlic bread on the pan. The creamy, buttery garlic-parsley mixture smeared over the inside of the French bread reignited the hunger in her belly. "That's all that matters."

"But I could be biased. Could you read it?"

"Sure." Indigo sauntered back to the oven. She let the heat warm her face and arm as she slid the pan inside.

"I mean later tonight." Tate delicately placed two wineglasses on the island. The way she held her waist as her eyebrows knitted together had him adding, "But only if you want to."

"I'll see what I can do, but I'm not making promises."

"Fine by me." Tate's lips curved up as he studied the wine bottle. "When did you start drinking chardonnay?"

"Trying something new." Indigo hopped onto the barstool at the island with another yawn. Reading the chapter later tonight was a serious no-go. All she was going to do was chow this food down then collapse in bed. It would have to be tomorrow, but she kept that to herself, or he'd start pouting.

Tate held the bottle at arm's length as if he needed his glasses to decipher the words scrawled across the label. "Alcohol-removed. What possessed you to buy this?"

"I said . . ." She glared at him sharply. "I'm trying something new."

"Mm-hmm." He twisted the corkscrew in the cork, and with a loud pop, the bottle was opened. Gambit, well acquainted with the noise, didn't stir.

"You're withholding something, but I'm going to find out."

"There's nothing to find out." She held out her hand. "Just give me my glass."

Tate gasped, holding her glass just out of arm's length. "Indigo Opal Clark! Are you changing yourself for one of these dudes? Did they say something about you drinking wine?" He narrowed his eyes on her. "What the hell is going on?"

"Nothing." Indigo lifted her butt off the stool to grab the stem of the glass, but he pulled it back. "Uh-uh, stop playing!"

"Then stop trying to be like one of those women."

"What women?"

"The kind that changes themselves to suit a man."

"I'm not changing—" She stopped because the word left a bitter taste on her tongue. "Alcohol . . . technically isn't good for you. It deteriorates the liver. Do you want my liver to die?"

Tate swirled the liquid around in the glass. "You nurse one glass of wine a night." He chuckled. "Your liver ain't dying from that. Plus . . ." He lifted the glass to his mouth. "Wine has antioxidants."

Indigo slid off the stool and wrenched the glass out of Tate's hand. "Thank you!" She grinned up at him before taking a long sip.

"You know, just because you're about to be the big three-oh doesn't mean you have to settle." Tate poured his own glass of wine.

Indigo lowered the glass from her lips. "And how do you know?"

"Since I'm your first kiss, last teenage boyfriend, and current best friend . . ." He matched his eyes to hers with a faint smile playing on his supple lips. "I know a woman like you should never settle."

"Um." Indigo's brain froze. The chilled glass did nothing to curtail the heat kindling beneath her flesh or the racing of her heart. She closed her eyes. "That's . . . um . . . Thank you." She peeked up at him with warm cheeks, slightly flustered, then averted her gaze—she didn't want him to know he could still have that effect on her after all these years. "I guess."

"No thanks needed." He grinned then playfully bumped his muscled bicep against her soft one. He sniffed the aroma circling them. "We should eat."

Indigo swallowed a gulp of wine, wishing it had alcohol. Of all nights, tonight had to be the one where she'd decided to try something new. "Most definitely."

Tate yanked open the oven door. "Damn! We burned the bread."

"Shit!" Indigo was happy to be talking about something other than her dating life. "Well, bread makes your butt big anyway." She shrugged. "And I don't need any more help."

"True." The corner of his lips lifted, but it wasn't from humor. His eyes glided over the curve of her hip and the smooth richness of her thigh not shielded by knit shorts.

"Hey!" She playfully punched his shoulder.

"It was a compliment." He held up his hands, toned biceps on full display in the loose black tank. "A big booty is a beautiful sight."

"Oh! I know you think so." She turned the oven off as he trashed the charred loaves of bread. "I bet you still have that collection of *King* and *XXL*."

"I—"

She looked at him pointedly with a hand on her hip. "Don't even try to lie."

"I'm not. I'm a grown man. I don't have to," he said coolly. "And I don't have them. They're at my parents' house, where I keep all my vintage things."

"Like your cello." She smiled fondly to herself, remembering those days after school when he'd practiced while she did homework on his bed. Those were simple times; she missed them. Things had been less complicated then. Easy.

"It's still there," he told her, grabbing two plates from the cabinet near the pantry. "Along with my baseball equipment, skateboard, and yearbooks."

"Haven't flipped through one of those in years." She took a sip of wine, still getting accustomed to the tart taste. "It might be fun to revisit."

All of her and her siblings' childhood and teenage keepsakes had been stored away in her parents' garage when her mom redecorated, turning one of their old bedrooms into a nursery for her grandchildren.

"They're coming back from Bahia soon; you can come with me to their welcome-home dinner."

"Isn't that for family?" She grabbed a pair of forks for them, moving around the kitchen as if it were her own.

"You're the daughter my mom wished she had." Tate placed the plates of steamy, mouthwatering spaghetti in front of the barstools.

The comment made her smile.

"She'd love for you to be there," Tate continued, claiming the barstool next to her. "Plus, it's always more fun when it's the four of us instead of just three." He bumped his shoulder into hers.

"Well, I love your parents. So, I'll be there, but you're driving."

"I wouldn't have it any other way."

"Good." She stabbed her fork into the hill of noodles. "Now, let's see if this is tasty."

"Everything I make is tasty."

"Let me be the judge of that, *Tasty Tate*," she joked as she spun the fork around, collecting a mouthful.

She closed her eyes to appreciate the bite, emitting a soft "Mmm."

"So, it's tasty, right?" Tate's husky tone made her eyes pop open.

She swallowed, fighting the urge to grin. "Don't get cocky."

"Too late." He shrugged. "Let's eat."

"Damn!" She slapped her hand down on the counter. "I've created a monster."

They both laughed then went back to eating. The leisurely conversation and frequent bouts of laughter reminded Indigo of one of the things she wanted in a potential partner: someone who made the simplest moments memorable.

Chapter 22

"You're going to be a good boy, you hear me?" Gambit's pink tongue hung out of his mouth as they stood on the doorstep of a breathtaking modern home with sharp lines and curb appeal. "No jumping. No begging." Gambit's marble eyes connected with hers, and she knew he understood. "Good boy." She patted his head before knocking on the frosted glass door.

It was a little past seven, and the summer heat was less intense. Still, she'd decided on shorts—a yellow floral pair that accentuated her sepia legs. A warm breeze brushed against her cream silk spaghetti strap blouse as she brushed her hand down the braid she had constructed.

Just as she smoothed her glossed lips against each other, trying to decide if she should knock one more time, the door swung open. "Hey!" Diego's chocolate eyes gleamed, causing her heartbeat to rise slightly. "Come in."

Indigo let Gambit enter before her. The canine sniffed the travertine floors. "Beautiful home." She stopped in the foyer by the floating staircase, viewing the leather couch in the living room.

"I'm leasing it." He shut the door behind them. "You can let him loose." He pointed to the black leash in her hand.

"You sure?" Indigo gawked at him with disbelief.

"Of course." Diego knelt, gliding his hand down Gambit's wide back, the pooch not paying him any mind as he sniffed all the scents lingering on the floor. "He's a good fella. Plus . . ." He stood. "We have a date. He's just along for the ride."

"Man, are you serious?" She side-eyed him, not really buying it. He was completely fine with two hundred pounds of furry muscle running around a house that was probably in the million-dollar price range? Exquisite artwork hung on the wall, so there was no telling what other delicate big-ticket items there were around of the house. "You don't have to front for me."

Diego waved off her words. "Girl, I'm not fronting. It's just a house, and he's an indoor dog." He leaned over and quickly unlatched Gambit's leash. "Go, boy! Frolic!"

"Don't!" She shoved his hands away, but it was already done. Gambit was free of his leash and following his nose down the hallway. "You jackass." She slapped his shoulder.

Diego found humor in her sharp tongue. "Are you ready to see what I have planned?" He slipped his hand into the pocket of his dark khaki chino shorts and suavely strode over to her. His lavender-patchouli scent was intoxicating, and the Isley Brothers harmonizing in the background wasn't putting out the sensual fire blazing within her.

Indigo blinked. "It better be good." She slid her gaze down his dreamy eyes, broad nose, and full, kissable lips. "'Cause you have a lot to make up for, you know."

"Don't fret." He reached over, locking his fingers on the intricate weaving of her plait. "I'll blow your mind." Indigo slapped his hand off her tresses with a tsk, and he chuckled. "Feisty. I love it."

The last thing Indigo would have imagined upon stepping out

into Diego's backyard was the scene that was laid out before her. It all came together—the text bombs of random questions he'd been sending her, inquiring about her top two favorite movies, indoor or outdoor, turkey or beef, chocolate or vanilla.

"Backyard movie!" She followed him over to the blanket flooded with plush pillows. "Did you do all this yourself?" she asked, lowering herself onto the blanket, her eyes on the massive screen with *The Others* inscribed across it.

Diego's confident smile was grand as he flipped open a wicker basket. "I'm a man of many skills." He handed her a sandwich wrapped in wax paper. "Turkey-tomato panini with avocado mayo."

She said with a trace of disbelief, "You made this?"

"Woman, take the sandwich." He peeled her hand off her knee and set the sandwich in her palm. "I got talent." He grabbed his sandwich out of the basket.

"Mm-hmm." She folded her legs underneath her bottom as Gambit dropped his big body beside her thigh. "So, what else is on the menu?" Even though the basket was at his side, she could tell it wasn't empty.

"Popcorn." He gestured to the screen. "And dessert." He pulled a small yellow cake box out of the basket. "Someone told me cara-mel cake is your favorite."

"Someone." She nudged Gambit's mouth off her knee. "Stop," she told the pooch. "You mean Harrison. 'Cause that's from his bakery. I helped him pick out the design."

"It is." He placed the cake box back in the basket. "But that's for the second movie."

Indigo nodded, raising the sandwich to her lips, positive that he was taking credit for a sandwich he'd picked up. She sank her teeth into the toasted bread. It didn't matter if it was homemade or store-bought—it was delicious. "Mmm," she hummed at the seasoned turkey and mozzarella.

Diego didn't speak a word, just gave her a gratified, close-mouthed smile then started the movie. After the food was finished and they'd drunk up all the blackberry-mint spritzer, the space between them dwindled. A mound of pillows held up their backs, bodies angled toward each other with their bare knees slightly touching.

Although Indigo's eyes were on the screen, her mind was deliberating. She didn't know what it was about him, why he had her pulse quickening. This shouldn't be happening, not with a man like Diego.

She was a woman well versed in her weaknesses, and her Achilles' heel was a debonair, well-spoken, intelligent man who wore suits and smelled of vanilla and patchouli. Her heart flipped, and her mouth grew dry. Then she skittered her eyes over at him and pondered whether maybe he was different. Maybe he wasn't like the others.

By the second movie, they'd both found their voices. "I can't believe *Boomerang* is one of your favorite movies." Diego fell back on the pillows after putting the disc in the projector.

"Why?" She sat up abruptly, staring down at him in his relaxed position. "You don't like it?"

"Out of all the millions of movies in the world, *Boomerang*." He shook his head with a laugh. "I'd pick *Boyz n the Hood* and *Takers* but—"

"But that's you," she interjected, stacking more pillows behind her before lying back. "Me." She pointed to herself then to the screen. "This is my jam."

Indigo felt the heat of his gaze, but she kept her eyes ahead.

Diego rumbled out a chuckle. "Let me stop." He slid closer to her no matter how tightly she folded her arms. "I like this movie too. Watched it like forty times." He slung his arm around her shoulder, drawing her near.

She wanted to pull away, thought about it, but the stoutness of his chest lulled her. His masculine scent enveloped her. With Gambit curled up in a ball at their feet, they watched, entertained by Eddie Murphy and Robin Givens. They both laughed at the same parts and commented during the same scenes.

Until a provocative moment sprawled across the screen. Indigo tore her eyes from the movie, not needing to add any more lighter fluid to the fire burning within her from the beating of Diego's heart against her back.

Indigo ripped herself out of his embrace.

"What do your parents do?" She quickly asked the question to eradicate the sexual tension erupting around them. "You grew up in Dallas, right?" She folded the extra blanket near Gambit's head and spread it over her legs. "Have you been back to see them?"

"That's a lot of questions in one breath." He smirked. "My parents are judges. They still live in Dallas, where I grew up, and no, I haven't been to visit them."

"Okay." Her eyebrows rose; she wanted to ask more but didn't want to appear nosy.

"You're wondering why." Diego sat up, turning his body toward her. He held her gaze for what felt like minutes then asked, "Aren't you?"

"Yeah."

She wasn't the closest to her mom, and they had their disagreements, but she still talked to her at least four times a week, and that didn't include the game and movie nights. She was curious and wondered if it was among the reasons her mom didn't want her fraternizing with him.

He chuckled. "Don't look so serious." He softly tapped the bottom of her chin with his knuckle. "I've just been busy starting a new job, getting acclimated to a new city. Too soon to go on vacation."

She nodded.

"And they understand I'm trying to make partner." He glanced down at his watch but didn't linger to read the time. "Being in the law profession, they understand the time constraints and dedication it takes to achieve that goal." He gestured to her. "And I'm sure it's something you understand too, being an entrepreneur."

"I do." She scooted closer to him, loving the connection he'd made with their professions. Even though she hadn't done the extra three years of education after earning a bachelor's degree, she'd still put in many years of hustle, hard work, and determination. "Being your own boss requires a lot of time, but now I've finally set up a system and hired the right people so that I can have the weekends off."

She even scheduled social media posts so she didn't have to manage those on the weekend.

"Weekends off." He glanced down at his lap with a faint shake of his head. "It may be a couple years, if I'm lucky, before I get to have every weekend off." He propped his arm on the stack of pillows with a grin on his handsome face. "But I do a lot of living in the hours I have free."

"And what are the things you like doing?"

"Since I'm in Houston and spending time with you," he said, taking her hand in his, "anything you want us to do."

"We're an 'us' now?" She chuckled, liking the way her hand felt in his.

"Anytime we're together, we're an us," he declared before placing a soft kiss on the back of her hand. "How do you feel about that?"

"I feel . . ." She paused to think about what she was feeling. Her body was pumping an array of emotions from thrilled to uncertain. Diego was growing on her, which didn't surprise her because she had been attracted to him the first time she saw him. It was his arrogance that had rubbed her the wrong way, but even that had toned down the more they talked. "That we could be a lot of things with more time."

"I don't have much time . . . but," he said, interweaving their fingers, "whenever I'm in town and have no obligations, I'm yours, and we can see where that takes us."

"Sounds doable," she admitted.

He looked at her with a fierceness that made her skin scorch and her cheeks flush, then, as his eyes dropped to her slightly open lips, she let out a slow stream of air. He pulled her closer to him and brushed his lips against hers, igniting a spark of passion that had her begging for more. She hooked her arms behind his broad neck, and he claimed her mouth as his feast. Her breath hitched as his hand slid up her thigh.

"Tell me if you want me to stop," he whispered huskily near her ear as he wrapped her leg around his waist.

Indigo bit her lip as his mouth found her collarbone. Words escaped every space of her mind as his soft lips peppered kisses up her neck. She gripped his shoulder as his hand glided down the bare skin of her thigh, sending a chill up her body. Lust blazed in her core.

Just as she let out a sultry moan, Gambit barked, snatching them out of their haze of attraction. Their dazed eyes shot to the pooch standing in front of them as if he was their chaperone.

"Uh . . ." Indigo put some space between her and Diego, slightly grateful for her four-legged friend bringing her back to logic. Sex would complicate things, and they were already complicated enough. "The movie ended."

"Yeah." Diego hopped off the ground. "I'll be right back. Restroom break."

"Okay." She nodded as he trotted back to the house. Once he disappeared inside, she glanced up at the starry sky, faintly fanning herself. "Shit, that was close."

. . .

Mondays were always busy at Adorn, especially the third Monday of the month. All day, repeat customers had streamed into the boutique with the 20-percent-discount card they had received in the mail weeks ago. Sure, 20 percent probably didn't seem like much, but a hundred bucks off a five-hundred-dollar price tag was still a deal. Well, that's how Indigo's customers felt, and she had made sales the entire day.

"You always want to do it the way you want to, but I don't like it like that." Indigo stopped typing numbers into the spreadsheet. "I'm not playing, Sax."

"Because your way's wrong," Saxon said in a singsong through the speaker of Indigo's cell.

Indigo frowned at her phone. "If you mess up my burger, you're going to be the one eating it." Her stomach groaned in protest. She pushed her laptop forward and leaned on the checkout counter.

The store was closed for the day, and if she hadn't been waiting on Nathan to stop by, she would have been updating Adorn's books in her office, sitting in her tufted swivel chair, not leaning on the metallic counter on the sales floor.

"Please, don't ruin my night. I'm hungry." She went over the dollar amounts in her spreadsheet.

"Fine. Toppings at the top and patty at the bottom. Do you want fries?"

"Duh." Indigo stopped nodding her head to Aaliyah's melodic voice streaming from the store's speaker system. She was the only one in the boutique, and the music consoled her.

Saxon chuckled. "Don't take too long. You know Harrison loves tomatoes, and the fries go fast."

"Yeah." Indigo's mouth slanted up in a half smile at the sight of Nathan standing at the locked doors. "I'll be there as soon as you get off the phone. Bye." She rushed the words out and hung up the call before Saxon could add her au revoir.

Indigo felt nervousness swell in her stomach as she headed toward the door. She didn't take pleasure in causing others pain, and Indigo feared what she had to say would do just that. But being truthful was best, right? It was what her parents had told her. Always tell the truth. They were probably right. She had lied before, and it had caused the person pain, then when the truth came out, they were hurt even more.

She twisted the lock and swung open the door with the warmest smile she could muster. "Welcome to Adorn." She fanned her arm out, gold bangles jangling as she gestured to the sales floor.

"Snazzy." Nathan nodded, entering the store. As she locked the door behind him, he took it all in—the unstained wooden floor, navy leather-tufted benches, and glass shelves full of luxurious shoes. "You did all this by yourself?" He lifted his sights up toward the elegant, modern crystal chandelier.

"The design? Yes." The light fixture, she'd bought at an estate sale. "This place used to be a candle shop. It was open for about a year then put up for sale. Emery told me about it, and when I saw it . . ." She remembered the days when she'd scavenged garage sales for deals on furniture and decor and the nights spent on DIY projects.

"The park across the street plus the great natural light . . ." The golden sun was still beaming down on the people visiting the lush yard. "I fell in love with it."

Nathan sidled next to her. "How are we? I mean . . . are we still a 'we'?"

"Oh, man!" She stepped away from him, folding her arms over her head.

Nathan rubbed his stubbled chin, his eyes widening slightly. "This doesn't sound good."

"A lot can happen in a week, you know." She whirled back around, her champagne shirtdress billowing out. "A lot happened last week."

"What happened?" He inched closer to her but stopped. The sun's glow highlighted the outline of his strong frame.

"I did this thing I do, which you probably don't know because we haven't been dating for that long." Indigo gestured, and her words came faster than her mind could string them together. "I analyze things to determine if they're cost-effective, but before we met, my sister told me to follow my heart, and I did that . . ." Her gaze drifted from him as "4 Page Letter" played over the speaker. "I felt something for you that I haven't felt for many guys at first glance—"

"Our affinity for vintage things?" He shrugged, his burgundy shirt clinging to his torso without being too tight—it was just right.

"No." She glued her eyes back to his face. "Comfortable. You made me comfortable."

"Made? As in—"

"It took me a week to go over all these things . . . how you make me feel, your addiction and the uncertainty of it—how it scares me a little. But I keep coming back to the same realization. I just like you." She shrugged haphazardly. "I really like you, even though my brain isn't fully on board." She wrapped her arms around her waist, a serene smirk tugging at her mouth. "I enjoy your company."

"Ah." Nathan clutched his chest. "I thought you were cutting me loose." He closed the space between them with a pleased smile. "But I get it. This is all new. Alcoholism is a little heavy, but I got it all under control." He tentatively looped his arms around her waist. "And I'll show you that . . . but it's barely been two months, and we're still figuring it all out. Dating-wise."

Dating. Nathan said it with so much ease that he caused her to blink. It felt like gambling to Indigo: investing time and emotions without being sure if it'd all work out in the end. However, she'd made her lists in the past, examined her old relationships before committing to those men, and they hadn't worked out, so maybe she needed to do things differently. Go with the flow. Figure things out along the way.

"Right." She twisted her mouth to the side with a crinkle in her nose, clinging to his arms. "And in the name of dating and keeping things transparent, I . . ." She leaned back, bracing for a shift in his demeanor. ". . . I went on a date. With someone else." Surprised that his shoulders didn't tense up after his chest rose from the deep breath he took, she continued. "And I have another one."

"Damn." He shifted back, letting his hands sit around her waist.

"What?" She bit her bottom lip. "Too much?"

"Nah." His eyes left her face, scanned her curvaceous body, then moved back to her face. "I'm not surprised. You're a beautiful, successful woman. Your phone's probably filled with dudes' numbers and texts."

That would be incorrect. Indigo's contact list was concise, with only business, family, and friends' numbers. There was only one other guy: Diego. "Intimidated?"

"Pssh." He pulled her back to him, tightening his hold around her waist. "Not at all. Competition is healthy. Anyway, he'll just prove that I'm the guy for you."

"Confident." She rose on her tiptoes, locking her arms around his neck. "I like it."

Chapter 23

It was May 21, and she probably should've had her birthday dress picked out already, but it was the last thing on her mind, which was saying a lot for someone who loved fashion.

Currently, she stood barefoot on a pedestal in a white ball gown that made her feel like a stunt double for Anne Hathaway in *Bride Wars*. Mirrors didn't lie, and the three she was peering into were telling her the abundance of tulle, taffeta, and satin was activating her gag reflex. At every angle, the dress was hideous.

"Phenomenal," her mom praised, perched on a beige settee with her legs crossed. Indigo inwardly cringed as her mama tipped a half-filled champagne glass toward the eager saleswoman. "What necklace would you suggest?"

What necklace would you suggest? Indigo thought to herself as she picked at the satin bodice. *This sack is staying here.*

The saleswoman, wearing all black with a sugary smile, walked across the room behind Indigo, appraising. "Some people would go with a choker, but I'd personally . . ." She looked between Stella and an interested Indigo. "Nix the necklace."

"Really?" Stella's head reeled back.

"Yes." The saleswoman nodded, happy that someone was engaging in conversation with her since the store was relatively quiet for a weekday at noon. "With an off-the-shoulder dress, that'll be too much going on. A beautiful woman like your sister—"

"Daughter," Stella quickly corrected.

Indigo rolled her eyes as the woman laughed off the mistake. Flattery might get you everywhere, but it wouldn't get Indigo to pull out her credit card. "Necklace. No necklace. I don't care. I look like a marshmallow." She brushed her hands down the pounds of tulle, but the skirt remained steady in its place. "I'm not wearing this dress. This is for a birthday. Not a wedding."

"Okay." The saleswoman's expression dimmed. "I can go pull something else from the rack." She jutted her thumb to the rows and rows of high-end designer dresses.

Indigo turned up her nose, examining the rack of dresses she'd already tried on—all duds. "Don't bother yourself . . ." She paused to read the name on the silver name tag pinned to the woman's shirt. "Florence. Can you just help me out of this prom dress so I can get back to work?"

Florence looked over at Stella as if she needed permission. Maybe she did, since Stella was the one who had scheduled the appointment. Indigo, however, didn't need permission. She pulled her phone out of her purse on the other end of the settee. There were three texts and one missed call, not bad for a Wednesday. Indigo read the texts in order. Emery wanted to know if she was still coming to the baseball game; Saxon had sent her a funny dog video her son showed her; and the last one was from Nathan, asking if she wanted him to pick her up for their date or if she wanted to drive herself.

"I didn't raise you to be rude." Stella snatched the phone out of Indigo's hand. "I don't care how old you are. That woman was doing her job." Her mom pointed to the spot where Florence had once stood. "And you dismissed her."

"Mama." Indigo paused to ponder her words. She wanted to remind her mother that she worked in customer service and had honed the talent of being courteous. She knew how to deal with people without appearing sanctimonious, but the crease in her mama's forehead insisted she take a different approach. "I wasn't dismissing her. I was releasing her so she could help someone who actually needs her help, and I already have a dress better than this." She frowned down at the gown.

"You have a dress?" Stella's voice died as her eyes lowered to the vibrating phone in Indigo's hand and she took it. "Had fun last night?" Her hard eyes bored into her daughter, and when Indigo reached for the phone, she pulled it back. "Is this why you missed family game night? Because you were having fun with Diego?"

Indigo stuck her hand out, waiting for her phone. "Missing one game night isn't a crime, and neither is me dating Diego."

"So, you're dating him now?" Stella's head tilted in that you-don't-know-everything-about-everything way Indigo was used to. "And he told you his life plans?"

"Mama, we're dating. Not engaged." She observed her mama's unchanging features. "We're still learning about each other, but we do have a lot in common."

"Is that so?" Stella set the cell in Indigo's palm.

"Yes!" Indigo's voice raised, and her mama's heated glare informed her of the shaky ground she was treading on. "Excuse me for my tone, but I won't apologize for enjoying the company of a charming, hardworking, resilient man." She grabbed her purse off the settee. "You've never agreed with any of the choices I've made, and you know . . ." She shrugged weakly, feeling tears sting the back of her eyes. "When I was younger, it used to eat me up inside, but now—" She flung up her arms as she backed away. "It doesn't faze me. I'm the disappointing daughter."

Indigo turned before her mother could speak. She didn't need to hear any more or be cross-examined. Nope, she didn't need to hear how it had been a mistake to turn down Dartmouth for a state school. Or how being a boutique owner didn't hold the same prestige and clout as a legal eagle. Or that being single and childless, unlike Saxon, was a blemish on the Clark name.

• • •

Indigo's stomach was still in knots as she peered down at the steaming container of orange chicken at her desk. Her phone sat next to her keyboard, since she knew what was coming next—a call from her dad. The expert mediator always called to hear her side of the story and find a plan to resolve the conflict. Indigo just didn't know if she and her mama could iron out the issues between them this time. Apologies and dinner at one of the swanky, pretentious restaurants her mama always insisted on wouldn't cut it.

"What's wrong with you?" Hazel was sitting on the other side of the desk with her bare feet propped up on the other chair and her food on her lap. "How can you be in a shitty mood after shopping?"

"With my mama," Indigo said, delicately mixing the syrupy mandarin sauce into the fluffy jasmine rice, "the possibilities are numerous." She reflected on their many shopping excursions over the years.

Clothes shopping had always been a tug-of-war between Stella and Indigo Clark. Where Stella colored inside the lines, wishing to remain conservative, Indigo wanted to take risks—show a little midriff, subtract some inches off the skirt that sat at the knees, wear heels with shorts.

"She liked something. I didn't. I voiced my opinion. Boom!" Indigo dropped her fork, devoid of an appetite. "The fatal flaw . . . thinking I have an option." She sulked back in her comfy chair.

Remorse painted Hazel's features. "Thank God my mama hates shopping." She dipped her spring roll in some sweet-and-sour sauce. "But you're turning thirty . . . wear whatever you want. As long as it's not a T-shirt and a thong, they should be happy."

Indigo snorted out a laugh as she collapsed back in the chair. "Oh, Hazy, you have a way of making things simple."

"I know. It's my superpower." She grinned, grabbing another spring roll from one of the four take-out containers on the desk.

For the life of Indigo, she couldn't understand how Hazel could put away so much food and remain the size of a string bean. Maybe she had a tapeworm? But most likely it was her metabolism and high energy level.

Downing the spring roll in two bites, Hazel snapped her fingers in her friend's direction. "Didn't you have a date the other night?"

Indigo leaned back over her food, finding her appetite. "Nuh-uh."

Hazel dropped her feet off the chair. "Spill." Her mouth opened with an airy gasp. "You had sex with him!" She sprung from the seat. "Tell me everything!"

Indigo slowly chewed the tangy yet sweet chunk of chicken. "A lady doesn't kiss and tell."

A packet of duck sauce flew past Indigo's head and smacked her chair.

"Elaborate." Hazel demanded. She checked the gold analog wall clock. Their lunchtime was a couple minutes from concluding. "'Cause I know it's good from the way you're avoiding it." She propped her elbows on the desk and held her face like a child waiting for story time.

"It was . . ." Indigo tilted her head, contemplating the exact word that would encompass all the emotions she had felt last night. "Let me start by saying Diego surprised me, you know? After he canceled our first date."

Hazel eagerly nodded, scooting up a bit.

"The amount of thought and planning that went into the evening, it was just . . ." She beamed a bright smile.

"Shit." Hazel slapped the desk, looking over Indigo's elated features. "You're digging this dude."

"After the BS he caused here and the overall arrogance he exudes, I assumed he was a chauvinistic playboy. But during our date, he showed me a side of himself that was warm, beautiful, and endearing."

"You still didn't answer my question." Hazel peered at her sideways with narrowed eyes. "Did y'all do the *nasty*?" She sang the word, standing to wind her small hips.

"We didn't," she finally answered. "I don't want to muck up my mind even more."

"I don't know." Hazel shrugged. "But then maybe you're right. Diego does have big dick energy." She held up her hands in surrender. "And he might know how to use it." Her eyes went back to the clock—the minute hand was past the six. "Time to get back to work. You and Nate still on?"

"Yeah." Indigo snapped the plastic top over her food. Her hunger hadn't come back. "Why wouldn't we be?"

"You might feel differently now."

"Nope." She stood up from the chair, fixing her blouse. "If anything, I'm more confused than before. But, um . . . this . . ." she said, gesturing between the two of them, "stays between us. I know you and Nate are cousins, but—"

Hazel stopped at the door. "Girl code." She patted her heart.

"But the minute there's penetration, you have to let him know."

"Of course." Indigo nodded, wondering if her heart counted.

Chapter 24

Saturday, Indigo found herself at Calder's, a little pub near the field where Nathan and his team had been massacred just twenty five minutes ago in an intramural soccer game. Conversation, laughter, and upbeat music filled the atmosphere. Some people were at the bar, with hands on beers and eyes on the flat-screen as commentators debated NBA trade deals, while other people were scattered around the tables. Sitting in a booth by the window, surrounded by three recently sweaty men, Indigo tapped her mouth in contemplation.

"Let me get this straight." Indigo pointed to the man across from her. He had a grass-stained yellow shirt, clean-shaven head, and a full beard wrapping around his face. "Ash, from Phoenix, moved to Houston because you got a football scholarship at U of H, and you're an accountant for Walcott Bank and Trust—where you met Freddie . . ." She moved her index finger to the man with the curly fro wearing a gray hoodie and sitting next to Ash. "Financial examiner who grew up in Fifth Ward, graduated from Prairie View, and is getting married in four weeks. Right?" She smiled, hoping she'd remembered the things they had told her before the game.

"That's right!" Freddie returned her smile and reached his fist over the table. Indigo pounded her fist to his.

Ash swallowed a swig of beer. "Damn, Nate! About time you bring a smart girl around."

Nathan's cheeks began to flush as he rubbed his hand down his face. "Hey, Ash, if you don't want me to bring out your skeletons, you better stop broadcasting mine."

"No!" Indigo playfully slapped Nathan's arm. "Ash, please tell." She pushed over the fried pickle slices and inched closer to the table with a toothy smile.

Freddie shrugged as Ash slid his eyes over to Nathan.

"Look at me." Indigo snapped her fingers at Ash, pulling his gaze to her. "Don't look at him!" She put her hand in front of Nathan's face.

Nathan grabbed her wrist and planted a kiss on the palm of her hand, earning a coy smile from Indigo. "You don't want to hear about my exes." He interlocked their fingers and rested their hands on his thigh. "They're irrelevant anyway."

"He just doesn't want you to know about the stripper," Freddie spilled with his eyes glued to the TV, watching Curry throw the ball up for a three-pointer.

Silence claimed the table as a wicked smile spread across Indigo's face, and Nathan glared at Freddie. Then Ash's hyena-like chuckles engulfed them.

"Dude!" Nathan tossed a balled-up napkin at Freddie.

The napkin popped Freddie on the forehead, and he finally tore his eyes away from the screen. "Bruh, what the hell!"

"You told her about Cinnamon?" Ash snickered at Freddie's bewildered face.

"I did?" Freddie slouched back in the booth. "Did I?"

Nathan took the beer out of Freddie's hand. "You have had one too many."

"I only had two. Man, stop playing." Freddie reached for the half-empty bottle.

Nathan pulled the amber-tinted bottle farther out of his friend's reach, and Indigo couldn't help the tightness constricting her insides. She didn't want him tempted to set his lips on the bottle. "I'll take it." She circled her fingers around the sweating neck of the bottle.

"I'm good." Nathan slipped the bottle out of her grasp with an austere glint in his eyes as he held her gaze for the briefest of seconds; it was gone before he turned back to his friends' bantering.

"You better slow down." Seriousness claimed Ash's face. "'Cause you know if you go home wasted, Aisha will kill yo ass."

Freddie waved off Ash and picked up his now cold chili fries.

"So . . ." Indigo pulled Nathan's arm onto her lap. "You heard T-Pain's song one too many times and fell in love with a stripper."

He huffed amusedly. "Something like that."

"I heard she's a nurse now," Ash offered with a mouthful of food.

Nathan rolled his eyes at his friends, one entranced by the television and the other eating like he had just finished a juice cleanse, then placed his eyes back on Indigo. "Are you ready to go?"

"Um . . ." She wiped her hand down her blue-jeaned thigh, removing the moisture but still feeling coldness nipping at her palm. "Yeah. Let's go."

She wondered why the topic of his ex-girlfriend had changed his mood so abruptly, but she knew there were some dark parts of his past that he didn't like revisiting. She understood that. There were moments in her past she hated revisiting.

. . .

After Nathan changed out of his dirt-stained clothes, they were rolling down the highway in his vintage Buick. A warm breeze washed over Indigo's naked face through the open windows, rays of sun stinging her bronze skin. The tires pounded against the concrete and lulled Indigo into a relaxed state as she gazed at the sky.

Although she'd grown up in a suburban enclave miles away from 610, the city of Houston was her backyard. She'd spent twelve years at Holy Baptist Preparatory, a stone's throw from her parents' firm and where most of the children of the professionals in the area were taught. At ten, she and her siblings had walked to the zoo and spent hours observing animals and mimicking their sounds only to lose Harrison and later find him outside riding the mini-trains and licking a lollipop. At sixteen, her car had died on Allen Parkway when she and Tate were en route to Corpus Christi for spring break.

As the song ended and Nathan stepped on the brake, viewing the slowing traffic ahead, she twisted toward him. "So, tell me, how did the boy who wanted to be in marketing start his own car shop?"

"My mom." A slight smile crossed his lips as he stole a look at her before focusing back on the freeway. "She left me her dad's old car . . . this car."

"You did this," she said, rubbing her hand down the smooth leather of the passenger seat, "when you were twenty-one." She already knew the story of his mother's death and how he'd gotten the call when he was in class—he told her during one of those nights where neither of them had wanted to get off the phone. "And dating Cinnamon."

"Don't." He softly clenched her fleshy thigh. "It's not what you think."

"Hmm. It's just . . ." She studied the stubble along his jaw and the effortless way his hair hung when he didn't use any products. "I told you about all my exes . . . even the con man. I don't . . . I wouldn't care," she said, setting her hand on her chest. "It's just that we shared a lot but not that. Not your relationships."

"I don't like talking about Cinna—" He paused; the traffic was moving at a tortoise's pace, so he was able to fix his gaze on her for longer than a second. His current look wasn't as harsh as the one at the restaurant, where it had looked like he was warring with both pain and regret. "About Christina. I was a part-time bartender at Lady Ophelia's. We dated. My mom died. I remedied my sorrow with vodka. We broke up. That's it."

She nodded. "Lady Ophelia's." The corner of her mouth quirked up. "Very Shakespearean for a strip club. I like it."

"Not really." He matched her levity with a small smile, the first since she'd brought up the topic. "The owner was just a lady named Ophelia."

"So . . . back at Calder's, when I offered to hold the bottle for you, you practically gave me the evil eye." She looked away from the Fiat trying to bogart its way into the lane of a monster truck and peered at him. "Why?"

Nathan's grip loosened around the steering wheel. "I wasn't trying to be rude." He glanced at her with sincerity flooding his features. "They just don't know about everything in my past."

"They don't know . . ."

"No, and I don't want them to."

"Do you think that's a good idea?" She positioned her braids over one shoulder, her opinion audible in her words. "They could help you stay on the wagon . . . be successful."

Nathan shook his head as the wind played games with his tresses. "They're my homies, but I don't need them all in my business that much. My sponsor helps me out. Emery and Hazel and my sister keep me straight. I've been good for years. No need to change the plan now."

Family having your back—she couldn't disagree with that. "Well, like they say, if it ain't broke, don't fix it."

"Right." He tapped the gas pedal to keep up with the sluggish traffic. The freeway was a parking lot. "Know what?" He turned on the blinker then investigated the view in the side mirror. "I know a faster way."

"No." She settled back in the seat, not worried about the congested traffic. "It's just slow from the merging lanes. Once we pass those, it'll pick up." She turned the music up a little, nodding her head along with the infectious beat. "Anyway, there'll be thirty minutes of previews. We have time."

He shook his head adamantly. "Nah, we're not going to be late." He quickly merged into the next lane. The sedan he overtook drowned out their music with its horn. "Watch this."

Watched it, Indigo did. She watched as they got stuck in an excruciatingly long line with a traffic light that only remained green for thirty seconds. Once they crossed that threshold, they had to wait behind five more just like it. As they sat at the fourth traffic light, stranded in a sea of cars on the frontage road, he realized she was right. The brisk pace of vehicles on the highway up ahead backed up her words. She didn't gloat, though, just listened to Kool & the Gang with a smirk.

Chapter 25

"Eat up," Indigo said, setting the plate of food in front of her nephew.

She'd planned on cooking up more than a chicken sandwich and some fries she found in the freezer, but once she walked through the front door, the thought of standing in the kitchen chopping, dicing, and stirring didn't seem appealing. Fortunately, River wasn't a hard sell on her change of menu. He'd rather eat zesty curly fries than the pasta she had planned, anyway.

Having company was another thing Indigo hadn't planned on, but during her commute home, he'd sent her a text asking if he could come over, needing refuge from a crying baby and noisy little sister. By the time she pulled her truck into the driveway, he was sitting on her porch with his eyes in a book.

River took a long draw from his straw with a hum, then said, "Aunt Indie, you're my favorite aunt in this entire dimension."

"So, you mean I have competition in the other dimensions," she stated, squirting tartar sauce next to the ketchup on his plate. The pairing was her fault. She took full responsibility for it.

"You're my favorite here." He dipped a fry in the sauce. "But I must meet and greet everyone in that dimension to see how they hold up."

"So, I'm the paradigm?" she asked with a hand on her hip.

River's eyebrows wrinkled, and his head tilted with confusion. "What does that mean?"

"It means . . . uh . . ." She gesticulated, not quite remembering the dictionary meaning herself. "The model, the standard by which you measure other things."

River nodded, his eyes shifting from right to left as he committed the word to memory. "Yeah! You are." He tossed a fry into his mouth. "I'm yours, right? Your paradigm for a kid. Not Adira."

"Don't be like that," she said as a rap of knocks sounded against the front door. The noise roused the dog from his nap into a barking fit. "Y'all are both great little people," she said, trotting to the door.

"I'm better," River quipped, feeding Gambit a piece of chicken while his aunt's back was to him.

"Who is it?" she asked before the person knocked again.

"It's me!" exclaimed a male voice from the other side.

She knew who it was, but why was he at her door? "What business do you have here, sir?" she joked.

"Important business," Tate replied, and they both laughed at the same time. "Are you letting me in?"

Indigo stepped to the side and opened the door wider for him.

"I was looking for something in my garage, and guess what I found," he started as he entered the house. He toted in a massive photograph of her, dwarfing his statuesque frame. "What was your influence for this picture?"

The glossy photograph reminded Indigo that Tate wasn't the only creative person in his family. His mom, Beatrice Larsen, was an artist in her own right, and her books were highly coveted for the exceptional images she captured of majestic landscapes all around the world. Indigo remembered the day she'd posed for the photograph: standing in the lavender fields of Blanco with contemplation on her face and a golden horizon behind her. It was for the grand opening of Adorn; she hadn't had enough funds for a photographer, and Mrs. Larsen had done the shoot free of charge.

The visual didn't just remind her of the reason she'd posed for the image; it also reminded her of what had happened between her and Tate that night. She wondered if the thought had crossed his mind when he'd stumbled upon it. She shook the notion out of her head as she closed the door.

"Your mom's an artist," she affirmed with reverence, locking the door. "I let her creativity lead her to the best decision."

"I'm an artist," he declared, leaning the artwork against the wall in the living room. "But when I suggested red walls, you shot me down."

"Because my name ain't Carrie." She tried to lift the picture to put it in her office, but the frame was heavier than she'd expected, like it was actual gold. She left it where he'd placed it. "What's my name, River?" she playfully asked the boy who was munching on fries and watching them like a movie.

"Aunt Indie," he gleefully answered once he swallowed a fry.

She dropped her head, and her curly ponytail flowed forward like spiral strings of a pom-pom. It had happened: she was relegated to a title, but it was one she loved, so she accepted it.

"What's a Carrie?" River asked, sitting backward on the barstool.

He was too cute to even put into words, but she knew if she told him that, the nine-year-old would get bashful. Of course, he didn't know the movie or Stephen King's novel. Saxon hadn't allowed him or Adira to consume anything scarier than *Hocus*

Pocus. To Indigo, that was tragic. She remembered watching *Fright Night* at the tender age of nine, and it had turned out stellar. Well, at least she thought so. She still enjoyed having a hallway light on, but who wanted their entire house pitch-black at night?

"It's a movie about a girl who seeks revenge," Tate said, sliding into the barstool next to the boy. "When you hit teenhood, I'll show it to you."

River shook his head then held up his half-empty glass of root beer float. "This is stupendous. You should sell 'em at your store."

Stupendous. Must be another spelling word. School was out, but Saxon never stopped being a teacher.

"I'll get on that." She winked at him. "Does this mean you're on my team?"

"What team?" Tate asked.

"Aunt Indie thinks root beer floats are better than milkshakes," River explained before taking another sip of his dessert in a cup.

"You just said it was *stupendous*," she reminded her nephew.

"But not better than milkshakes," River reiterated while taking another sip of his float.

"That's a hefty claim, though." Tate leaned on the island. "Maybe I should try one of these 'floats,'" he said, air-quoting, "to see how it stacks up against the creamy, thick deliciousness of a chocolate milkshake."

"You've already started wrong because a chocolate milkshake could never compete with a strawberry milkshake." She threw up her arms as if she'd given the winning statement. "Chocolate ice cream is a mistake. It just makes you thirsty."

Both man and boy glared at Indigo as if she had lost her mind, but she folded her arms and stood by her words.

"Don't look at me like that," she said. "Chocolate is better in a cake or cookies but not ice cream."

Tate turned to River. "Your aunt slips in bouts of crazy. Just nod and smile."

River nodded and laughed.

"Go ahead and joke. I'm an individual, anyway." She reached for her dinging phone and read the text. "Your mom said to send you over."

"Do I have to?" River pouted, slumped back in the chair.

"Yes, child," Indigo told him with humor in her voice. "Being the oldest has its cons, but it'll get better. Just remember what I said."

"I know," he said as he slunk out of the chair. "Love your siblings, and kindness over taunting."

"And what else?" she asked as she strode to the living room.

"I'm not a snitch, Auntie," he affirmed, fitting his backpack over his shoulders. "I never had ice cream and fries. You gave me a sandwich and tea. *Green tea*." He grinned. He gave the dog a quick pat on the head then headed to the door. "Bye, my people. Pray for me."

"I will," Indigo said, pushing down her laugh until he closed the door behind him.

The smile on Tate's face as he peered at her warmed her cheeks, and she asked, "What?"

"I'm still waiting on my float." He tapped his hands on the counter. "I'm sure you're wrong, but it's been a while since I had one."

She narrowed her eyes at him. "Reverse psychology doesn't work on me, Tattie Tate."

"It doesn't?" he inquired with a quirk to his mouth as seriousness filled his eyes.

"No. It doesn't," she said, spinning on her heel to open the freezer. "What flavor do you want?"

He shrugged. "Surprise me. I trust you."

Indigo hovered her hand over the cartons of ice cream, realizing that like her nephew, she too had a paradigm: one for the type of partner she wanted, one that she measured all the men she dated against.

. . .

"This one's good too," she said, showing Tate another hairstyle on her Pinterest to toss into the mix. She had a hair appointment coming up and needed to decide on the style she wanted.

"Fantastic," he told her from his cozy corner of the couch.

"Okay." She turned the iPad back to herself. "I get it. I'm boring you."

"No. You're not," he swiftly retorted, sitting up. "I'm just trying to picture it. In my head." He gestured to his face. "Which one does Diego or Nathan like?"

"I haven't asked them." She swiped her finger across the glossy screen, the light gleaming in the dimly lit room, and wondered why the thought had never crossed her mind.

Maybe it was because they were still new additions in her life, and Tate had known her through most stages. When they'd first met in third grade, he'd stolen her pencil and claimed he found it. Her immediate reaction was to plow her fist into his eye. The incident caused each of them to give the other an apology before he and his parents sat down to have dinner with her family. Strangely, after dinner they became fast friends over a mutual liking for *Crash Bandicoot*.

Tate nodded. "Hmm."

Only the rays from the moonlight leaking through the open blinds and the shine from the TV screen lit the room. Tate's gaze drifted over the living room, taking in the subtle touches of gold and lilac sprinkled throughout the room. Her half-read book sat on top of the coffee table next to their emptied glasses of root beer float. A cream fleece blanket was draped over one of the side chairs, and she wondered if he was contemplating spending the night.

Then his eyes went to the TV. "Did you watch *The Harder They Fall* without me?"

"Uh." Indigo scratched at her eyebrow.

He flung a pillow at her, and Gambit lifted his head; when Indigo giggled, the dog's head fell back down with a huff.

"Just the first thirty minutes." She hugged the ivory pillow. "You were at the lake house, and I . . ."

"So, it's my fault."

She nodded, grinning. "Absolutely."

"Then I forgive you." He side-eyed her as he relaxed back in the couch's corner, stretching his long legs out as far as he could without kicking Gambit. "And I think you should pick whichever hairstyle you feel most comfortable in because honestly you look stunning in any style, but I love you in braids."

The way his voice went smooth and husky as he spoke those three words—*I love you*—struck a chord deep in her heart.

"Thanks." She shook her head, not sure if that was the right reply, but it was the only word that popped into her mind. "Um . . . so . . . I still have to decide who's going to be my date for my b-day, but what about you?"

"What about me?" Confusion washed over his face.

She sighed audibly. "Are you bringing a date? When are you going to start dating again?"

"I don't need to bring a date. Plus, I don't date while I'm writing. I don't have the time to get to know a new person when I'm working." He sighed then reached over and grabbed the remote off the coffee table. "I'm pretty sure the person for me isn't out there."

Indigo's mouth opened, but words didn't come out. *Who's the person for you?* The question weighed heavy on her tongue, but her voice abandoned her. She didn't know what muted her voice, confusion or fear.

"We're starting from the beginning," he said as he selected *The Harder They Fall*.

"Fine by me," she replied, sliding to the floor with a pillow in tow.

He chuckled, doing the same. There was no space between them as they sat on the floor with their backs against the couch. She could feel Tate stealing a peek at her and wondered what he was thinking, while another part of her was too afraid to acknowledge that she knew the answer.

• • •

Indigo hummed, completely content as sleep faded and her mind awakened. Her eyes remained closed, not ready to vacate the comfort of the body enveloping hers. The notes of bergamot, apple, lavender, and patchouli merged, flooding her with a tranquility that eased the stress teeming within her mind and lulled the worry in her soul. Indigo was at peace. A haven no storm could entrench. She was at home in his arms.

His breaths evenly inhaled and exhaled as his chest expanded against her back, and a slightly larger than usual bulge prodded her backside. He was content too, and a slight curve etched its way across her mouth. She contemplated chasing the lingering embers of sleep, but the erection she leaned back into awoke a hunger in her.

She stroked her hand along the arm draped across her waist, holding her close, and he let out a low moan.

"Can you stop?" he grumbled, moving his arm. "I'm horny enough."

Wait. What? She most definitely wasn't dreaming. *Where am I?* Her eyes sprung open.

"Tate!" She jumped up too fast. The world around her spun slightly. She held her temples, trying to remember the events of yesterday.

The fog of sleep was dissipating, and images of last night played vividly in her head like the show they'd just binged. Kernels of popcorn were sprinkled on the floor, from the handful she'd tossed at him for teasing her when she'd yelped at a jump scare in the horror movie they'd watched after finishing the western.

"Get up!" she said, flinging a decorative couch pillow at him.

He groaned with his eyes still closed. "Just another hour." He held the pillow she'd thrown like it was his favorite childhood stuffed animal. "I was having a pleasant dream."

She muttered grumpily, ambling to the kitchen as Gambit moved away from his spot behind Tate's back, sniffing the kernels of popcorn on the floor then eating them.

She needed coffee and a pastry to subdue the nausea and guilt that was forming in her gut. She'd assumed the erection she'd ground against was a figment of her imagination and not her best friend. This wasn't good. It was terrible. She needed Tate and his hard dick to go back across the street. ASAP.

Indigo busied herself making coffee and steaming her plant-based milk after letting Gambit out to do his morning business. She didn't even hear Tate shuffle over to the kitchen island and take a seat. She was deep in her head as she stirred the warm milk into the coffee. When he cleared his throat, she jumped.

He chuckled. "Still thinking of zombies?"

"Ugh," she grumbled, turning to face him, cupping the toasty mug that did wonders to quell the goose bumps that threatened to form on her forearms.

She didn't know why they were forming. Maybe it was from the previous incident or the way Tate's half-closed eyes stalked her. The way he was peering at her tugged at the door holding back trapped emotions she'd locked up years ago.

What are you doing? she mentally hissed at herself as she put the mug on the island. *Stop thinking about that. Tate is old news. You have dates with* two *great men. Don't fuck things up for an old flame.*

"Um, do I get a cup?" He looked around her at the coffeepot full of java.

"Tate," she said plainly, narrowing her eyes. "Go home. I've got to get dressed for work. We'll talk later."

He nodded. "Always." He patted Gambit's head and left.

She let out a heavy breath once the door closed behind him then climbed the stairs. She knew they were just friends, but the cold shower she stepped into implied the opposite. Maybe these emotions were just because they shared a chemistry that was palpable—there was no denying it. And besides, those residual feelings would fade like they always had in the past. Things would go back to being purely platonic.

They were great as friends. She was sure of it. *Right?*

Chapter 26

Indigo nursed a grapefruit-rosemary cocktail while enjoying an exfoliating apricot mask on her face and soaking her feet in warm water infused with seaweed and Himalayan sea salt. After a long day of work, her body was on cloud nine, but her mind was roaming like the Road Runner. This morning's slipup with Tate had her overthinking. Three questions ping-ponged in her mind: *Why am I so relaxed in Tate's arms? Should I entertain the thought of us trying to be more than friends and commit to a real nonplatonic relationship, or am I just overreaching? Are my knotless braids too tight?*

"Where's my Lemonheads?" Hazel asked, walking in from the kitchen on her heels so as not to disturb the foam toe spacers.

Emery didn't budge from her relaxed position on the couch, her legs dangling over the arm with her foot tapping the air to the serene R & B streaming from the speaker. Her coffee table was spread with healthy snacks she'd prepped before the ladies arrived at her house.

If her eyes hadn't been closed, she would've seen Hazel's slap to her knee coming.

"What the hell!" Emery squawked from the sting of the smack. Her gray, black, and white cat, Calico, leaped off her stomach, not caring for his owner's abrupt movement. "Why'd you do that? I was zoning out."

"Come back to reality," Hazel ordered, falling back in the armchair opposite Indigo. "Did you forget them in the car?"

"Forget what?" Emery asked, using her elbows to prop herself up.

"My Lemonheads."

Emery shook her head then lay back down. "This self-care session is sugar-free."

"You know, strawberries are sweet." Hazel pointed to the bowl of fruit on the coffee table.

"Fructose doesn't count," Emery countered, taking in her cousin's annoyed disposition. "They're high in vitamin C, which encourages radiant skin and helps produce collagen. Don't you want *radiant skin*?"

Hazel rolled her eyes. "My skin stays gleaming." She looked over at Indigo and asked, "What's up with you? You're mighty quiet over there while this woman's going to starve us with this frenzy of fruit."

"Just mentally going over last-minute birthday things." Her birthday party was in a couple weeks, and she still hadn't chosen the shoes she was going to wear, which had never happened before. Picking shoes to wear with an outfit was her gift. She'd used her talent to create a profitable boutique. But the ability was failing her for a significant milestone. She couldn't decide what shoes to pair with her metallic-gold A-line dress, nor could she decide who was going to accompany her to the party. "No, that's a lie." She rubbed her face, slumping down in the chair.

"Spill," Hazel insisted right before biting into an avocado

hummus–dipped carrot, causing a loud crack that made Calico hiss.

"You know he doesn't like sharp disturbances," Emery chirped.

"He literally gifts you mouse heads, but he's afraid of noises." Hazel gave the majestic cat a long stare. "Act right because I scratch back."

"Leave him alone," Emery told her then turned back to Indigo. "I'm sensing tension leaking from your aura." She held up her hands as if they were chakra detectors.

Hazel and Indigo both glared at her, but only Hazel spoke. "You read one book and now you're a guru." She snickered then added to Indigo, "But you do look worried."

"Yesterday . . ." Indigo let out a deep breath. "Tate and I were binging movies, and apparently we fell asleep on the floor because in the morning I woke up in his arms, and . . ." She paused, wiggling her toes in the warm water, easing the tension in her calves from standing in heels most of the day.

She tried to think of the best way to say this, but these were her girls, so she decided to give it to them unfiltered. "His dick was hard against my ass, and I grinded on it, and it felt good." She dropped her head back against the chair. "Damn, what's wrong with me?"

"Nothing," Hazel said, holding the carrot stick like a cigarette. "You're just horny. All these dates and no dick would drive any sane woman crazy."

Indigo turned to Emery, waiting for a difference of opinion, but Emery peered at her blankly.

"I know I don't say this often, but," Emery said, half shrugging, stressing the last word, "she's right. It's a normal reaction when you're in the arms of a man you share history with. Who you're attracted to."

Who you're attracted to. Yes, Tate was attractive, but was she still attracted to him? She couldn't avoid the three-letter answer. Her reaction to him this morning was evidence that her body still enjoyed being next to his.

"How big was it?" Hazel asked with her head tilted as if she was wondering. "He has big dick energy. Right? I know I'm not the only one that feels that energy."

"I'm not discussing my best friend's package," Indigo told them.

Indigo was well versed in the length and girth of what Tate toted around in his pants. A shiver traveled down her spine as warmth heated up her body.

"Hazel, you're right." Indigo nodded her head. "I just need some rosé and my rose."

"Some R & R." Hazel tipped her carrot to her.

"Exactly," Indigo added.

But Emery wore a questioning look as she studied her friend, keeping her lips sealed.

. . .

After a night of R & R and a day without being in the company of Tate, Indigo's world was back on its proper axis. She heard the front door slam over the music as she stood in her closet, shimmying her freshly showered body into a dress. She would've been alarmed if she'd heard Gambit barking and snarling, but there was none of that, so she twisted her arm behind her back and pulled up the zipper.

Indigo pranced out of the closet to find Tate sprawled across her bed eating the fruit salad she had made yesterday, with Gambit intently begging him for it.

"Don't give him any of that." She settled in front of the floor-length mirror. "He'll get gas." She sucked in her stomach, checking out her frame in the red dress.

She saw Tate's contorted face in the mirror. "What?" She turned toward him, slapping her hands to her hips. He didn't respond, so she asked again. "What!"

"Nothing." Tate investigated the glass bowl, smeared white with Philadelphia cream cheese. "It's just, I thought you and Diego were going to the ballet and . . ." His eyebrows went up. "That dress doesn't say ballet."

"Then what does it say?" She spun back to the mirror, hoping to translate into words what her bodycon red dress was giving off.

"It says . . ." Tate stopped scraping the bottom of the bowl with the spoon and glided his eyes over Indigo's small waist, wide hips, thick thighs, and ample derriere. "Are you going to use your hands or your teeth to rip open the condom?"

"No, it doesn't." She scowled at him.

"Yes, it does," he countered.

"Well, maybe that isn't a bad thing." She looked back at her reflection in the mirror, rubbing her hands down the smooth red fabric. She didn't just look sexy. She felt sexy, and the way his eyes scrolled over her body reassured her. She contemplated the way his gaze lingered on every inch of her as if he wanted to commit it to memory.

"Maybe." He dropped his eyes to the bowl, scooped up the cherry in his spoon, and tossed it into his mouth. "But you're going to be in a theater, and you know how you get cold. That's a lot of skin to get goose bumps, but it's your prerogative."

"Hmm, you might be right." She pranced back to the closet, unzipping the dress. She did the same shimmy to get out of the dress that she'd done to get into it. "What time do we have to meet your parents tomorrow?" Her voice was muffled as she pulled the cloth over her face.

Indigo heard the spoon clack against the bowl as Tate began to speak. "Five, but they canceled the reservations at that fancy new place on the south side because my mom wants to cook instead."

"Sounds good." She strutted out in an emerald midi dress with spaghetti straps. "You like?" She twirled with her nude pumps in hand. "It has pockets!"

"Sexy yet warm." He gave her a thumbs-up then set the bowl on her nightstand.

"Home-cooked meal." Indigo crossed the room to her dresser, redirecting their conversation back to the dinner with his parents. "Which means you don't need to wear something nice."

"All the stuff I wear is nice." He pulled his legs onto the bed, lounging back on her plush pillows. "I always look decent. Plus, they don't care about what we're wearing. They're there for the conversation. Speaking of which, I missed you yesterday. You should cancel on Diego so we can have another movie marathon . . . I'm thinking Wes Craven—Freddy Krueger."

She stopped fishing in her jewelry box to give Tate a once-over. He sat there with his chestnut locks finger-combed out of his face, wearing a striped white-and-yellow shirt and muted green shorts that showed off his lean, muscular thighs. He was the picture of effortless allure, something he pulled off well. Every muscle in his face told her he wasn't playing. He did want her to call off her date with Diego.

Even Indigo couldn't deny it—she wouldn't have minded ordering various dishes from various eateries and staying in, but she was looking for a partner who would one day be a husband, not just a best friend who would just be a friend.

"Absolutely not." Indigo slid a gaggle of gold bangles over her hand. "Number one, that's rude."

"But didn't he cancel on you before?"

"He had work-related reasons." She pointed a stern finger toward him that had even Gambit sitting at attention. "My bestie wanting me to hang out with him is not a good reason."

"I think it is." He scratched at his eyebrow. "I'm more fun anyway."

Indigo dropping a long gold necklace around her neck. "That's what you think."

"It's true." He interlaced his ink-stained hands together, watching her spritz perfume on her neck.

"You know what you should do?" Indigo said. "Download Tinder and go on a date also."

"I don't want to waste time with a random hottie." He jumped off the bed and sidled next to her in front of the dresser. "I want to spend time with you."

She glanced at his face, picking up the subtle traces of sadness in his brown eyes. But there was another emotion mingling with it she just couldn't place, which was peculiar because she could usually read his facial expressions like it was her second language. Was it frustration? Jealousy? Maybe confusion about their relationship if she entered into a serious relationship with Diego or Nathan?

"You're not a fan of Diego. I'm aware." She thought about the one opinion he'd voiced about her suitor. "But he's growing on me, and I want to see where this might go."

"Fine." Tate turned away from her, rubbing a hand over the smooth hairs of his beard. "But you don't have to."

Indigo shook her head at him, then read the time on the clock resting on her nightstand.

Tate peeked out the window; a black SUV had pulled into her driveway. "Your date's here." He turned back to her as she slipped on her heels. "You and Diego. I would've never guessed it. You're not the kind of girl he dates."

"And what type is that?"

"Young and 'eager to please.'" He air-quoted the latter attribute.

"Well, Tattie, people change." She quickly grabbed her purse and cardigan and rubbed Gambit's head vigorously. "You two be good." She crossed the room. "There's actual food in the fridge; help yourself." She gave Tate a friendly peck on the cheek before prancing out the bedroom door with Gambit trailing behind.

"Don't rush out there!" Tate called out, following the procession. "Make him knock."

• • •

Indigo didn't rush out the door, but she didn't wait until Diego knocked. Saying that she was keen for the evening was an understatement. She was giddy with excitement. It surged underneath her skin like electricity. Diego had lit the spark earlier that day with a call that took her by surprise since he had told her yesterday that he'd be stuck in court all day. He was quick and to the point, no time for small talk. He had just one question—did she like ballet? That was an easy question for her. She positively loved ballet. She'd be a ballerina now if her mama hadn't deemed it frivolous and enrolled her in piano lessons instead. As she inspected her lipstick in the hallway mirror before heading out the door, she still had the same cheery smile that had graced her lips at the end of that call.

The performance didn't disappoint, and neither did Diego. As soon as she slid in the passenger seat of his tinted-out Mercedes, she felt like the luckiest girl in the world. For a couple of seconds, she turned her nose up at the thought of getting dreamy about a guy because he was devilishly handsome in a black suit. She was an independent, levelheaded, grown woman, not a starry-eyed girl untrained in the wiles of a suave, slick-talking gentleman like Diego Simpson.

Still, his easy conversation and hearty, sexy laugh ignited an ardent attraction in her that she hadn't felt since the guy she'd dated the summer after graduating from high school. They were falling into an effortless groove. It was a fact Indigo couldn't deny. Neither could she deny the faint echoes of suspicion in the back of her mind. Was this all real? Was Diego legit? With her hand firmly in his as he guided them down the theater aisle in search of their row, she wished, hoped, and prayed he was.

The show was a delight. However, Indigo's attention wasn't entirely glued to the stage. Who could blame her? Diego had leaned into her more times than she could count, whispering in her ear about the beautiful costumes and captivating set design. Her attention continually drifted from *The Merry Widow*'s flaw-lessly precise principal ballerinas executing elegant footwork and whimsical twirls to the effervescent music. She was pleased that he didn't fall asleep on her shoulder like Corey or snore like Darius, nor did she have to twist his arm like she would have with Tate. Diego was thoroughly entertained even though Indigo wanted to grab his hand, find a vacant balcony suite, and do things that would have made Madame Bovary blush.

Once the last step was planted and the final note played, they headed out to the valet to begin the next phase of the date. La Plaque Rouge was a quaint, exquisite restaurant that had to be exclusive from the way the maître d's phone frequently rang. The callers' hopes must have diminished when she told them in her hushed French accent that the schedule was booked solid well through August. The hostess, with her chignon and her voguish black dress, led them to an intimate table away from the other diners. Indigo didn't need to wonder how Diego had acquired the reservation. Stewart & Snyder's lawyers had perks. She could remember the countless times her parents had received VIP tickets and all-inclusive passes to exclusive events from the partners to woo clients.

The moment they settled into their seats, they were handed a menu. Indigo was happy to discover that the owner of the establishment didn't assume everyone who came to the posh French restaurant knew the romantic language. Before they could thoroughly peruse the menu, a waiter appeared at their table.

"Bonsoir, Monsieur Simpson and Mademoiselle . . ." the lanky waiter with whirly raven curls enunciated in the same accent as the hostess. He halted, wearing a benign smile on his flat lips.

"Indigo," she hurriedly uttered, stifling a yawn with the back of her hand. "Excuse me. Long day." He gave her an understanding nod that she matched with a smile. "I would love a cup of coffee."

"This late?" Diego inquired, pulling his eyes away from the leather-bound menu to study his Everose gold Rolex. "You'll be wired all night. Bring the lady some hot Earl Grey."

"Right away, sir," the waiter chirped.

"Huh." Indigo's head cocked to the side, allowing her to stare at both of the males in her presence. "The lady—i.e., me—wants a coffee." She glared at Diego to see if he would rebuff her. "Two cubes of sugar and a teaspoon of cream."

"As you wish." The waiter gave her a cursory nod. "Are you all ready to order an appetizer?"

"Yes." Diego closed his menu. "I'll have my usual, and she'll have . . ." He gestured to Indigo.

"The beetroot carpaccio with goat cheese, citrus honey, and figs." She handed the waiter her menu, already knowing the next dishes she wanted to try.

The coq au Riesling served with pomme purée wasn't as delectable as the first time she had devoured the meal in a little corner bistro near the Eiffel Tower. Her sixteen-year-old self and Saxon had discovered the bistro while accompanying their dad on a trip. But the creamy, rich entree did hit the spot quite nicely and had her contemplating booking a flight to Paris to see if the chef there was still churning out masterpieces.

"I'm not eating that," Indigo declared, scrunching her nose up at the spoon Diego had in her face.

"I thought you were a foodie."

"I am." She smiled her thanks as the waiter refilled her glass with red wine. "But I draw the line at escargot."

"How do you know it's not tasty if you haven't tried it?" He balanced the escargot in the spoon near his nose. He inhaled a whiff of the gastropod snug in its shell, which no doubt gave off a succulent aroma due to the butter, garlic, and parsley sauce drowning it. But that wasn't enough to sway her.

"Baseless claim." Indigo sliced into the tender chicken breast. She held her fork over the table. "Here, taste this."

He glanced around the dimly lit room, light coming only from the chandeliers hanging over each table. As a Bach concerto played softly, no one at the distant tables cared about the happenings at theirs, so he opened his mouth and let her set the slender slice of chicken on his tongue. He chewed the morsel. "Hmm." He swallowed. "Good, but it's not better than this." He gestured to his steaming bowl of beef bourguignon.

Indigo licked her lips. "That does look good." She twisted her mouth to the side. "Can I have a taste?"

"No." Diego dabbed the corners of his mouth, removing nonexistent food, then flashed a smug grin. "You ordered that . . . smothered chicken."

"Be a jackass about your little food." She shrugged, slicing into her chicken.

Diego's eyes showed that he finally realized that he might have upset her. "Fine." He stabbed his fork into the juicy chunk of beef. "Taste it. You'll love it."

"Too late." She dipped her herbed stewed carrot in the pomme purée. "Moment passed."

His arm wavered there, across the table. "You're really going to hold a grudge?"

"Not a grudge. I'm just not one of the young girls you usually date." She shrugged then bit into the carrot.

"Hmm." He drew back his arm, setting his fork back on the plate. "Tate's been educating you on my past." He huffed. "So, you two are very, *very* close."

"Childhood best friends," she said, elation flooding her body knowing how hard they'd worked to keep their friendship strong throughout all the difficult trials they'd faced. "BFFs since elementary."

"And that's all?" he inquired.

"Since we were in college." She twirled the wineglass, watching the red liquid dance. "Friendship works best for us."

He nodded with an arrogant smirk.

"So just know that I know some things about you, Diego," she teased, raising her eyebrow as he sat back in the leather chair with a hint of concern over his features. "Don't look so scared. You have exes. We both do."

"They didn't suit me." He leaned closer to the table, sliding his hand closer to hers until their fingertips met. "Not like you. You're the type of woman I need in my life." He held her hand as she peered into his chocolate eyes, seeing nothing but admiration. "You make me want to do better . . . be better." He briefly looked down with a chuckle. "You're stubborn and a challenge. You keep me on my toes. I like that."

"Good." She pulled her hand out of his grasp. "Now, eat before your food gets cold."

He did as instructed, sitting up in his chair. "Yes, ma'am."

"What do you hope to be doing in ten years?" Sure, it was a bland, overused, generic question, but she still needed to know. They had a passionate attraction that thrilled every synapse in her body; however, she needed to see if their goals matched. She didn't want just great sex. She wanted a man she could build a long-lasting relationship with, like her parents, like Saxon and Xavier. She wanted a Sunday morning kind of love—easy, soothing, and abiding.

"In ten years . . . I hope to be a partner at the firm, with a family." He nudged his bowl across the table. "Have a taste." He watched Indigo glide her fork into a beef chunk. "What about you? What's your ten-year plan?"

Indigo let the morsel hover in front of her lips. "I'd have another Adorn opened, near the suburbs." Her lips started to curve. "And once I've clocked out, I'll go home and spend the evening with my husband and our kid or kids . . . and, of course, Gambit."

"That's some dream, Indigo Clark." Diego dipped his spoon in the translucent brown broth. "I guess you want it all."

"Is that a problem?"

"Not for me."

Chapter 27

Indigo was late, but who could blame her? She'd been working all week, had gone on a date last night, and waking up at 7:00 a.m. on a Saturday disagreed with her circadian rhythm.

Fortunately, the Summer Extravaganza was teeming with hordes of people by the time Indigo and Tate arrived, and she was no longer sluggish. The fundraiser, held by Saxon's school district, was an event to help supply materials to schools with students from lower-income neighborhoods. It was a cause that Indigo loved to participate in—even if it meant she had to wake up at the crack of dawn.

"You know how many kids have been waiting to get their faces painted?" Saxon squirted globs of paint on a wooden slab.

Indigo judged the line of kids and their parents forming behind the orange cone. "I'm assuming a lot." She tied the same off-white paint-stained apron she had used last year around her neck. "Give me that. You're doing it wrong." She snatched the bottle of red paint out of Saxon's hand. "It's supposed to be ROY G. BIV, not . . . BOY V. RIG." She bumped her sister with her hip, hoping it would get her out of her workspace. She wasn't the best painter, and the critical eye Saxon had on her was not going to help keep her hand steady. "Go man someone else's station."

Saxon peered out at the festival grounds—a massive patch of land made up of concrete and grassy meadows bordered by pine trees and a man-made lake. Upbeat popular music played as people visited the various wooden booths, from ring toss to balloon darts.

"It's my first year as coordinator, and I just want it all to be a success." Saxon took a deep breath, looking away from Xavier manning the grill at the hot dog stand and Tate supervising the dunk tank. "Some of the teachers couldn't make it. I had a hard time finding the powder for the color fight. We might not have enough syrup for the snow cones. There was a chance of rain. And—"

"Just breathe," Indigo interjected, gently holding Saxon's shoulders to bring her racing mind back to earth. "It's all going to work out. Look around you. The sun is shining. The sky is clear." They both looked around. "Everyone's having fun, and if we run out of syrup, I'll just go buy all the ice cream and sorbet at Costco."

"You'd do that?"

Indigo grinned. "You know, like Martin, I love the kids." They both laughed, and she was relieved that her sister could take a calming breath. So what if she'd have to drop a grand on dairy products? Students were going to have the materials they needed for the upcoming academic year and go on a field trip or two. "Now begone so I can turn these children into lions and tigers."

"Zebras too."

"Zebras too!" With a firm hand, she guided Saxon out of the booth and got to work.

Morning turned into afternoon, and Indigo had decorated more tiny faces, turning them into cute critters, than she could count. Her hand was beginning to cramp around the paintbrush. Indigo was thrilled when a teenager relieved her of her duty.

"Corn dog for the lady." Tate held out a lump of battered, lop-sided meat on a stick in front of her.

"Thank you, kind sir." Indigo lifted her hands, clean of all the paint she had marred them with, out of the bowl of murky water.

Tate waved his Popsicle stick like a magic wand. "Are you ready to postpone adulting and be a kid again?"

Indigo thought about it as she chewed the warm, crusty, buttery batter. "I'm a Toys "R" Us kid. I ain't never growing up."

Be kids again, they did. The flick of Indigo's wrist helped Adira win a giant stuffed goldfish at soda toss. Tate's agility and height gave him a slight edge in the sack race. She tried to keep up with his hopping, but she couldn't stop tripping over herself. Tate laughed all the way to the finish line. Even Indigo's niece and nephew got a kick out of it. Indigo planned to seek revenge in Skee-Ball. She racked up a triple-digit score, did a victory dance, and minutes later was defeated by a snaggletoothed eight-year-old with a quick arm. Too heavy for the rock wall, they jumped their hearts out in a *Moana* bounce house, ignoring the neighborhood moms' disapproving stares. After funny faces in the photo booth, it was time to fill their bellies with cotton candy.

"Where to next?" Indigo looked from booth to booth, mentally crossing off the ones they had already been to and those with crazy long lines. "Hole in one?"

Tate took his eyes off his phone. "Harrison's back with pie. Wanna go back to the table for a slice?"

"Nah." She sidestepped a cluster of teens who were comparing their rainbow hair and shirts after a rambunctious color fight. "Actually, we should probably head out." She peeked down at her watch. "It's three, and I need to shower before getting dressed." She was beyond sweaty, and her floral scent was long gone.

"Huh?" Tate swung his arm around her shoulders and drew

her against his side. "Still avoiding your mama?"

"I'm not." She threw his arm off her and used her hip to bump him out of her space.

Not buying it was written all over his face, but he shrugged away the urge to push it. "You really want to leave without riding the Ferris wheel?"

Indigo rolled her eyes at the ginormous red spoked wheel. "I despise Ferris wheels."

"Right." Tate's lips quirked as their footfalls stopped a few yards away from the entrance, joyful children swarming around them with excited voices. "Just because you got community service for one midnight Ferris wheel ride doesn't mean you have to write them all off. Plus . . ." He playfully bumped her shoulder with his fist. "Criminals are sexy."

She guffawed. "Quoting *Transformers* isn't going to get me to change my mind."

"The line's not even that long," Tate went on.

"Indigo!" A voice boomed her name.

She whipped her head around and searched the crowd for the familiar face. A slow smile slid up her face as a surge of warmth flooded her chest. "Nathan! What are you doing here?" He'd told her he was going to a car show.

"Freddie's sitter got sick." Nathan jabbed his thumb toward the man buying tickets for a little boy who looked to be about seven. "He needed something kid-friendly." His gaze briefly brushed over Tate. "I remembered this was happening today, so . . . here I am."

"Well, hey!" Indigo brushed her hand over the frizzy flyaway that had gathered around her hairline. "Glad to see you."

Bewilderment washed over Nathan's face. "Are you sure?" He gestured between her and a texting Tate. "Aren't you on a da—"

"No!" Indigo blurted out with a nervous laugh. "This is Tate."

She slapped her friend's arm, pulling his attention away from the screen. "My homie."

"Oh!" Elated relief replaced Nathan's confusion. "Nathan." He held out his hand. "The boyfriend."

Tate's eyes immediately went to Indigo while her chin quirked up at Nathan's words. *Boyfriend?* She'd thought they were just dating. They hadn't had the exclusivity talk yet. She watched the two men shake hands.

"Tate. Just Tate." He pulled his hand away from Nathan after two pumps. "I've heard a lot about you, though."

"All good, I hope."

"Well . . ." Tate paused, feigning skepticism. Mortification washed over Nathan for the five seconds he stood waiting.

"Stop playing." Indigo pushed Tate with a shake of her head. "He's just messing with you." Indigo set her hand against Nathan's chest, bringing a light smile to his kissable lips. "He's a jackass like that. He writes horror."

"Oh, you're the writer." Nathan snaked his arm around Indigo's waist, pulling her closer to his side.

"Guilty as charged." Tate held out his arms with a chuckle. "Need me to sign anything?"

"Doubt it," Nathan said. "I don't get much time to read."

Indigo peered up at him, leaning back. "We're going to have to do something about that. Reading is fundamental."

The two friends laughed simultaneously, leaving Nathan out of their little inside joke.

"As you wish." Nathan dipped down for a taste of her lips.

The sensual kiss had Tate clearing his throat. The sound caused the lovebirds to disconnect. "You don't have to read it," Tate said. Indigo's eyebrows furrowed, and Nathan's eyes were tinged with hardness until Tate added, "You'll be able to watch it soon."

"What?" Indigo stepped closer to him, Nathan's hand still hanging on her hip.

"I was going to tell you this later with my parents, but . . ." He combed his hand through his hair with a glance at Nathan. "A deal was reached. In a year, we'll be bringing *Chronicles of the Undead* to a major streamer."

Indigo squealed with excitement, lunging forward and enveloping Tate in her arms. "Congrats, buddy!"

"Yeah." Nathan gave him a clipped nod. "Congrats, man."

"I love it." Indigo pulled her arms away from Tate. "I can't wait."

"Me neither." Tate's smile was soft as he gave all his attention to Indigo.

"Hey . . ." Nathan wrapped his arms around Indigo's waist, setting her back against his chest, getting her to refocus on him. "You want to be cheesy and make out at the top of the Ferris wheel?"

Indigo clutched his wrist, the embrace now feeling slightly awkward with Tate in their presence. "I wish."

"You still want to swing back by your house?" Tate held up his phone so that she could see the time. "For that shower?"

"Oh, Nathan, we gotta go." She twisted in his arms. "Having dinner with his parents. They flew in yesterday." She rose on her tiptoes for a peck on his lips. "Call you later."

"Sure thing." Nathan tipped up her chin for another kiss, and when they broke apart, Tate was no longer in earshot. "Are you sure friendship is the only thing he wants?"

"I'm sure." She glanced over her shoulder to see Tate talking on his phone. "We're friends, that's it."

They kissed once more, and then she caught up with Tate. She hoped Nathan believed her. Trusted her. There was no way she and Tate could ever be anything but friends. What she'd done years ago had made sure of that.

Chapter 28

Indigo hadn't seen Tate's parents since Mr. Larsen had retired in January and taken his wife on a vacation that spanned multiple continents and ended in her home country of Brazil. She envied them just a little but didn't fret since she had her own vacation planned to Antigua in July. And once she stepped into the house where she and her siblings had spent the majority of their days after school, it felt like old times. She kicked her heels off in the foyer and surrendered to the ease of the environment. Her bare feet led her to the same place they always did—the kitchen.

Music echoed through the rooms, floating on the warm afternoon breeze that flowed through the open windows. Whitney Houston and no AC was Beatrice Larsen's homeostasis. "You Give Good Love" played as Indigo's mouth watered at the sight of a fluffy slice of cake, shining from a sweet, sticky passion fruit glaze.

"Go'n girl. Eat," Mrs. Larsen said, her accent resurging after spending a month with her family. Her thick, curly black hair was held out of her face with a maroon scarf. She sighed. "Don't tell me you're on a diet."

Indigo shook her head, her braids swaying in an updo that had her looking like Janet Jackson's double for *Poetic Justice*. She picked up the plate and a fork.

"I thought you were practicing the ways of my son." She threw up her hands. "I leave for a couple of months and he's thinner. Look at him. Has he been eating?"

Indigo swallowed the piece of cake before looking over her shoulder at Tate standing next to his dad in the backyard at the grill. Her eyes canvassed every inch of him in the fading sunlight, from his gleaming, wavy hair resting just past the collar of the crisp white button-up shirt that matched the pair of Air Force 1s on his feet, to his sun-kissed skin, to the dark-blue chino shorts that gave her a slight view of his toned thighs.

"He looks good to me." She took a deep breath then quickly turned back to see the woman eyeing her quizzically. "I mean, h-he looks healthy, like low-cholesterol healthy. I'm healthy. He's healthy. We eat."

She glanced down and abruptly put another bite of cake into her mouth to stop the rambling.

"Together?"

"Sometimes," Indigo told her, watching the woman maneuver around the kitchen like a gazelle. "Are you sure you don't need help?" She drummed the fingers of her right hand on the granite countertop, trying to fight the urge to act as sous-chef. Afro-Brazilian food wasn't her specialty, but she was acquainted with the cuisine.

"I've been cooking for you lot since the nineties." Mrs. Larsen hoisted a Dutch oven from the oven. A plume of steam rose to the ceiling as she uncovered the pot, and Indigo's mouth watered once more at the sight of the black bean stew. "I don't need help now. Plus, you're a guest."

She set the top back on and turned her attention to the frango com quiabo simmering in a cast-iron skillet. "And I'm sure you're tired from all those dates I hear you've been going on."

She cast a smirk in Indigo's direction.

Indigo's fork stopped sliding into the cake. "He told you about that?"

"He tells me about his life, and," Mrs. Larsen said, turning the dial on the stove down a degree and moving back to the island, "you are a part of his life."

"I understand." Indigo nodded. "He's a part of mine too."

"Mm-hmm." Mrs. Larsen eyed her with suspicion. "So, how are these dates going? Found someone you love?"

Indigo's eyes widened at the four-letter word. "I haven't found that yet, but the potential for it is there." She grinned, thinking about Nathan and Diego, how both of them had the qualities of the type of man she was searching for.

"But do they treat you like my son treats you?"

The grin dropped from her face. Her lips parted, and she gasped in a gulp of air, but it felt like all the oxygen had been sucked out of the kitchen.

"They—" She didn't know what to say. Her voice departed from her as one two-letter word took up all the space in her mind.

"You're an adult now, so I'm going to talk to you like a woman." Mrs. Larsen rubbed her hands down the vibrant apron shielding her blouse and jeans. "I don't know what you and my son have going on. Y'all say it's friendship, but—"

"It is friendship," Indigo said, finally gaining control of her voice. "We work best as friends."

"Hmm." Mrs. Larsen slowly nodded. "I get it now, but he . . ." She looked past Indigo, letting her sights land on her son. "He loves you. And not like a friend."

"He told you that?" Indigo's words came out breathless.

"Baby." Mrs. Larsen leaned closer to her. "He don't have to." She straightened her posture. "I knew he wasn't going to play cello all through high school, knew he wasn't going to practice law even though he graduated law school. I know him. He's my baby. So, I'm saying this with love for you and for him . . ." Her hand went to her chest. "If you don't love him like he loves you, let him know, so he can move on and find someone who does."

"I—" This time, fear rendered her silent.

"What are y'all up to in here?" Tate asked with humor in his voice as he strolled to the fridge, but the elation quickly vaporized when he examined their faces. He gave an inquisitive nod. "You okay?"

"I'm fine," Indigo said quietly before sliding off the barstool. "Going to the restroom."

"Kebabs are done," Gregory Larsen announced, entering the kitchen with a platter of grilled beef and vegetables.

As she exited the kitchen, she heard Mr. Larsen ask what was going on, and his wife simply replied with, "Just an honest conversation."

· · ·

Neither of them uttered a word the entire ride home. She didn't know why he was silent, but the reason for her silence weighed heavy on her heart. The discussion with his mom had made her build a wall of standoffishness between Tate and herself. Indigo's arms were folded tightly against her body; she wished she'd brought a cardigan, but she knew the chilliness she felt wasn't just from the air-conditioning. It was from the way Tate's eyes left the road to steal glances at her and how he clenched his jaw in deep contemplation and confusion. She'd thought having dinner with his parents would be fun, but it had just reopened old wounds.

Tate eased his dark Audi into his driveway, shifting it into Park and turning down the music in one seamless motion. Neither one of them moved to unbuckle their seat belts. This time, Tate let his eyes stay on her for more than a second.

"What did you and my mom talk about in the kitchen?" He gestured to her erect posture. "Something has shifted in you."

She glared straight ahead, fidgeting with the lotus ring on her finger. "Nothing."

She'd told two lies tonight, which was rare from a woman who loved to keep things honest—the first during her conversation with Mrs. Larsen.

"Bullshit," Tate hissed, killing the headlights and shrouding them in darkness. Their neighborhood was disturbingly quiet for a summer night.

"You can't say that." Indigo stopped playing with the ring. "You don't know how I feel."

"Then tell me." His voice raised with frustration. "Because before we got to my parents' house, you were laughing and happy, but over dinner you were distant. Not at all like my Indigo."

"I'm not your Indigo!" She jerked her head in his direction. "I'm not yours. We're not a couple. We're friends, and I need everyone to get that. I need your mom to get that!"

"Everyone knows that."

Indigo dropped her head against the leather headrest, smashing her curly mane. "We just let everyone believe that distance is what ended us."

Their brief romantic relationship, spanning the summer after graduating high school to their freshman winter break, had been more intense than any of her other relationships. It was a connection of mind, body, and soul that mere distance couldn't break. But that was the very thing he'd let his parents believe. Indigo had told her parents they'd broken up to focus on their studies, which was partly true.

"Ended *us*." Tate's voice was cloaked with pain that still lingered, raising the hairs on the back of her neck. "*We* didn't end us. You did."

Indigo peered out the window at the stars, glimmering up high in the massive sky. "This isn't supposed to be happening." She turned toward him with stern eyes; for a second, she lost her words, seeing the turmoil and sadness written on his face. "We decided never to talk about it. The breakup. The baby." Her eyes burned with unshed tears. "None of it."

"Another one of your decisions."

Indigo scoffed, unbuckling her seat belt. "Oh! Yeah! Getting an abortion at eighteen was at the top of my bucket list." She flung open the car door then glanced back at him. "I made a hard choice."

"This is—" he started to say, but she was already out of the car. He fought with his seat belt and leaped out before she could make her way down the driveway. "This is not about that, and you know it." He waited until she twisted back around to face him. "After the abortion, you shut me out. Me!" He rigidly tapped his finger to his chest. "I didn't do it on purpose. You know that. I didn't mean for it to break."

"I know that." Indigo shook her head, inhaling a breath in the hopes that it would defuse the hurt and sadness swarming underneath her skin. "We should call it a night."

"Or maybe you should tell the truth instead of trying to avoid this conversation?"

"I told you the truth. I've never lied to you, ever."

Tate laughed mirthlessly. "I'm not Nathan or Diego. I know you, so do me the courtesy of not standing in front of me and lying to my face."

"I'm going home." She stabbed her clutch to her chest. "You can stay here in the driveway putting all your business in the street."

"There it is!" Tate's thunderous claps cracked through the quiet neighborhood.

She looked at their neighbors' homes, lights still on, knowing someone was going to hear them. She closed the space between them with a few steps. "Hush! Before you bring everyone outside."

"Fuck these people!" Tate furiously waved off her words. "But, of course, you care. You always care what people think. It's why you're doing what you're doing right now. God forbid you turn thirty and not have a man on your arm. What will everyone think?" He covered his mouth, feigning a gasp.

"Fuck you, Tate," Indigo hissed under her breath, no longer able to hold it back. "This was a mistake."

"What? Dinner with my parents or us being friends?"

Her eyes stung as hurt gripped her heart. She let anger and pain fuel her words. "Both!"

"Then maybe we shouldn't be friends." A sheen of mist in his eyes shone under the moon's glow.

"Maybe." She quickly turned around before the tears sprung from her eyes. "Good night, Tate."

"Good night, Indigo."

It was a simple expression, but it didn't feel like they were parting for the night as she walked across the street. It felt like the end of a relationship.

Chapter 29

From the window of her study, Indigo watched Tate toss his duffel bag into his trunk and drive off. She assumed he was headed to his cabin. There was no way either of them was going to get a good night's sleep after that argument. Part of her wanted to go outside in her lace pajamas and make sure everything between them would be okay. The other side of her, a loud voice in her mind, cursed out her heart for feeling sentimental and reminded her of all the things they'd said.

She turned back to her laptop, plunging back into revamping Adorn's blog. Her life was a mess, but it didn't mean her website couldn't be flawless. Or her closet. Or her kitchen. Or any other square inch of her property. Her Sunday was planned. She was going to organize the clutter and clean out the junk. She was going to avoid the world and everybody in it, one chore at a time.

Nathan called. She ignored it.

Her dad called. She didn't answer.

Emery and Hazel tried to FaceTime her. She declined.

Diego called . . . more than once. She let it go to voicemail.

Saxon texted. She paid it no mind.

Harrison DMed on Instagram, noting if she was on the phone, she could answer his call.

She spent most of the morning color-coding her clothes. Too many dates and family engagements had wreaked chaos on the spare room she'd renovated into a walk-in closet. Shorts were scrambled in with dresses and pants mixed in with shirts. But by the time ten o'clock rolled around, Indigo's closet could have put any department store to shame.

Gambit rose from his nap and trotted behind her as she set off on her next mission. The backyard. Indigo's lawn needed to be mowed. Why wait for the landscaper to come by on Wednesday when she had a mower sitting in the garage? The angelonias and celosias in the flower beds needed to be pruned, and as she ripped weeds out of the dirt, she forgot that she couldn't do the same with the problems in her own life. Her issues were ignored as Indigo plowed the earth with her fingers in the sweltering sun. The only thought that snuck in was the thirst on her tongue.

She discovered the answer hanging on her lemon tree. She pushed herself off the ground, remembering the adage "When life gives you lemons, make lemonade." She didn't stop at lemonade. She squeezed enough of the citrus fruit to make a dozen lemon-poppy muffins and a lemon custard pie with some to spare. So, she decided to whip up some lemon-garlic chicken. While she was halfway through making fresh pasta, an art she had picked up from one of the cooking classes she'd taken last year, her music was interrupted by the ringing of her doorbell. She planned to ignore it. She had flour on her hands, and surely whoever it was would get the message when she didn't come to the door.

Unfortunately, the person on her porch wasn't the type of person to catch a hint. They harassed her doorbell enough times that Gambit howled out his frustration. Indigo couldn't hope them away. She washed her hands and dried them on her apron as she trekked to the door with slow steps. She wanted to spit out a sarcastic comment, but on cracking open the door, Emery's blotchy face and Hazel's doleful expression wiped the snark from her.

"What's going on?" Indigo's tone was soft. She released the door so it swung wider, and Gambit no longer had to peek around her leg to see who was visiting.

"Is your phone off again?" Hazel asked. She looked like she had just hopped off a treadmill, in gray running shorts and a sports bra showing off her toned midriff. "We need a sister circle." She nodded to Emery.

"We broke up," Emery said, sniffling. "Last night."

Indigo circled her arms around her. "It's going to be fine." She stroked Emery's quivering back as fresh tears fell on her shoulder. "Come on in." She broke away from her friend, ushering them into her house. "I've got goodies inside."

• • •

"This is good," Hazel complimented, stabbing her fork into the piece of lemon custard pie on her dessert plate.

"Don't sound so surprised," Indigo said, no longer bothered that Hazel always sat on the countertop swinging her legs. "Harrison isn't the only one who knows how to bake." Before her little brother could tell the difference between a teaspoon and a tablespoon, the siblings had helped her granny in the kitchen. Her dad's mother had watched them when their parents were at work, and Indigo had loved playing sous-chef. It was all an adventure, with Nana telling her stories about the simpler times when she was a child, shucking corn and snapping green beans.

"Hmm." Hazel licked her fork, eyeing the carved-up pie,

probably wondering if she should have thirds. "What's got you in lemon land?"

"Now isn't about me," Indigo quickly diverted, dropping the pasta into the pot of boiling water. "Em, what happened?"

"Cancun." Emery kept her eyes cast down at the untouched slice of pie on her plate. Sleep deprivation and crying had stained her eyes scarlet. Her elbow sat on the island as she rested her cheek on her chin. "You remember he was supposed to take me?" Indigo nodded, and Emery continued, "He said he had business, and I couldn't go alone, so we planned something else, and he flaked on that too."

Hazel dropped a muffin on her plate, her sweet tooth not yet satisfied. "The man does have to work. What do you want him to do? Quit and leech off you?"

"That's not what I'm—" Emery stopped, her cheeks flushing. She let out a breath, sitting erect on the stool. "I don't want him to be unemployed. I just want to be treated like the woman he says he loves and not a flyover that fills his belly and gets him off."

Indigo nodded, lifting the pot of water. "I get it."

"Then, damn," Hazel started, hopping on the stool next to her cousin, "stop cooking for his ass and fucking him regularly. He's comfortable, and he ain't gotta do shit to get 'good man' privileges."

"That's why I broke up with him last night." For the first time since sitting down, Emery picked up her fork. "But I miss him."

"It's still fresh." Indigo shook the al dente noodles in the colander. "Give it some time. Maybe he'll come around." As soon as the words left her mouth, she wondered if she was talking about her own situation.

"Now, spill it," Hazel said with her sights on Indigo. "Why are you avoiding people, lemon lady?"

"I'm good." Indigo awkwardly shrugged as the steam from the

hot water gave her a facial. "I just needed to use them before they went bad."

"Mm-hmm," Hazel muttered around her mouthful of muffin.

Emery cocked her head, disbelief written all over her face. "This is a safe space. You can tell us."

Indigo couldn't help but chuckle at the side-eye Hazel gave Emery. "Fine, but this stays between us." Both the women agreed to secrecy, and Indigo let out a breath before continuing. "Em, you weren't the only one having drama last night. Tate and I got into a blowout."

"Why?" Emery asked.

"Are we finally going to find out what really went down between y'all and not the summary?" Hazel scooted closer to the island, getting prepared for what was about to be said.

"I went to dinner at his parents." Indigo whirled around to the stove, grabbed a mitten, and removed the iron skillet from the burner. "But I forgot how much his mom loved us being together." She set the skillet on the pot holder. "And they don't even know the reason we broke up."

"I mean . . . we don't know the reason." Emery gestured between herself and Hazel. "And I was your roommate when it happened."

Indigo massaged a muscle in the crook of her neck that seemed to grow tighter as they peered at her, waiting for her to disclose more. But she didn't want to; she already felt terrible, and she didn't want them to look at her differently. She knew how people felt about people who did what she'd done, but she was also tired of keeping that portion of her life a secret, fearing the day someone would find out.

"I—" She cleared her throat, trying to find her voice. "I had an abortion, and I didn't tell Tate until after the procedure."

"No. No." Emery blinked with a shake of her head. "I would've known. You were never sick. Indigo, why didn't you tell me? We slept in the same room, ten feet away from each other."

"I was ashamed." She tried to push back the tears that welled in her eyes. "And you had that new boyfriend, plus I didn't want anyone to know that I got knocked up by the kid down the street." She wiped the tear off her lip with the back of her hand. "I was mortified, and I had final exams. We were eighteen." Her voice wobbled. "I saw my future flash before my eyes, and a baby wasn't a part of it . . . not at the time."

Indigo wrapped her arms around her waist, looking up. She was nauseous and light-headed, heartbroken and scared—all the same emotions she had been racked with as she sat in the clinic's waiting room years ago.

"Sometimes things don't go as planned." Hazel's clear, steady voice broke through the silence. "And even though you have the final decision, he was there when it happened too."

"I should have told him!" Indigo said with her sight blurring and chest heaving. "I made a mistake. People make mistakes."

"Yes, they do," Emery said, rounding the island and wrapping her arms around Indigo. "Don't they, Hazel?"

"Of course." Hazel nodded briskly. "Just last week I made a mistake . . . then I made it again and again . . . and then four more times again." She cocked her head, her eyes fixed in reflection. "Last night, actually."

Indigo sniffed. "What are you getting at?"

"I . . ." She shook her head as if to get her thoughts back in the right order. "Nothing." Her eyelashes fluttered.

Emery's hold slacked around Indigo. "I wish you would've told me so I could've been there for you."

"Yeah." Indigo freed herself from Emery's embrace. "I just wanted to fix things quickly. Be normal again."

"I get it." Hazel nodded. "And you don't have to be ashamed around us. That's real-life shit, and we're real-ass friends."

"I know." Indigo genuinely smiled, grateful to have a pair of great girlfriends. "I know. I promise to be completely open from this point on."

"Good," Hazel replied.

"So . . ." Emery grabbed three plates from the cabinet. "What are you going to do about Tate?"

Indigo didn't have an answer to that question. She had spent all day trying not to think about the state of their relationship. Could she and Tate move forward, repair their friendship? Or had they both been naive, thinking that exes with a history like theirs could go back to being friends again?

"That's a riddle for another day." Indigo watched Emery plate the food as if she was going to be critiqued. "But I have decided which guy I'm bringing as my plus-one to my thirtieth."

It was one of the things she'd thought about last night. It had been a difficult decision to come to until she'd related each of the guys to shoes. Nathan was a strappy sandal with a block heel: summertime fun with an easy flow. Diego was stilettos: sexy, confident, and exuding power. Tate was a pair of Air Force 1s: reliable and goes well with everything.

She looked good with all of them, was comfortable with each. One she admired, one she adored, and one she loved deeply. But she knew she could have only one, which made her hopeful and heartbroken at the same time. Excited for the adventure and possibility of a new relationship but sad about the ending of an old one.

"Who?" Hazel yanked her eyes away from the text she was composing.

Emery stopped scooping out chicken. "Nathan or Diego?"

Indigo smirked. "I was afraid of how much I liked him . . .

afraid to commit to someone like him, to trust him with my heart, but after last night, I realized that basing it on fear is the wrong way to make a decision."

She thought about how she'd been afraid to tell Tate she was pregnant, how her parents would have reacted if they'd known their child was with child, and what people would have thought about her being a mother out of wedlock. Running away from those fears hadn't given her what she wanted. Back then, she'd been a teenage girl in love with the boy next door who wanted to marry her, but now she was a grown woman, and she wasn't going to let fear stand in her way.

"Bitch, who?"

"Hazel!" Emery said with a roll of her eyes. "Don't do that, but really, Indigo . . ." She turned back to Indigo. "Who?"

Chapter 30

The previous night had been a blur of dishing about man trouble and emptying wine bottles. Indigo rose at five in the morning with a splitting headache and a crick in her neck from sleeping on the couch. She didn't remember either Hazel or Emery going home after they'd polished off the last of the custard pie and Blue Bell ice cream, but when she woke up, they weren't there.

The last thing she had on her mind that morning was clothes. She shimmied into a pair of white jeans, threw on a tank, slipped on some loafers, and grabbed a blazer. She had two important things to do that day, one of which was taking Gambit to the vet.

It was past ten by the time traffic cleared up, and going back home to drop off Gambit after the vet was out of the question. As Indigo rolled by the mangled Fiat, she knew it would be a bring-your-dog-to-work day. She got a couple of turned-up noses and twisted faces as she strutted into Adorn with Gambit trotting beside her.

"He's trained," she offered with a reassuring smile that did nothing to ease some of her clients' tension. She stopped behind the checkout counter, where Hazel was bagging a middle-aged woman's stilettos. "Good morning, Mrs. Reynolds."

"Morning, Indigo, darling." Mrs. Reynolds received her card back from Hazel. She fitted the plastic in her leather wallet then peeked around the counter at Gambit. "Such a good fella."

"Yeah." Indigo patted his head, and he leaned against her leg, loving the affection. "He is."

"I hope everything goes well at your daughter's wedding," Hazel said as she put the receipt in the shopping bag and handed it to Mrs. Reynolds with a dazzling smile. "Don't forget to come back and tell us how it went."

"Oh! You know I will." Mrs. Reynolds set her purse strap on her shoulder, returning Hazel's smile. "And with pictures too."

"That's what I like to hear!" Hazel chuckled with a couple of claps as the woman headed out the door. Her jovial excitement faded once her eyes met the stoniness of Indigo's. "What?"

"Loose lips sink ships," she started, flipping through the schedule binder for the page with the current day's date. "Last night—or this morning—you and Emery didn't sneak off and tell Nathan—"

"That you're about to break up with him?" Hazel sprayed cleaner on a cloth and wiped the fingerprint smudges off the store's iPad. "No. I asked Harrison to pick us up on his way to work."

"Hmm." Indigo smirked. Harrison kept a strict schedule, since owning a bakery meant very early mornings. He was usually at home by nine and in bed by nine thirty. "Things are really serious between y'all."

After Indigo had gotten all her truths off her chest, Hazel had made a confession of her own. Indigo continued, "Mr. Eight Hours of Sleep Is Essential for a Healthy Mind and Body would never disrupt his sleep cycle for anything other than an emergency."

Hazel shrugged, but the smile she wore and the sparkle in her eyes gave her feelings away. "I wouldn't go tossing around that L-word yet, but it is definitely more than like."

Indigo's shriek drew the attention of the customers perusing the shelves and trying on shoes. "We're going to be sisters!"

"Whoa!" Hazel held up her hands, halting Indigo's presumption. "Slow down. No one's jumping any brooms. We're just . . . dating."

"Ugh," Indigo groaned. "I'm starting to hate that word."

"It's almost twelve." Hazel patted Indigo's back then held out her hand for Gambit's leash. "Go ahead. Monay's is a few blocks away, and you know how traffic gets."

Indigo handed Gambit off to Hazel, knowing that this lunch date couldn't be canceled, just like the pooch's appointment. Last night, after she'd told the girls what she'd decided, she'd sent Nathan a text asking to meet up for lunch. Unfortunately, now she was feeling queasy and a bit anxious. She liked Nathan. She really did. But it was just something in the back of her head, like the feeling you get when you're on your way to work and you wonder if you turned off the coffeemaker or remembered to lock the door. In her brain, she and Nathan felt right, but her heart wouldn't agree. It kept whispering that something was off.

"Fine. I'll get going." Indigo reluctantly shut the schedule binder and slid it back on the shelf behind the counter. "Just put him in my office. He'll take a nap and . . ." She read her watch. "Lula needs to go on break soon."

"Got it. Now, go." Hazel shooed her out.

Indigo grabbed her purse but spent a little time conversing with the clients in the store. She had some time to spare, so why not build a rapport with her customers, make them feel special before she went and ruined someone else's day?

· · ·

To Indigo's amazement, the traffic wasn't as monstrous as she'd expected. She arrived at Monay's with a couple of minutes to spare. The hostess offered to sit her at one of the best tables in the house since it was Monday and things were a little slow. Indigo politely declined. She didn't want to sit in the middle of the restaurant. It was too close to the space where she and Nathan had had their first drink together.

She snatched up a table by the window with a prime view of the sidewalk. She wanted to be able to prepare herself for his arrival. She needed to be able to compose herself and remember the speech she had prepared in the truck during her drive over.

Noon rolled around, and she was still nursing a sweet strawberry iced tea while partaking in a competitive game of *Words with Friends 2* with her nephew. She was beginning to wonder if the kid's vocabulary rivaled hers or if he had a dictionary by his side. Ten minutes later, tables started to fill, and a hum was present in the restaurant, but there was still no Nathan. Not even a call or a text.

Five minutes later, she received dirty glares from the sidewalk from those who wanted a table in the upscale Cajun restaurant. She knocked back the last chunk of ice in her glass and headed across the street to his shop. Inside the vintage dealership and repair shop, Indigo discovered Nathan wasn't there either. Not only had he missed work, but he also hadn't informed anyone where he was. She was more worried when she learned that neither Hazel nor Emery knew what was up with him. A bad feeling came over Indigo, so she went to the only place she could think he would be if he wasn't at work—his loft.

• • •

It must've been the robust, earthy aroma of percolating coffee that made Nathan push back the covers and climb out of bed. Or perhaps the sunlight bleeding through the blinds—slightly slanted as Musiq Soulchild serenaded him about love.

"What happened last night?" Indigo was surprised she'd managed to keep her tone steady as she turned toward him from her spot in his kitchen, pot in hand.

"How'd you get in?" He glanced over his shoulder, looking past the whirling ceiling fan and trail of clothes on the ground to see that the front door was locked.

"You don't answer a question with a question." She scooped a mass of buttery oatmeal into a cereal bowl, inwardly cringing at the statement her mama had frequently used on her as a youngster. "You answer. Any answer would suffice." She slid the bowl across the counter, and thankfully his reflexes weren't impaired by sleep. "What did you do last night?" She didn't deposit her serving of the breakfast cereal in her bowl. Her appetite was gone. Indigo knew the answer to her question by the stench of liquor oozing from his pores.

"Freddie's bachelor party was last night." He kept his eyes down as he gingerly stirred the oatmeal. "I have it under control."

"You're serious." Her words brought his gaze up to hers. "You honestly think this is under control?" She dropped the pot in the sink with a loud thud. A fiery rage rushed through her. "Either you're lying to me or you're lying to yourself. I don't know, but you need to figure it out." She hurried out of the kitchen into the living room.

"Wh-where are you going?" He spun around on the stool then stood up. "Just believe me." He advanced toward her. "I know how to fix this."

She quickly stepped away from his embrace. "You're relapsing. You told me you had a system." She gripped her purse strap as he peered at her with a sad, remorseful look. "What did your sponsor say about partying? Hanging out in places where alcohol is in limitless supply?"

"It . . . uh . . ." He roughly rubbed the smooth flesh over his collarbone. "It . . . didn't come up in the meeting."

"You mean you didn't tell him." She threw her arms up weakly. "You are a businessman. People count on you having your life together. They're working their asses off. Do you know how I know? I went there looking for you." She pointed at him. "You can screw around with your livelihood but not theirs."

"Look, Indigo. I know my body." He slapped his palm in his other hand emphatically. "It's gonna take more than one night of too many beers to push me off the wagon. This wasn't a drunken binge fueled by an argument or some other emotionally devastating event. It was just one fun night out with my boys." He spread out his arms with a twisted smile. "I can manage this. I got this. And look at me." He brushed his hands down his scruffy face and then looked over his own appearance—black boxer briefs, no shirt, bloodshot eyes, and rumpled black locks. "No shakes. I'm not craving a drink." He chuckled, stepping closer to her. "Let's eat our breakfast and talk about our plans for later."

"It's one p.m." Indigo held up her hand with a shake of her head.

He looked over at the microwave clock. The neon-green numbers glared back at them: 1:12. "Babe, I'm sorry."

"Don't." She fished her hand around in her purse in search of her keys.

Her eyes filled with tears, but she didn't understand why. Why was she getting emotional when she had been going to break things off with him earlier today? The answer made itself known from the deep pang of worry in her gut. He might not be the right choice for her, but they'd built a friendship over the last few months. She cared for him and his well-being. The man standing before her was a ghost of the man she'd given her business card to at Monay's.

"You're playing a dangerous game." Her hand stilled in her purse as she trained her gaze on him. "You can't be two versions of yourself. The one that's responsible and in control with me, Emery, Hazel, and your sister, and then another one that cuts loose and gets drunk with his friends. That's not how alcoholism works!"

He flinched at her tone, taken off guard. They'd never had anything to argue about. She hadn't meant to raise her voice, but it was the only way she was going to get the words out; frustration clung to her throat, strangling her.

"I know how alcoholism works."

"Then act like it. I know you don't want your friends to know," she said with sincerity, causing his features to soften. "But this sober-lite routine you're working isn't going to last, and you're going to lose all the things you worked so hard for. And I don't want that for you."

He nodded. "Me neither."

She grabbed his dead phone from the bar countertop. "You have everything inside you to be a great man for someone one day . . ." She nodded as a tear rolled down her cheek. She knew it was true from the way he cared for his sister and the comforting, courteous manner he had with her. He just had to conquer those demons that haunted him. "Really . . . you will, but that someone isn't me. It would be best if you focused on yourself. Heal you." She handed him his phone. "Charge it and call your sponsor. Be the person I know you can be."

"Indigo." He closed the space between them, staring down at her tearstained face with a chagrined look of his own. "I'm sorry."

"I know." She gave him a hug then pulled out of his weak grasp.

"Goodbye, Nathan." She sniffed, widening the gap between them. "Be well." She left him standing in the living room alone. The moment she stepped into the elevator, she called Emery—told her everything, and that she should probably check on him.

Chapter 31

"I like it." Hazel fawned over Indigo's newly straightened mane. She tucked a strand behind Indigo's ear, letting the sun radiate through the diamond stud in her earlobe. "Madam C.J. Walker would approve."

Indigo didn't know how she felt about it. The person staring back at her in the floor-length mirror in her office didn't look like her. She hadn't rocked a straight hairdo since college, though since then, her face hadn't changed much. No wrinkles, just faint laugh lines around the corners of her mouth whenever she curved her lips. She still looked like that twenty-two-year-old who didn't know what the next step in her life was. It was eerie and unnerving that seven years had passed since she had last seen that girl but that she still was uncertain about her future.

"I'm just keeping it like this for the party." Indigo plucked her hair from behind her ear and combed the glossy tresses over one shoulder. "Then I'm jumping in the pool."

Hazel sauntered over to the door, laughing. "Girl, you a trip." She twisted the knob and whipped the door open. "Now, let's go get this day over with so we can get our nails done."

"Agreed." Indigo turned away from the mirror. She wasn't big on going to the salon—she usually preferred painting her nails at home on a quiet Sunday—but after her altercation with Nathan yesterday, she felt like being pampered. "Clock in this second half."

She followed Hazel out of the hallway. Indigo fiddled with her blush pants and white blouse, her matching pumps clicking. With every step of her strut, her confidence rose. A smile slid across her lips as she brushed her eyes over the sun-drenched store. It was a little past two, and customers were still coming through the door after the lunch rush. Lula was ringing up three pairs of Ralph & Russos at the counter for an elegant, suit-wearing woman. Hazel was explaining the importance of having a pair of ballet flats in your closet to a stiletto-clad real estate agent, which meant the young woman who'd just walked through the door was Indigo's.

"Hi! Welcome to Adorn!" She pranced over to the woman with an outstretched hand. "I'm Indigo. Shopping for anything special today?"

"Indigo." The young woman shook Indigo's hand with an infectious smile beaming on her face. "That's your name, really?"

"Yes. Really." It never got old, seeing the expression of bewilderment and wonder at the utterance of her name. "My mama wanted to travel to India before having babies, but her plate was full, so she gave me a name that wasn't just a childhood friend's name, but also a symbol of her wanderlust."

"Neat backstory." The woman nodded, running her hand through her raven silk-pressed mane. "I'm just Monique, after page thirty-three in a baby naming book."

"Metaphorical traveling or picked from a list . . ." Indigo slipped her hands into her pockets as another customer breezed in. "It doesn't matter how we got our names—it's what we do with them."

"Wow! Are you a poet too?"

"No, but I know one." Indigo's smile faltered just a sliver thinking about Tate, whom she hadn't heard from since Saturday. "Writing isn't my thing. Style is."

"Good!" Monique rubbed her hands briskly together, moving over to the glass shelf of Louboutins. "'Cause my boyfriend and I just got over a rough patch. He's taking me out, and I need something that screams sexy."

Indigo grinned at the woman, who towered over her in espadrilles. "Red bottoms are sexy, but to help you pick out the perfect pair of shoes, I need to know a little more about the outfit you have planned and the place y'all are going to."

"Uh . . . I'm thinking about wearing this black lace McQueen dress I picked up in Tokyo." She toyed with the diamond eternity band on her ring finger, tilting her head. "And we're going to see *The Merry Widow*."

"Aw, I just recently went on a date to see that myself." She watched Monique pick up a black Pigalle.

"Did you like it? I'm more of an opera kind of girl." She held out the shoe for Indigo to inspect her choice.

"It was funny and captivating. You'll love it." Indigo set her hand under the foot of the pump and took hold of the heel, knowing she'd have to buff out the smudge Monique had just put on the patent leather. "Classic black is beautiful, but you said sexy . . ." She set the shoe back on the shelf and picked up the one next to it. "And with your long legs, these red ones will make it almost impossible for him to keep his hands off you."

"Mmm, a little fondling." Monique's shoulders danced as Hazel strolled to the back for a green flat in size nine. "Absolutely!" She unzipped her wallet and handed a card over to Indigo. "Here, and keep the tab open. I see a pair of Giuseppes that are calling my name. I was in Milan for a shoot but didn't have time to shop. Shame, right?"

"A horror," Indigo murmured, running her eyes over the name on the platinum card. Her brows knitted, chest tightened, and stomach knotted at the twelve letters spelling out the first and last name of a man she knew: Diego Simpson. She held up the card. "Is this the . . . um . . . your boyfriend?"

"Yeah." Monique's smile faltered as her hand clung to a green strappy sandal. "I'm looking for shoes to go with a green leather miniskirt I just picked up." She spoke as if she was talking to herself. "I had something, but he returned my shoes." She glanced around to see if she could spot them on one of the shelves. "Do you have them here? I hadn't even worn them. He always overreacts like this. I don't even know why—" She shielded her mouth with her hand bashfully. "Overshare. I'm so sorry."

"No . . . um." Indigo blinked and looked back at the svelte woman who couldn't be more than twenty-three. Her mind froze on what to do next. Should she tell Monique that she'd been dating her boyfriend, that he was cheating on her, or should she keep it to herself?

Indigo's lips moved before her brain could catch up, or maybe it was the other way around—maybe her brain was working on autopilot, and her lips were just following along. "That date I went on to the ballet . . . it was with Diego." She swallowed hard as the woman stared blankly at her. "Simpson. I completely apologize." Indigo's hands fluttered by her chest. "I didn't know he had a girl-friend. I would've never entertained him if I'd known."

"You are straight out of *Steel Magnolias*." Monique wore that cheery smile again. With a flick of her wrist, she continued, "Whatever Diego does in Texas is his business. I'm his California girl. Now, if you two skip yourselves to the Golden State, then that's a completely different situation, that would be my time with him, unless . . ." She smirked, stepping back to run her eyes up and down Indigo's frame. "Unless we're talking about a ménage-type thing. Those are always fun."

Indigo blinked. Then she did the only thing she could do—she threw her head back and guffawed. She gripped her waist, emitting a laugh so loud the other customers, as well as Lula and Hazel, looked her way. They didn't know she had to laugh to stop crying.

Indigo's laughter died as she turned to Lula at the counter. "I need you to finish assisting Ms. . . ." She gestured for the woman to fill in her surname.

"Williams," Monique said. She reached out, laying her hand on Indigo's arm. "You don't have to feel weird about this. It works really well. And I'm good at sharing."

"You probably are, but I don't want a man I have to share." She gave Monique a clipped smile then handed Lula the credit card.

Indigo dashed back to her office, muttering, "Shit" under her breath. Hazel followed her.

Anger, fiery and spiky, shot through Indigo. She grabbed the purse off her desk, running down a list of things Hazel had to keep an eye on while she stepped out. She did not speak a word to any of the clients. Nor did Indigo tell Hazel where she was going. She hopped in her truck, swerved out of the parallel parking spot, and skidded across the intersection before the yellow light flashed to red.

Before Indigo knew it, she was at the law firm. She hadn't had enough time to form a polished speech, so she went for the first words sitting on her tongue.

"You son of a bitch!" The statement spewed out like venom once she stepped foot in Diego's office. His hands went slack on the keyboard. His eyes widened, then just as his lips parted to speak, she cut him off. "No! It's not your mama. It's just you." She twisted on her heel as she dashed to the door, abruptly shutting it without a sound. "You're the bitch!"

"Are you losing your mind?" Diego slunk toward her with his palms up. "What's the matter with you?" he hissed, glancing over at the glass wall to see if anyone was in the hallway eavesdropping. He turned back to her, rolling his eyes over her locks. "Your hair's nice, though." He reached for the long strand framing her face.

Indigo smacked his hand away, and he hissed from the sting. "You would like it, since your girlfriend's rocking the same style."

"Eh?" He casually slid his hands into his pockets. "You met Monique?"

"Yes. Yes, I met Monique." She took a step back, her eyes narrowing into hard slits at the coolness of his tone and overall nonchalance. "You have a girlfriend in California. I can't believe this." Her shoulders hunched as she held her face. There was a dull ache in her heart as the acid bubbling in her stomach made her queasy. "I picked you. I chose you over—"

"Who told you to do that?" he quickly interjected.

Indigo's hands slithered down her face. "Silly me. I thought we were moving toward something."

"We are." His voice rose a bit. "We're two responsible adults who enjoy spending time with each other . . . when we have time."

"Oh! I get it. You want a part-time woman. One who runs when you call her." She nodded, remembering that most of the dates they'd gone on had fitted around his schedule whenever he was finished with a case or didn't have to review contracts. "Company, so you're not bored and lonely in a new city. Is that what you think of me as?" She stabbed her fingertips against her chest. "A plaything that you pick up when you want a relationship with no commitment?"

"It's an open relationship." He sighed as if she was being unreasonable. "And yes, there is commitment. I'm committed to you on the days that I have time to deal with this." He gestured to her. "And the days that I don't, you're free to do whatever you want."

Indigo tsked. "And you thought this was cool with me? After I told you marriage is what I want?" She held up her finger as he moved to speak. "And as I remember, you told me the same thing."

"True." He shrugged. "But I also said I want to be partner." He strode back around his desk, smoothly dropping his body into the leather chair. "And I can't possibly perform at the high level that I need to if I'm busy tending to your needs, wants, and wishes twenty-four seven." He pulled his chair closer to the lavish mahogany desk. "Your parents are lawyers. You should know this."

"You said . . ." Indigo remembered the words he'd said to her at the French restaurant then chuckled, even though inside, she wanted to cry. "You know what I do know, Diego?" She set her clasped hands under her chin. "The type of man I want is someone who won't see me as a chore or a hindrance standing in the way of professional goals. I'm not a hobby or a trophy. I'm a woman with her own ambitions, dreams, and goals, and I want someone who'll fight for me like I'll fight for him and love me unconditionally like I'll love him and . . ." Her eyes grew misty as she glared at him straight on. "You're not him." She sniffed then cleared her throat. "Not at all."

She darted out of the office, raced down the hallway, and hurried into the empty elevator, where she cried alone.

Chapter 32

"Boo!" Harrison heckled from the middle seat. "This ain't a sing-along. Can I watch *Sparkle* in peace?"

"No," Indigo said, hopping up and hustling in front of the massive screen, mimicking Lonette McKee's dance moves to "Hooked on Your Love."

He flung a pillow at Indigo. She swatted it to the floor before it hit her in the face.

"Hater," she said with a shimmy of her shoulders before snatching up the pillow.

Saxon stopped laughing and said, "You sure you ain't related to Lucky Lips?"

"Shut up." Indigo hit Saxon with the pillow then collapsed next to her on the couch. "Neither of y'all better start singing when *The Five Heartbeats* is on."

Harrison huffed. "I can carry a tune."

"To hell," Saxon added.

Both of his sisters laughed as Indigo gave Saxon a high five. The trio had been at their parents' house all Friday, having a classic movie marathon and only getting up for food, restroom breaks, and when one of the children needed something—which was seldom since their grandparents were also there. Frost was the only one who truly required Saxon's attention.

A day with family was what Indigo needed to heal the sting of heartbreak. She'd thought Diego had the potential to be a great match for her, but she was wrong. She'd been wrong about a lot of things. She'd been wrong about Nathan and about her ability to move past her history with Tate.

The movie continued to play in the dim theater room.

"How are you doing, for real?" Saxon asked. She must have picked up on the shift in Indigo's mood.

Indigo shrugged. "I'm fine. A little hurt but fine." She grabbed one of the other decorative pillows and hugged it tight. "I thought I picked better this time."

Harrison nodded, but not Saxon.

"Did you, though?" Her sister turned to her, the baby monitor still in her lap. "Don't get me wrong, they seemed like fine guys from what you told me earlier on, but it just felt like you were settling for good and not great."

Indigo's head tilted to the side. "Is this about Tate?"

"Oh, you see that," Harrison jumped in, gesturing to her. "She didn't even bring him up, but you did."

"Can you chill, Dr. Phil?" Indigo held up her hand. She let out a heavy breath. "After breaking things off with Diego, I did a lot of deep thinking."

Saxon propped her arm on the back of the couch. "And what realization did you come to?"

"I realized . . ." She paused, tucking a clump of hair that was already beginning to curl up behind her ear. "I picked men that

I vibed with, men that I could like and learn to adore but never actually have that mind, body, and soul love with." She tried to sniffle away her emotions, but her tears still fell.

Saxon held her hand. "I'm sorry, baby. If I knew you were still hurting this much, I wouldn't have pushed you to start dating again."

"Same," Harrison chimed in.

"But I'm not hurting," Indigo clarified, wiping away the tears. "I healed from the pain of my breakup with Tate. We healed our friendship. But I'm still scared to love someone with the ferociousness that we loved each other with. Because it's the type of love that hurts to the core when it doesn't work out."

She hadn't told them about the abortion yet. She wanted to tell her mom first.

"I understand that," Harrison said. "I don't know what Hazel and I have yet, but I do know that it's not something I've experienced before. She's the first person I want to talk to when I wake up and the last voice I want to hear before going to sleep."

"Baby brother." Saxon peered at him softly. "Are you in love?"

He dropped his back against the chair. "I might be."

Indigo agreed with a faint nod. However, her situation was different. There was no uncertainty for her. She knew she was in love; she just didn't know if she had the strength to confess it.

• • •

The movie marathon had ended hours ago, but instead of going upstairs and sliding into bed like the rest of the family, Indigo sought refuge in the sitting room on a comfy chair underneath a cozy blanket with Gambit curled in a ball by the ottoman. The conversation with her brother and sister was still heavy on her mind. Her eyes lifted from the photo album in her lap, landing on her phone on the coffee table. She knew what she needed to do but still needed to muster up some courage.

She shook her head at herself, looking back at the photos. "I'm supposed to be a *boss-ass bitch*."

"Don't call yourself a bitch again."

Indigo's head whipped toward the door. Gambit didn't stir. "Mama. I thought you were asleep."

"Hmm." Stella entered the room in her red satin robe and matching headscarf. "Is that why you're in here cussing at yourself?"

"No," she said, setting her attention back on one of the hundreds of pictures her parents had taken of her and her siblings during their childhood and teenage years.

Stella sidled next to her chair. "I hope it's not because of that man."

"Diego?" Indigo peered up at her mama.

"Yes."

"Definitely not."

"Good." Stella smoothed her hand over Indigo's head.

Indigo didn't disagree with the gesture or fuss about her mom messing up her hair. It was already tangled with stubborn curls. A blowout during a Texas summer was a bad idea.

Once her mama's hand dropped from her head, she asked, "Are you going to tell me *I told you so*?"

"I'm not petty," Stella affirmed. "Just want to look out for you." She lifted Indigo's chin so she could look her in the eyes. "I don't care that you're turning thirty this week, you're still my baby, and I want the best for you. A man who's ruled by ambition, power-hungry, and indifferent to the importance of family isn't a good partner for you. Makes for a good lawyer, though." She released her chin and took a step toward the door. "Don't stay up all night. I know you're already beautiful, but you do need rest."

"Yes, ma'am," she uttered then called, "Mama," stopping the woman's footfalls out of the room. "I'm sorry for how I acted."

"No need." Her mom smiled softly. "You were raised to be outspoken and speak up for yourself."

Indigo agreed and echoed her mama's good night before she left. In the silence of her room, her mama's words stayed with her. *Be outspoken. Speak up for yourself.* It was time for her to be the type of person she'd been raised to be . . . in every aspect of her life.

Chapter 33

Three days later, Indigo found herself sitting stiffly on the settee in her bedroom. Her brown eyes were trained ahead, but her thoughts weren't on the gold stilettos on the dresser. She was going over the past three months. The impressive dates she'd gone on, the wonderful conversations and sensuous interplay. She'd been sure she'd find the right guy, adamant about it. But now, as she sat in her room, she knew she'd been wrong.

She'd thought she had figured out dating. She had been sure Nathan and Diego were promising suitors. She couldn't understand what had gone wrong. Was it her, like Saxon said? Did she really not know how to pick a good guy? Diego had it all. He checked off all the boxes on her list—intelligent, cultured, hardworking, and handsome. She'd had an inkling Diego was a player but not an unrepentant one. She'd assumed he really wanted her and just her. She was wrong about that one.

Then there was Nathan. After the dust settled from her confrontation with Diego, she'd thought about him. In the quiet of her living room two days ago, her finger had hovered over his name. She'd wanted to call him, see how he was doing, but she couldn't work up the nerve—not after calling things off with him. Maybe that was the mistake she had made. Had she thrown in the towel too soon? Maybe she should have driven him to rehab and not Emery. She didn't know if what she was feeling was regret or desperation. She did feel something for him, but was it love or like? Was it a passion so intense that she could wait for him to wade through his problems and get his life back on track? That was simple for her to answer. No.

"Indigo!" A voice called her name with a tinge of urgency.

She thought about saying something, but her jaws refused to move, and her voice fled. Her eyes followed Gambit as he jetted out of the room, wagging his tail. She wished she were as jovial as her furry friend. It was her birthday, after all.

She should've been jumping for joy. She'd been on this planet for thirty years, she still had the energy of a teenager, and no grays had sprung up in her scalp. However, a cloud of melancholy hung over her.

Tate came into the room, holding a flat white box at his side.

"What's wrong?" The playful smile he wore slowly disappeared. "Why are you crying?"

Indigo wiped her face and looked at her fingertips, annoyed that she was still tearful. "Nothing." She shrugged, wiping away more tears she didn't remember shedding. "I'm fine." She tried to switch the conversation. "You cut your hair."

"Yeah, creative process complete." He spoke nonchalantly, sitting next to her. "If you're fine, look at me."

"I don't need to look at you." Her voice began to crack, so she stopped, took a deep breath, and slowly exhaled. "I already know how you look."

"Humor me." Tate placed two fingers under Indigo's chin and

turned her head toward him. She closed her eyes. "Come on," he urged, but she squeezed her eyelids tighter together. "Don't make me start singing. 'Cause I'll start singing 'Never Too Much' until you look at me, and you know I will."

Oh, yeah, she knew. She'd been victim to the sharp, tone-deaf screeching of his singing voice before. It was a torture she didn't wish to endure again. She opened her eyes and drank in the sincerity swelling in his dark eyes and subtle smile.

"That's my girl," he whispered as his fingers abandoned her chin and swept across her cheek. "What's wrong?"

She pulled her face away from him, blowing out an audible breath. "I broke up with Diego." Her shoulders slumped, causing her silk robe to open, displaying a sliver of her black lace bra.

"Just now?" He gawked at the phone in her hand.

"No," she whined, regaining her posture. "Last week."

"And you're just telling me." He nudged her shoulder.

Feeling the air-conditioning kick on, she shrugged weakly, a cool burst of air blowing across her damp face. "I didn't think you wanted to talk to me."

"Well, that's stupid."

She cocked her head and glanced at him from the side. "Are you calling me stupid?"

"I'm calling the idea of you thinking I don't want to talk to you stupid."

"I just . . ." She stopped to remember all the harsh words they had spewed at each other in his driveway. "We fought, and you left without saying anything. Then when you came back, you didn't break the silence, so . . ."

"You know, Indigo . . ." The sun through the bedroom window rained across him, making the gold in his chestnut tresses shimmer. "Everything is not about you."

"Is that so?" she mocked, feeling the ache of heartbreak fade slightly.

"Yes." He nodded. "I was in the zone." He tapped his hand on the flat white box resting on his lap. "And I finished it."

"Your book!" She reached for the box, but he stopped her hand midair.

"It's only the first chapter, and it's your birthday present. You can't open it until after the party."

Indigo grinned, taking in his appearance: his disheveled mane, nicely pressed black suit, white dress shirt stretching across his expansive chest, and gold tie. "I don't think I'm going." Her eyes drifted to the glimmering gold body-hugging dress zipped in the plastic bag draped over the chair. "I don't feel like being around all those people, talking about my lackluster life and answering their nagging questions about my marital status and uterus."

"Stop lying." He shook his head. "Your life's not lackluster, and if you don't want to answer questions about your . . . um . . . uterus, do what I do. Plead the Fifth."

Indigo gave her first genuine smile in days. "You get questions about your uterus too?"

"Funny, but you know what I mean."

"Yeah, I do." She glanced at the box on his lap. "So . . . can I open it now? Please." She pouted. "Pretty please?"

"Fine." He handed her the box. "Just don't get your hopes up."

"Hopes regulated." Indigo quickly opened the box with a full-fledged smile. Her eyes slid over the Times New Roman script of the cover page, which read *The Courtship of Charisma* with Tate's name underneath it. Her left eyebrow kicked up. "Is this about me? I feel like this is about me."

"You are the inspiration, yes." He stood, fiddling with his tie. "But it's all fiction."

"Uh-huh." Indigo delicately lifted the neatly stacked sheets of white paper from the box as if they were porcelain. She pulled the first sheet off and placed it back in the box facedown. She rubbed her hands over the centered, italicized words: "'To the girl who gave me a black eye.'"

"Do you have to read it out loud?" he muttered as his shoulders rose and his nose bunched.

"Yes." She didn't look up. "'The woman who broke my heart and the best friend who put me back together with conversations and leftovers. My love for you is deep and unchanging.'" She lifted her head as fresh tears streamed down her cheeks. "I love it."

He looked coy. "You haven't even read the story yet."

"I don't have to. You wrote it. I know it's brilliant."

Tate combed his hand through his hair. "I just hope the story has the same effect on Hiran."

"It will." Indigo bit her bottom lip, thinking of doing something she probably shouldn't do, but every fiber in her being urged her to follow through. Her hand grew clammy against the paper, and her stomach twisted with nervous excitement. It was a bold move, but it was her birthday. "I'd like to give you my thank-you."

"You're welcome." He ran his hands down the buttons of his shirt.

"No. I wasn't saying thank you." She stood, adjusting her silk robe around her. "My thanks is something I have to give." She took a few small steps to close the space between them as he narrowed his eyes at her.

He chuckled nervously. "Wh-what are you doing?"

"Being thankful." Indigo rose on her tiptoes and wrapped her arms around his neck.

For the slightest of seconds, Tate froze, staring down at her like a deer in headlights, then he circled his arms around her back, pulling her closer. Chest to chest, body to body, their warmth surged together, sparking a fire underneath their yearning flesh. Tate's head fell into the crook of her neck as his hands rose along her back then inched back down to her waist.

Indigo's lips rested at his ear as she shakily breathed in the earthy bergamot cologne that was seeped into his pores, reminding her of the first bottle she'd ever bought him. Her heart pounded like a drum getting ready for battle, banging against her rib cage as she twisted her arms tighter around his neck. She licked her lips, finding her voice as he squeezed her like he was a man going off to war.

"You were right. I wasn't honest." Indigo's voice came out huskier than usual. It was probably because Tate's hand had found its way to the top of her ample derriere. "I was ashamed, and I couldn't bear telling my parents that I got knocked up, seeing the disgust in their eyes." She breathed him in once more. "And I really, really didn't want to ruin my life . . . and yours."

Tate pulled back with a pensive look that made her draw in a ragged breath. "You could never ruin my life, Indigo." He delicately brushed the stray tendrils of hair away from her face. "You didn't have to be ashamed. I would've had your back and been right by your side."

"I know you would've, and," she said, leaning into the embrace of his hand, "I never blamed you. I pushed you away because I felt dumb and irresponsible for getting pregnant." Her throat burned as tears streamed down her cheeks. "I made a mistake . . ." Her hands fell from his neck, settling on his biceps. "And I'm sorry."

"Indie." He leaned in and gently kissed her forehead. "I'm sorry. I should've been more careful. I should've never put you in that situation. I should've had the right condom . . . one that wouldn't break. And you've never been dumb or irresponsible."

"Oh my God!" She laughed weakly, rubbing the tears from her face. "We're an after-school special."

"Uh . . ." He chortled. "You know how to kill a mood."

She shrugged. "It's my specialty." She pulled out of his embrace and scooped the gold gown off the chair. "Let me put this rag on so we can go."

"Cool." He patted his thigh, summoning Gambit out of his slumber. "I'll be waiting."

As she retreated into the bathroom, those three words lingered in the air around her. *I'll be waiting*. She wondered if that's what he'd . . . they'd . . . been doing: waiting. Waiting for the right time. For the right moment. For closure. Just waiting on each other.

Chapter 34

This is good shit, Indigo thought to herself as she took another sip of champagne. She didn't know where her mama had procured the sparkling elixir, but she needed to figure it out. The bubbles danced as the notes of peach, almond, and white cherry harmonized on her taste buds. She examined the crystal flute as the humid night air rejuvenated the curls in her hair. All she discovered was that her glass was almost empty.

"Hmm, I should've swiped a bottle," she whispered to herself, her eyes drinking in the sight of her family, friends, and friends of the family chatting, dancing energetically, and feasting on the Southern comfort foods waiters whisked around on their platters.

She'd snuck away after blowing out the solitary candle plunged into the middle of the caramel cake Harrison had brought out of the house. Under the twinkling lights strung over her parents' backyard, she'd fought the urge to join in as everyone sang Stevie Wonder's rendition of "Happy Birthday."

It was official. Indigo was thirty, and although she'd woken up that morning with a knot in her stomach and a bittersweet pang in her heart, she was no longer melancholy. How could she be when she was driving another forkful of caramel cake into her mouth?

"Are you still avoiding me?" her mama asked, advancing toward her like a gazelle with a champagne flute in each hand.

Indigo swallowed the buttery, sweet bite of caramel cake before saying, "No." She smiled warmly as her mama approached her. "I'm just taking it all in." She waved her fork at the merriment unfolding on the dance floor as the deejay entered the new jack swing portion of the playlist. "How'd you know I like this song?" She started nodding her head to the beat.

"Girl." Her mama gave her an "Are you serious?" look as she sat down on the bench beside her. "You played that song every night for a month. I was starting to despise Tony! Toni! Toné!"

Indigo gasped.

"Yes!" Her mama handed her a fresh glass filled with bubbly. "But it's your birthday, so . . ."

Indigo clung to the flute, eyeing her mama suspiciously. "Really?"

"Yes." Her mama tore her gaze away from Harrison teasing Saxon's dance moves. "I want you to be happy."

"Is that why you wanted me to wear that taffeta nightmare?"

Her mama shook her head with a smirk. "You make it sound worse than it was. That dress was lovely." Indigo gagged. "Stop exaggerating. You love ball gowns."

"Yeah, when I was eight and wanted to be Lisa from *Coming to America*." Her mouth curved up, matching the smile on her mama's face. "But that's not what I want anymore. I don't want to be a princess or shout out 'I object,' and I know that upsets you, but I can't be perfect like Saxon."

"What?" Her mama's face flinched, and her arched eyebrows snapped together. "I don't want you to be like Saxon. Where'd you get that idea from?"

"Come on, Mama," Indigo drawled, her shoulders sagging slightly as she turned toward the matriarch. She was old enough. She could take it. She didn't need her mama coddling her feelings anymore. She could just come out and tell her how she really felt. "I know you favor Saxon more than me. She does everything the right way, while I—"

"Let me stop you right there." Her mama held her hand out. "I don't favor any one of y'all over the other. I don't love Saxon more than you or you more than Harrison."

Indigo's mouth tugged to the side as her heartbeat quickened. "But I disappoint you?"

"No."

"Yes, I do." Indigo let out a frustrated grunt. "You don't have to protect my feelings. I'm a big girl." She gestured at the party. "I'm an adult. You can be honest with me."

"I'm being honest with you, baby girl." The older woman's face was blanketed with sincere concern. She took Indigo's hand in hers, holding it tightly as if for dear life. "You have never disappointed me."

"But I went to the wrong school."

"Yes." She lightly nodded her head, her sleek mane of gray hair in intricate twists. "I wanted you to go to Yale or Dartmouth and not a state school, but once you were there a semester, I realized why you'd picked it."

"Why?" Indigo narrowed her eyes at her mama suspiciously, waiting for the answer.

"Because you three are close." Her brown eyes glided over to Saxon and Harrison, goading each other on the dance floor—the cheerleader versus the class clown. "We raised y'all that way. To have each other's backs, so . . . no, I'm not upset that you wanted a school closer to home."

Tears pricked at the bottom of Indigo's eyes. "But I'm not a lawyer . . . after taking all those prep courses in high school and shadowing you and Dad, I didn't follow through."

"You followed your passion." Her mama patted her hand. "Was I surprised that you changed career paths? No. It was a child's plan. I didn't place too much stock in it."

"But when I moved back home after graduating, you always brought it up." Indigo remembered those evening discussions around the dinner table. They used to cause her so much concern that she'd eat dinner at the Larsens' before her parents got home so she could avoid the ritual. "'Why don't you just try your luck at the LSAT'? 'Law school is just three years'?"

"I wanted you to have something stable. A career you could depend on. And now, you do." Her mama stroked her cheek. "And I couldn't be prouder."

"You are?" she whispered, then tried to sniff back her tears, but she was too late—they glided from her eyes and rolled around her mama's thumb.

"Tremendously." Her mama wrapped her arm around Indigo's shoulder and pulled her into an embrace that had Indigo feeling like a kid again. "You have matured into a woman I admire. I love you, Indigo. I never want you to be like anyone else. Or mimic anyone else's life. I wouldn't have given you a unique name if I wanted you to be ordinary." She stroked Indigo's back as her tears dripped on her shoulder. "Nothing you can do will ever make me disappointed with you, ever."

Indigo knew one thing that might. It blinked in her mind like a marquee in Vegas. Indigo knew her conservative, proper, by-the-book mama would be stunned by the one confession Indigo had yet to make.

"But I . . . um . . ." She gripped at her mama's sides, clinging to her black dress as if this was going to be their last hug. "At . . . eighteen, I had an abortion."

Silence. Her mama's hand stilled on Indigo's back. Indigo knew it. That was the one unforgivable thing. There was no coming back from it. It was out. She couldn't pull it back even if she wanted to.

Indigo sobbed harder, and then something surprised her. Her mama didn't slink away from her or curse her name; she wrapped her arms around her tighter and kissed the side of her head—mussing up her styled locks.

"It's going to be okay. It's going to be okay," her mama reassured her with a swaying rock.

The years of regret, guilt, and shame melted away as her mama held her. She cried until she had no more tears left to cry, and after what seemed like forever, Indigo untangled her arms from her around her mama and stood up straight.

"Do you feel better?" Her mama's voice was soft, and Indigo noticed the pinkness in her eyes.

She nodded, drying her face. "I do." She inhaled a deep breath and then breathed out, her chest deflating as if this was the first easy breath she'd taken in a while. "So much better."

And she truly did. Sure, she was aware she and her mom needed to have an honest and open conversation, but that would have to come later, when they had privacy and quiet.

"Now, tell me, when are you going to be that grown woman you keep telling me you are and . . ." She smoothed her hands down Indigo's hair. "And tell him you love him?"

She followed her mom's gaze toward the dance floor, where family and friends danced. Her eyes easily found Tate in the middle, twirling Adira as if she was a princess at a ball.

Indigo bit down on her lip, casting her eyes up at the starry sky. "I—" She lowered her gaze back to her mama. "I need a minute."

She nodded, and her mama echoed her gesture then stood and walked away.

. . .

Indigo walked away from the melodic tunes, energetic conversations, and jolly partygoers all there to celebrate her existence. She abandoned it all for the solitude of the gazebo. Her focus was on the man-made lake at the end of her parents' property, but her thoughts weren't on the beauty of the moon's glow reflected off the placid water. Her mama's words felt like the code to the safe-deposit box that locked away all the emotions she had for Tate.

Old memories washed over her like a tsunami.

It was the day before high school graduation. A simple day of catching up after avoiding each other to study for finals before the craziness of graduation day. It might not have been Halloween, but they had a Freddy Krueger marathon anyway. Scary movies were their thing: *Darkness Falls*, *Dawn of the Dead*, and *Gothika* were just some of the movies neither of them had had to persuade the other to see at the theater.

That day she brought the movies, and he supplied the snacks. The Larsen house was the perfect spot since his parents were away. As soon as the DVD slipped into the player, they got cozy on the couch, and by the third movie she drifted to sleep until the deep, robust stroking of strings willed her awake. She followed the sound up the stairs and found herself in his room.

Her eyes went wide, taking in the sight of him in a chair with his cello between his legs and his eyes closed, moving the bow delicately over the strings. The vibrations bounced off the walls and stroked her skin. He'd quit orchestra freshman year to focus on soccer. She hadn't known he still remembered how to play, but he did. He even remembered the notes of her favorite song.

As she leaned against the doorframe, she wondered how she'd missed it. When did the stubble sprout around his chin? How did his shoulders get broader? When did his arms get sculpted, and dear God in heaven, when did he get abs? When did her heartbeats start to flutter from the sight of him? The questions ran through her mind but ceased when the music stopped, and his eyes met hers. She smiled at him, and he did the same back as if he knew all the answers to the questions she was asking herself.

"What are you doing out here?"

The humor in Tate's baritone sent a shiver down her spine. She tried to blink the mist from her eyes, but the water just slid down the side of her face. She cleared her throat to remove the emotions clogging up her voice box.

"Contemplating." Indigo could only get out the singular word.

"About shaking your ass on a yacht in Dubai?" He chuckled, bringing up the TikTok she'd sent to him when he'd texted her about the probability of her brother giving her a Target gift card for her birthday.

She, however, remained silent as his footfalls struck against the dark-lacquered wooden planks. Her heartbeat quickened as he moved into the space next to her, and she was grateful for the warm, faint breeze that dried her face.

"Hey." He nudged her arm with his elbow, concern painting his features. "Are you okay?" He reached his hand toward her arm, and she abruptly slid over. "*Indigo.*"

"I'm thinking, Tate. Damn!" She gripped her waist tightly, feeling a slight shiver brush over her skin. She knew it wasn't the temperature but the man in her presence. She sniffed. "Go back to the party. Leave me. Let me think."

"*Leave you.*" He whispered the words like they were a foreign language from an ancient civilization. "Indie . . . talk to me. I can feel it like a porcupine needle lodged in my spine. What is it? Let me help you."

Although her eyes were watering, she could still see him clearly. She could make out his face through the darkness of night: the curve of his lips, the confusion in his eyes, his high cheekbones, and his jawline were all seared in her mind, tied to memories of a love she'd tried desperately to forget. She knew there was no way he was going to go away until she told him the thing that was upsetting her.

"I told my mama why we broke up," she started, fanning out her arms. "And she knew."

"About the pregnancy?" he interjected with a frown.

She shook her head. "No. About how I . . ." The words got caught in her chest. Fear teemed within her. "Feel . . . about you."

The music leaked over to them. Indigo didn't shift her gaze from him as he looked at her like she was a new book in front of him. She wondered what was in that beautiful, creative mind of his. Was it the same fears, wants, and desires racing though hers?

No, they didn't want the same thing anymore. She wanted to be friends, lovers, and everything in between. He wanted to be friends; his silence told her that. A fresh wave of hot tears streamed from her face.

"This is my fault," he said with a hand resting on his chest as if her tears were causing him pain. "You shouldn't be crying on your birthday. You should be radiant like sunshine. You deserve goodness, joy. You deserve honesty and love. I'm sorry I didn't tell you those things that day when you came back from the baby shower." He let out a breath. "I was a coward. I didn't want to rush you."

"No." She spoke up, stopping his words. "I was afraid of how deeply I love you, and trying again frightens me, because if we don't work out, it'll hurt worse than before."

"Why would you think that?" he inquired. "Immaturity and inexperience arc what broke us up the first time. I'm a grown-ass man now. I know how to take care of you, so I'm not scared."

"You're not?" Her words came out in a whisper.

"No," he replied immediately. "Do you trust me?"

"Yes."

"Then let me propose this." He stepped closer to her, removing the space between them, and set two fingers under her chin, lifting her gaze to him. "Date me, so I can show you that you have nothing to fear, because all those things you want are the same things I want—*with you*. I never stopped loving you. Never. You're my *love*."

"Tate," she said breathlessly on hearing the moniker he'd given her when they were a couple. "I never really stopped either."

"Then let's stop wasting time." He nodded, and she did the same, as if they were making a silent oath.

There was no longer a need for words. He matched his lips with hers, and it was like no time had passed between them. They kissed in a rhythm only they knew: soft, slow, and flooding with passion. She got high from the taste of him. All thoughts, fears, and worries slipped from her mind. It was just them. He was who she wanted. All she needed. And this time, she knew they were going to make it.

Epilogue

Sixteen months went by in a flash. The "I dos" were said, the cake cut, and the first dance completed. The wedding went off without a hitch since Indigo had her perfect groom: a best friend and caring partner combined into one.

And the help of her mama. Who would've guessed individual mother-daughter time would be just as important during adulthood as it had been in childhood? Not Indigo, but the change did wonders for her relationship with her mama.

"You are glowing," Aunt Maureen marveled in her mustard skirt suit and matching hat. "You sure you not pregnant? 'Cause Clark women get pregnant fast."

Indigo chuckled. "I'm pretty sure I'm not."

This wasn't the type of conversation she wanted to have at her reception, but she wasn't surprised that it was happening. The truth was, she wasn't sure. She'd stop taking birth control two months ago, and since she hadn't been nauseous and could still fit into her wedding dress, she'd just assumed she wasn't. But her aunt didn't need to know that.

"But we just got a new addition in the family," Indigo added.

"Have you seen Harrison and Hazel's fur baby, Truffle?"

The chocolate poodle wasn't the only change in her little brother's life. He'd bought a house and asked Hazel to move in with him. Although their mama didn't actually agree with the arrangement, their dad, being the peacemaker he was, reminded her that they were all grown now.

"Can I borrow her for a minute?" Tate asked, taking hold of Indigo's hand and leading her away before the woman could answer.

"Was she asking about your uterus again?" he questioned as they passed by the dessert bar where Emery stood letting Tate's cousin Afonso feed her a slice of cake.

Indigo grinned; her friend had been enjoying the single phase of her life since cutting ties with Hiran. She turned back to Tate. "Yes."

Once they made it outside, she knew they weren't going to return. The reception would be an event that lasted into the wee hours of the autumn night, but they didn't want to linger in the renovated barn with twinkle lights hanging from the rafters, doing the Cupid Shuffle. They only wanted to be in the company of each other, and she didn't fret about what people might think about it.

Before the chill of the night air pierced the bare skin of her arms, Tate set his suit coat on her shoulders. The sandy driveway was cool against the soles of her feet.

Tate claimed her hand again, twirled her, then pulled her into an embrace with her back against his chest. They peered out at the apple orchard, which filled the air with sweetness, and the moon's glow lit up the sky.

He rested his chin on the top of her head and whispered, "What's next, Mrs. Larsen?"

She snuggled into him, his body giving off more warmth than the coat. "You like saying that, don't you?"

"Yes," he replied. She could feel his smile against her cheek.

"Good." She clung to his arms, wrapped around her middle. "And as for what's next, I don't know." She shrugged. "Our honeymoon and maybe some babies. But for right now, can we just be in the moment?"

He kissed her temple softly. "If that's what you want, that's what we'll do."

Indigo let her eyes close, and they stood in the quiet of the night, not overthinking the past or worrying about the future but being in the present and enjoying a love that sated them mind, body, and soul.

Acknowledgments

The list of people I must thank is as long as a CVS receipt, but I'll try to keep it brief. The process of becoming a writer is a solo one, but the journey is made up of a plethora of people. It truly takes a village, and I have been exceptionally blessed along the way.

First and foremost, I have to thank God for planting the desire to write in my heart.

To my mom: I am the woman I am today because of her love, tutelage, and encouragement. I would have given in to my doubts many times over if it wasn't for her unwavering belief in me.

To my dad: he gave me the tools I needed to achieve my dream. His relentless grind and hustle to thrive in a world that didn't make things easy for him was the motivation I needed to not stay down whenever I encountered a setback or failure.

To my sister, April: my mouthpiece when my social battery has reached its limit and my main homie. Thanks for always having my back.

To my family: I thank you for all the support and inspiration.

To my editors, Grace Kabeya, Octavia Dosier, Whitney French, and Margot Mallinson: thank you for believing in Indigo's story and for your valuable advice along the way. The conversations and feedback helped mold *The Many Dates of Indigo* into a novel. It was a pleasure working with each and every one of you.

To Leah Ruehlickc and Deanna McFadden: thank you for believing in Indigo's potential when it was a rough cut.

To Austin Tobe: thank you for helping me navigate the world of publishing.

Every writer needs a clique of writers as a community in these publishing streets, and I'm grateful to have Danesha Little, Angel Hilson, J. F., Kimberly Wesley, M. Ray, Rena, Idris Grey, Katie Cruz, and Sondi Warner in mine.

To my Wattpad Peeps, who I don't call fans or followers but Sunshines: thank you for all the votes, comments, and reads. *The Many Dates of Indigo* is where it is today because of all of the love y'all gave it. I'm utterly grateful.

About the Author

Amber Samuel is a writer, a Wattpad star, and an elementary school teacher. Born and raised in Houston, Texas, she's a graduate of Sam Houston State University. She loves being a dog mom to a nap-loving dalmatian, strolling through nature, and baking sweet treats she can share. She lives and works in Texas. *The Many Dates of Indigo* is her first novel.

Turn the page for a sneak peek of

Available now,
wherever books are sold.

chapter one

LACEY

"I'm surprised you agreed to come with."

We had just left the 95 and branched onto Montauk Highway. It was official—I was back in the Hamptons for the first time in seven years. The plan was to never come back—too many memories, both good and bad, and all that hurt. My dad's surprise was nothing compared to my own. It was a last-minute decision. I literally halted his car as he tried to leave and threw my bags into the backseat.

"It's just for a few weeks . . . for Rachel. She came to Michigan after Knox and I split. It's only fair."

"They were together a long time. Right?"

The small talk was awkward. Unfortunately, we still had another hour before we arrived, and he was being chattier than usual. Any sort of discussion about ourselves would make this even more uncomfortable; so why not just discuss my friend's breakup instead?

"Three years."

"Wow. Were they engaged?"

I finally turned to look at him to see if he was serious. When his gray eyebrows lifted, waiting for an answer, I cringed. If Rachel had been here to hear that, she would have ginger-snapped.

"What?" Dad asked, shifting his attention between me and the outstretched road.

"She's twenty-two!"

"So?"

"That's way too young, and three years is not that long."

"I married your mother at twenty-one after knowing her barely a year."

"That's different."

"How so?"

"Because *yours* was love at first sight."

Silence fell, Dad pinched his lower lip as he agreed, albeit unspoken. It was one of Mom's favorite stories—her chem lab romance. It was their first day of class. She was the first one in the room; he was the last. The only seat left open was beside her, and she looked up at my dashing dad, whose grin instantly "melted" her. They had been midway through a failed lab that shot a pink, sweet-smelling foam from their desk to the ceiling, sending my mom into a serious fit of giggles. The professor asked how my dad had turned a green liquid pink, and my dad answered he had successfully made a love potion and could prove it. He then turned to Mom to share their first, earth-shattering kiss. He only broke it to announce to the room he'd fallen in love. A year later, they married.

"Anyway,"—I attempted to change the subject away from

Mom—"you can drop me off at Rachel's. We're going out tonight. Where will I be riding out my hangover tomorrow? Where are we staying?"

"With William Drake."

I choked on the Hot Cheetos I had just shoved into my mouth. It took a few smacks to my chest before I could breathe normally, but I still couldn't speak. My esophagus was burning, and my mind was too busy rushing in a million different directions. The one place I wanted to avoid was our old house, and this would put us way too close. Then there was the panic at the thought of seeing Luke . . .

"It's just for the weekend. He wants to talk business, but I haven't agreed to return to run the lab yet. I'm in no rush to work for him again." Dad peered to his right to gauge my expression, surely finding just what he was expecting. "Lucas lives in Chapel Hill. He won't be there."

With my relief came an eye roll. "Of course *he* does."

North Carolina was only the home of the number one pharmacy program in the country. Ann Arbor was no small feat, either, but it wasn't the same. Chapel Hill was the dream—my mother's alma mater. The place where my parents met. Even with my savings, grants, and letters of recommendation, it wasn't enough to land me a spot in the program. Apparently, if Daddy makes hefty donations, a spot is obtainable.

"You're going to own a company together someday," my dad reminded me. "Eventually, speaking to each other will be a requirement."

I sank farther into my seat, wishing this car ride and discussion were over. "*If* there's still a company to run by then."

The way I saw it, I wouldn't have to speak to Lucas Drake again for at least three years.

———

My buzz didn't stand a chance against Rachel's. We sat on the floor of her childhood bedroom, where she was now living again, and ate burgers from a local restaurant we'd loved as kids. We washed them down with wine from her parent's wine cellar—too much of it. Unlike my breakup with Knox last year, she seemed to take this well for a girl who had no say in the end of her relationship.

"You really don't know what happened?" I asked, sensing that she had been holding back from me all night.

Rachel shrugged as she twisted the corkscrew. "We made it too complicated."

"He broke up with you, but you say *we*. And you don't seem to be upset with Chris."

Her cheeks turned the color of her hair. The cork popped free just as she hiccuped and giggled. How was this the same girl who had called me sobbing a mere twenty-four hours ago, saying she'd *messed up*? What exactly had she messed up?

With a wineglass the size of my head in hand, she stood and opened the doors to a walk-in closet bigger than my college dorm. I had forgotten just how extravagant everything needed to be here. Just in my seven years away, the Meyer home had been renovated to keep up with today's trends—if you could call having every wall, floor, and piece of furniture white a trend. Even the bedroom looked different from when we had played here as kids. Out of all the friends I had made during our four years living here, Rachel was now the only one I still spoke to. Odd, with our lives being so different. I was on the college path, while she had opted for the partying route and skipped college altogether—much to her parents' dismay. If I had asked my ten-year-old self which friend I thought I would have for life, the answer would have been much different. In fact, Rachel and I didn't become close again until after my mother's accident. We'd had a long-distance BFF relationship ever since.

"This one." She pulled a silver dress free from the wide array of clothing. It hung by a string no thicker than a shoelace. It was sexy—a cowl neckline with just enough bunched polyester fabric to cover a bustline. Its shiny material looked like it was made of glitter. Rachel swung it around to show the open back. "Your legs and ass will look amazing in this."

"Mine?" I asked, now convinced she was drunk. No way could I pull it off. "That will barely cover my ass."

"That's the point. Duh." She shook the hanger to make the dress shimmer.

"Where exactly are we going tonight? I thought we were hitting the bars? I don't need to be practically naked for those."

"We have to go to Blue. You'll need to be practically naked there. It's more fun that way."

Blue. Only a club would have a name like that. The Hamptons wasn't exactly a beacon for nightlife, unless you counted cocktail and dinner parties to show off your umpteenth home renovation—I'm sure one was held for the Meyer home. This meant we were leaving the Hamptons tonight.

While I'm used to the partying scene associated with being a college student, partying with Rachel wouldn't be the same. This wouldn't be a college scene. It would be somewhere expensive. Not only would there be a charge to get in but the cost of drinks would likely be triple what I was used to. The entire reason for my dad being back here was a dwindling bank account. The money my mother had saved was nearly gone, and my college fees weren't helping.

"Stop counting dollar signs." The dress was thrown into my

lap. "If you wear that dress, you won't be buying your own drinks. The rest is on me. We'll use Dad's driver. We are both getting laid tonight."

I dropped my back to the floor and groaned. She was frustrating. "Rach . . ."

"Don't start with me." She cackled, returning to the closet to find her own ensemble for the night. "You need this just as much as I do."

Guys were so much work. Getting laid was that much *extra* work. And for what? Not one of them had ever gotten me off during intercourse; not even my ex. So, I was supposed to show myself off like a prized pony, hoping to be picked and taken back to his place just to go home and finish the job myself? My hand and I had a glorious thing going. It hadn't let me down yet—unlike every penis I had met.

Two fingers snapped in front of my face, bringing me back to reality, and I found my best friend bent over me with a new pack of Venus razors. "We are going to drink away the thought of every man who did us wrong until we are carried out of that club like the queens we know we are. Now, get your ass into that shower and shave *everything*."

I knew better than to argue with her. I took the razors, got to my feet, and took the dress with me.

By the time we were both ready and climbing into the car, it was nearly eleven. What little wine buzz I had had was long gone. The same could not be said for Rachel. I was certain the entire bottle had gone into the shower with her, which no one could fault her for. The girl was hiding just how broken up she was over Chris and was doing a shit job of it. We just didn't handle our breakups the same way. After Knox, I needed Rachel, a binge-worthy TV show with over four seasons, a tub of Ben & Jerry's, and a lot of tissues. Rachel needed dick, and I needed to support that.

She rattled off the address of our destination to her father's driver, confirming that we'd be leaving the Hamptons tonight. And while Rachel rehashed tonight's plan to the woman who would take us to Blue, I was busy watching the New York scenery change back from beach house mansions to the few rare skyscrapers of Long Beach, New York. The buildings only grew in height and width the closer we got. It had been so long since I'd been anywhere near here that it took a mass of traffic behind a stoplight for me to realize just where I was. After we inched our way up a few car lengths, we sat adjacent to a high-rise office building with nothing but windows for walls on its exterior. Its red-and-purple logo beamed so brightly from its top floors that it reflected in the sheen of my dress. Keeping my legs crossed and my dress as far down as I could get it, I scooted myself closer to the window so I could see my name reflected in the red letters.

DRAKE-MASON PHARMACEUTICALS.

It was my mother's legacy; it was my future. And beside it, I felt ridiculously small.

"How bad is it?" Rachel asked, just as the car moved again.

The LED lights left my view, along with the building I hadn't seen in years. "Bad enough they want my dad to reopen the lab."

"Would he seriously do that?"

I shrugged. I never thought so, but my dad was here and willing to discuss it. He had held a grudge against William Drake for years after the closing of the department he managed. The entire business had grown from the lab. Dad didn't speak about it much, but when he did, it came with a serious dose of pent-up hostility. Drake-Mason had begun with three people and ended with two. William Drake purchased Mason Labs, my father's research combined with my mom's pharmacy and business knowledge, and thus, Drake-Mason Pharmaceuticals came to be. In three years, I was due to inherit the shares my mother had set aside for me, along with her own, which were currently held by a trust. My dad's shares were long gone—sold to cover our bills throughout the years. As of right now, Drake-Mason was a sinking ship. I was close to losing another piece of my mother, and the thought of it made my stomach churn.

"You know what, Rach? Maybe drinks and someone to take my mind off things might be good after all."

Our car came to a stop. The change in Rachel's posture accompanying her excitement agreed. "Oh, you're going to thank me tomorrow after you get some."

We'll see. I wouldn't be holding my breath. If I got laid, great. If not, fine. Either way, I wouldn't go out of my way to impress any guy tonight. Rachel was right—they could come to me. And the way Rachel had dressed us, I was sure the only time I'd need my wrist wallet was for my ID.

We both exited from my door, stepping onto the curb outside a club labeled Blue but intentionally lit in neon pink. I was questioning their choice of signage while being dragged to the front of a line that currently wrapped around the side of the building.

"Meyer," Rachel said confidently as she strode past the bouncer, her hand still gripped tightly around my wrist and leaving me no choice but to follow. She didn't even give the guy a chance to look at the clipboard he was holding, but he also didn't argue with her. One look at Rachel and her last name were all it took to get us to the doors. "You're in for a treat, Lacey Jo!" she shouted.

I could already feel the pulsing beat of the music beneath my feet, and we weren't even inside yet. A second bouncer pulled one side of a double door open for us. My wrist was tugged again, and this time, Rachel turned to wiggle her brows just before entering a club of people swinging their bodies in a sea of blue lights. Now I understood the choice of my silver and her white dress. We were sure to stick out in the crowd.

"No Hamptons boys!" I yelled above the music while weaving through the dancing bodies that packed the place.

Rachel smiled wickedly ahead of me. "I didn't know their tongues felt any different!"

I was sure she was right, and they wouldn't feel any different. But I also didn't need those tongues using talk of their trust funds as a way into my bubble tonight. My mind needed a rest from the topic of money, and I knew a few drinks would give me that break. The offers began before we even reached the bar.